FUTURE WORLDS OF JJ GREEN

A Collection

J.J. GREEN

INFINITE BOOK

NIGHT OF FLAMES

THE BOOKS OF SPACE COLONY ONE

The Books of Space Colony One

Night of Flames

He was barefoot, and the strange, mossy turf of the new world was rubbery and cool against his skin. After the night lamps of the barn, the outside world was pitch black to his eyes save for the string of lights leading to the latrine. He strained to listen. He was sure he'd heard the thunk of something large hitting the ground, but now he couldn't hear anything other than the wind rustling the fronds of vegetation surrounding the camp.

Back in the newly built barn, the rest of the colonists slept soundly. More than two hundred men and women on rows of low cots, exhausted after a long day bringing down essential supplies from the ship. It wasn't surprising that no one else had heard the noise.

The sound was probably nothing. Maybe just a dying plant toppled by the wind. None of the probes had found signs of complex animal life, nor of plants capable of locomotion.

Holding up a lamp and peering ahead, he went on. The lamp's glow wasn't strong, and the moonless planet with its faint, unfamiliar constellations was a dark place at night, but he had an idea of the direction the sound had come from. His eyes adjusted to the darkness. Dim gray shapes came into view—the boxes of supplies piled in heaps around the compound.

Another thunk.

He stopped.

This noise had come from farther away than the first, from the direction of the comm module they'd set up to talk to the ship. He ran a hand through his hair and glanced back at the barn, tall and wide behind him, blacker than the sky. Should he tell someone? Dr Crowley, perhaps? One of the Woken, the doctor always seemed to know what to do.

No. The old woman needed her rest, and he was just a Gen farmer. What did he know? Besides, what else would you expect on an alien planet but weird noises? He would walk the perimeter fence and satisfy himself there was no cause for alarm, then return to the barn and his well-earned slumber.

A third thunk. Off to his right. *What the...?* He swung around and gazed into the night. Beyond the dim circle of his lamp's light was nothing but darkness. He hesitated on the verge of returning and waking someone in authority, but he was sure he was nearly at the fence. It would only take him a moment to have a quick look around.

A shriek splintered the calm of the night. The cry had come from the barn. *Lauren.* An almost inhuman howl of agony shot through with terror followed the shriek. He sprinted back the way he'd come, his bare feet struggling to grip the damp ground cover. He slipped and fell. The lamp sprang from his hand and skittered away.

He leapt up. The lamp could wait. The shriek had been joined by shouts and screams. The barn doors flew open and people poured out. *Lauren. Where was she?* The people raced off, spreading in disorder throughout the camp, pushing each other down in their hurry to get away. The fallen couldn't stand and others tumbled over them, crushing them in the stampede.

He was at the barn. He forced his way against the tide of escaping colonists. A woman came rushing toward him, her eyes popping and her mouth wide. She held up bloody, raw hands, palms out.

"Don't touch it," she wailed. "It burns." Then she was gone.

Behind the people rushing from the barn lay the object of their fear: A grayish-brown mass covered most of one of the cots, leaving only the cot legs visible beneath the misshapen lump.

A man ran past, colliding with Ethan's shoulder.

"We can't get it off of her," he said, his deep voice choked with barely suppressed sobs. "We've tried everything. I'm going to call the ship."

The barn was nearly empty. Only the brown thing remained and a young woman standing over it, hitting it with the broken leg of a cot, her face wracked with anguish and despair.

"Lauren!"

"Ethan." She threw down the cot leg, ran to him and grabbed his arms. "Where have you been? The others all panicked and ran away. Can you help? Only don't touch it, it—"

"It burns. I know. Someone told me."

He stepped closer for a better look. As he saw what lay beneath the thing, the strength went from his legs and he nearly collapsed. Poking out from the upper end of the creature were the head and shoulders of Dr Crowley. The alien life form was on top of her.

"We can't move it," said Lauren. "It's stuck to her like glue, and we can't even touch it because its skin is caustic."

Dr Crowley was still alive, barely. The shriek he had heard must have been hers. Whatever the creature was doing to her, it had nearly finished the job. The doctor's eyes were half-closed and her lips were blue. The organism was suffocating her or—he recalled that its skin burned—was it digesting her?

He turned to try to find something to lever the thing off. There had to be something no one else had tried. But the thought of what the creature was doing to Dr Crowley overwhelmed him. Blood drained from his head and he became dizzy. He fell to his knees, vomit erupting from his stomach.

"What?" Lauren asked.

He looked up. She was bending over Dr Crowley, trying to catch the doctor's words.

"Don't go near that thing." He forced himself to his feet and drew his arm across his bile-stained mouth.

"The what?" Lauren repeated. "The…the fence?" She turned puzzled eyes to Ethan.

The fence? The electric fence. How had the creature entered the camp? Why hadn't the fence stopped it? The thunk he'd heard must have been the organism hitting the ground. And he'd heard more of them. More of them were in the camp. Where were the rest of the creatures? And where were all the people who had run out of the barn?

"Lauren," he said, "we have to go. I think the fence might have shorted and there are more of those things inside the compound."

———

Dr Crowley was the only Woken he had come to know.

She'd been one of the first to emerge healthy and sound from her hundred and eighty-four years spent in a twilight state somewhere between hibernation and death, while the *Nova Fortuna* carried them to their new home. Just as the Manual instructed, the Gens had begun to revive the founders of the mission two years before Arrival. Of those they attempted to return to life, many didn't survive, and those they managed to wake suffered strokes and aneurysms, or had brain damage, or were blind, or their limbs turned gangrenous when blood flow could not be restored.

Dr Crowley had been standing in Main Park beneath The Clock when he first saw her on his morning run. She was looking at the glowing figures that counted down, not up. Figures that marked the seconds, hours, days, months, and years that passed on their deep space flight.

At the sight of the doctor gazing transfixed at The Clock, he had been reminded of the time when he found out what it was measuring. He'd been in kindergarten, and the teacher had explained that the children were lucky Gens. They would be alive when the *Nova Fortuna* reached her destination. Soon after they were grown up, the teacher had said, they would leave the ship and travel to a planet where they would live out the rest of their lives.

Dr Crowley's fascination with The Clock had made sense. The figures on its display had counted down nearly two centuries while she'd lain in her vat of frozen slush. Though he was usually a little intimidated by the enigmatic Woken with their odd dialects and distant eyes, he couldn't resist the temptation to talk to this one. She seemed more approachable than the others, who were aloof and stuck together.

He jogged over and stood next to her, joining her contemplation of the steadily counting figures of The Clock. The older woman seemed to sense his nervousness, for she smiled kindly. "Do you have any plans for Arrival Day?"

"I guess I'll spend it with my girlfriend. Unless there's something ship-wide planned."

"I don't think so. I believe the Leader intends for everyone to celebrate in their own way, as it will mean different things to different people. May I ask what your occupation is to be?"

He shrugged. "Just a farmer. I didn't do too well at school." He gave an embarrassed smile.

Dr Crowley frowned. "Forgive me for saying so, but you seem ashamed. Being a farmer's nothing to be ashamed of. Your job is just as important as anyone else's, Maybe *more* important than some. The colony won't last long without food."

When he didn't react to her words, she tilted her head. "Don't you want to be a farmer?"

He glanced around. No one seemed close enough to hear their conversation. He didn't like to express his discontent with his allotted role publicly. He wouldn't be punished as such, but failure to conform to the Mandate wouldn't do much for his reputation. "If I could have chosen, I would have been an explorer."

"Oh, now that's a fine profession. Why didn't you select it? Surely you don't need good grades to be an explorer?"

"It's a Second Generation occupation. Maybe if I have kids and they want to take over the farm when they're older I'll get my chance."

"No explorers?" Dr. Crowley exclaimed, loud enough to cause him unease that they would be overheard.

"No explorers until the Second Gen. It's in the New Manual."

"Hmpf. I'll have a word with the Leader about that. Old Manual, New Manual..." She waggled a finger. "There's only one Manual, and that's the one I and the other founders wrote before we departed Earth. There was no talk then of drafting an *updated* version mid-voyage. What do you pups know of settling a planet? Living out your lives on a starship is hardly preparation for..." She paused and took a breath. Her gaze flicked to him. "Forgive me. It's not your fault."

After she'd calmed down a little more, she gave a short laugh. "It's strange. You'd think that tens of light years would be sufficient distance to leave behind petty politics and meddling in the affairs of others. But wherever you go, there you are, I guess."

"Is...is that what you wanted?" he asked. "To leave all that stuff behind?" He'd had no choice but to be born aboard the *Nova Fortuna* and be one of the first humans ever to set foot on an exoplanet. But the Woken had chosen to risk their lives for the opportunity. That had always struck him as odd. He imagined that Earth must have been a terrible place for them to want to leave it so badly, despite the positives that the vids and books showed.

"Politics and more," the doctor replied. "Much more, though I don't know if you can understand. Truth be told, I feared for what would happen to humankind. We seemed not to be progressing, but regressing. It wouldn't surprise me if the technology of the *Nova Fortuna* were the peak of human achievement and everything went downhill after we left. But it wasn't only that. My eyes were on the stars all my life. I was glad to come along, even though I knew I might never wake up."

"You think technology might not have progressed on Earth in all the time that's passed since we left?"

"I'm almost certain of it."

"Why do you think that?"

"Mainly because in the years leading up to the departure of the

Nova Fortuna, we seemed on the verge of inventing a Faster-Than-Light starship engine. Sure, the popular trend was against anything *unnatural,* and there were protests and demands that space travel funding be cut because it was *wrong* for humankind to leave its birthplace, but the scientists were close nonetheless. So close that some of the founders even wanted to postpone the *Nova Fortuna's* leaving date. Why spend two centuries traveling by fusion propulsion when you could arrive within a few years?

"Yet here we are, and there's no sign of anything from Earth. If an FTL engine had been invented while we were traveling, it would have caught up to us by now. We wouldn't be trying to decipher scrambled Earth comms sent decades ago. The fact that another ship hasn't followed us tells me a lot."

He nodded. The Woken woman's way of explaining things made much more sense than many of his former teachers'. "What do you think Earth's like now?"

"So much time has passed…I really couldn't guess. Does it matter? We have a whole new future ahead for more than two thousand of us. The beginning of a new civilization." She returned her gaze to The Clock.

———

Lauren hadn't seemed to hear his words when he told her they had to check the fence. She was closing Dr Crowley's eyes. "She's gone," she whispered.

He heard her but he couldn't process the words. He swallowed. "The fence," he repeated heavily. "We have to find the switch." He took her arm. "Come with me. Get away from that thing."

But Lauren was shaking her head. "I have to find Belle. I have to make sure she's okay." Belle was Lauren's nursery-mate. They'd been inseparable since they were three years old.

"There isn't time. She could be anywhere. And there are more of those creatures out there. I heard them dropping into the compound."

"I have to find her. She'll be terrified. You go and check the fence. I'll meet you at the comm module. I'll be careful."

He closed his eyes. There was no time for him to think. There was no time for anything. "Okay. Okay. But please, stay the hell away from those creatures."

As Lauren ran off, calling for her friend, he forced his reluctant legs to move. He was terrified of what might happen to her, but he had to stop any more of the life forms entering the camp. He grabbed another night lamp and sped away on the quickest route to the fence. It had been the first thing to be erected after Arrival. The builders had sunk metal posts and fixed high-tensile alloy fencing to them four meters high and a meter below ground, enclosing the compound. But he hadn't been a part of the building crew. Where was the switch to turn on the electricity? He didn't recall seeing it.

Another shriek split his ears. The noise had come from somewhere to the right. Someone else had been caught by one of the creatures. Sweat ran from his pores at the memory of what had happened to Dr Crowley—at the thought of what was happening to another person. The shriek evened out to a long, howling wail of someone in terrible torment.

The horrible cry stopped abruptly. Had the creature moved onto its victim's face? Had someone put the person out of their misery? He steered his thoughts away from the idea. He had one goal: turn on the fence.

From out of nowhere, a child ran into his side and rebounded from the impact. The kid rolled to a halt and sat up, crying. He went over, crouched down to the boy and held his arms. "Are you okay?"

"Mommy! I want my mommy."

The child was only six or seven years old. He must have been separated from his parents in the mad rush from the barn. What was he even doing on the planet surface? He hadn't noticed the child during the day's work.

The boy continued to sob into his fists. Around them, screams and shouts were filling the air. What to do? He had to go to the fence, but he didn't want to leave the kid alone with those creatures roaming the camp.

"Come with me," he said, straightening up and holding out his hand. "Come on, we'll find your mommy."

The kid didn't look up. He buried his face further into his hands and shook his entire body from side to side, signaling his refusal of Ethan's offer.

"Come on. It isn't safe for you to be out here by yourself. Come with me. We'll find your mommy, I promise."

The kid lifted his head long enough to shout, "No, leave me alone," before he thrust his face into his hands once more and fresh sobs rocked his little body.

He didn't have time to waste. He reached down and grabbed the kid, intending to carry him over his shoulder while he continued his search for the switch. But the boy struggled and kicked as he lifted him.

"Whoa, take it easy," Ethan protested, trying to get a firm grip on the wriggling child. A small, booted foot struck him full in the stomach. He grunted in pain and dropped the boy, who landed on his feet and ran the second he hit the ground, quickly disappearing into the darkness.

Ethan ran after him, but he couldn't see where he'd gone. He stopped and called out, telling the kid that it wasn't safe and that he had to come back, but he heard no response. The child was nowhere to be seen. His heart weighing heavy, he returned to his quest to find the switch.

———

The boy's attachment to one of his parents—to the extent of refusing a stranger's offer of help—struck him forcefully. He couldn't guess how that kind of attachment felt. It didn't seem so long ago that he'd been the kid's age, but he'd had no mother or father.

His earliest memories were of playing with other kids at his nursery. The nursery workers had been kind. He even remembered a few of them hugging and kissing him, their eyes teary, when it was time for him to go to kindergarten. But he hadn't developed the bonds with them that families were supposed to have. None of the care givers had been like a mother or father, as far as he'd understood the role. The only person he'd had that kind of relationship with had been Dr Crowley.

He learned about families at school, and how the Manual instructed that, as Arrival drew nearer, Gens were to be encouraged to reproduce naturally and revert to the nuclear family patterns of human societies on Earth. The transition had to happen. The artificial reproduction tech was wearing out. It would be decades before they would be able to manufacture replacement parts.

Like the other Gen his age and all the babies decanted throughout the flight, his conception had taken place in vitro. Gen ova and sperm and stored and, along with frozen donations from Earth, were carefully selected and matched to ensure maximum diversity. With a Gen population of just two thousand, inbreeding had to be avoided as much as possible. Even more dangerous was uncontrolled reproduction. The ship's enclosed habitat could not sustain a population growth greater than ten percent, or roughly the number of preserved founders they were bringing.

The lost boy had to have been one of the first naturally conceived. The Manual stated that the move away from artificial reproduction and toward creating families should start seven years before Arrival. Gens of reproductive age were to get used to the new way of living. Dr Crowley had told him of another reason behind the Manual's directive: the founders' thinking had been that Gens' new lives would be so much harder than living aboard ship that they might need something to live *for*.

He and Lauren had talked about conceiving a child, but she'd shuddered while lying in his arms, saying the idea of something growing inside her was weird. Maybe she would feel different later.

———

A shape approached, long and low and moving fast. One of the creatures. He swerved and ran. For something as large as a man laid out and at least twice as wide, the thing moved quickly. He looked over his shoulder, but the life form was veering in another direction. It seemed to have given up pursuit, presumably in favor of slower prey. He remembered the boy and his stomach dropped.

The thing had scooted along the ground, its method of locomotion obscured by its overhanging bulk. But he had no time to puzzle out how the life form moved. He was at the fence. His gaze roved it. No switch was in sight. A scream from another captured victim spurred him not to catch his breath before setting off to find the switch. Shouts of terror, panic and despair resounded through the night and people cried out the names of their loved ones.

Fence wire and posts sped past as he ran. The dark scuttling figure of a creature climbing the far side of the fence flashed into view. Its scaly belly outlined with hundreds of insectoid legs reflected the light from his lamp. He stopped and pushed the lamp between the wires at the underside of the organism, but at the touch of the metal its legs wrapped around the fence wires and clung tightly. He couldn't move the creature, and he didn't have time to try harder.

A thunk sounded somewhere behind. Another one of the creatures had made it over the fence. He took off.

A flicker of something yellow appeared on the edge of his vision. He stuck his heels into the spongy ground and skidded to a halt. A plastic handle jutted out from a post beneath a yellow hazard sign. He'd found the switch, but something was moving on the wires above it. One of the organisms was crawling over the post. He raised his lamp to shine on the scrabbling life form. He had only a second before it would fall. He darted in and grabbed the switch.

But before he pushed down, he hesitated. What if someone were touching the fence? Turning on the electricity could kill them. He looked up at the creature about to drop. He couldn't help it. He had to take the chance. He pushed down the lever. As the electricity hit, the creature jolted, its legs jerking. It became rigid, and a terrible reek like burning rotten flesh assaulted his senses.

He'd done it. The electrified fence would prevent any more creatures from coming into the camp. But why had it been turned off in the first place? He shook his head. It was odd, but he didn't have time to think about it. He had to find Lauren.

Holding out his lamp in front of him, he set off to search the compound. He hoped that Dr Crowley was the only fatality, though going by some of the cries he heard echoing through the night, he doubted it.

It wasn't long before he came across the creature he'd tried to push off the fence. It had made it over and was lying inside the camp, but its back end had been in contact with wire when he had turned the electricity on. The life form was stiff, its thick hide was dark and charred, and it gave off a stench that made his stomach churn.

Liquid had spread out from the organism in its death throes. A puddle lay beneath it that had scorched the ground cover down to the soil. Pressing his elbow over his nose and mouth, he peered closer. The creature didn't seem to have any eyes, mouth, or other sensory organs. He shivered and drew away. How had the probes missed these life forms?

From somewhere to his left came the sound of someone running. He lifted the lamp as the person came into view. It was the Leader, though Ethan barely recognized the man.

His gray hair stuck out all over and his eyes were wild. He grabbed Ethan's arm, making the lamp swing crazily. "They're dead! So many people killed by those things. What can we do? Where can we hide? Do you know where to hide?" His fingers dug stiffly into Ethan's forearm, and his gaze darted from side to side. Sweat beads clung to the man's face despite the cool of the night.

"What the hell do you mean, where can we hide? We've got to find the creatures and kill them."

"We can't." The director's voice was wobbly and high, as if verging on hysteria. "Nothing kills them. Nothing. We've tried everything we can think of. And the comm module's dead. We can't contact the ship. They have no idea what's happening down here. We haven't any hope of rescue."

His grip on Ethan's arm was painful. He peeled the man's fingers from his muscle. "The comm module's dead?"

"Broken." The director's eyes seemed about to leave their sockets. "Someone sabotaged it. We have no comm. We're alone down here."

The fence, and now the comm module? A scream, piercing and tortured, made them both jump.

"We have to help, not hide," Ethan said between his teeth. He pushed the man out of the way and ran toward the scream.

How had their hopes of a new, wonderful life turned to darkness and slaughter?

———

He remembered the Leader as everyone had watched the counting down of the final two hours remaining on The Clock. After a long, arduously fought election—to be the Leader who presided over Arrival and the first settlement—the man had stood straight-backed and proud on the podium in Main Park. His hair had been perfectly groomed, then.

The countdown had been breath-taking. Main Park held all the Gens and the Woken. Some had even slept in the park overnight with the black, starry fake sky over their heads and the figures of The Clock glowing green in the dark.

The Clock spanned a wide section of the dome. As early as five or six years before Arrival, couples and groups had begun to stand beneath it and discuss their plans of what they were going to do when the *Nova Fortuna* reached her destination. Those who weren't drawn to The Clock spent hours watching vids on the planet. As the ship drew nearer, visuals showed continents and seas and water-vapor clouds that seemed to confirm that everything the scientists had said was true.

On the final day, the murmuring of the crowd in Main Park had grown louder as more and more Gens and Woken arrived. Excited chatter about the impending long-anticipated event rose, drowning out the circulation fans that whirred at top speed to renew and cool the air.

He could hardly believe it when the moment he'd been taught to anticipate all his life arrived. The final hour of The Clock flicked to zero, matching the year, month, and day. Only minutes and seconds remained. The noise of the crowd grew almost painful. Then, strangely, the volume subsided as The Clock marked the final minutes. When it hit the final seconds, until only the quietest of whispers sounded.

The last few moments of their long voyage disappeared. One hundred and eighty-four years of waiting was over. The work of tens of thousands of people, many of whom had never set foot on the *Nova Fortuna*, many of whom had lived and died aboard her, were finally paid off. An almost deathly hush fell.

Five. Four. Three. Two. One.

The Clock was a row of zeros. The device that had faithfully kept time for nearly two centuries stopped, its work done. Not a person in the crowd stirred, as if no one could quite believe they had reached this point—that the ship was in geosynchronous orbit above the place that was soon to become their new home.

Brilliant lights exploded across the surface of the dome, accompanied by ear-splitting bangs and whistles. The Gens stared up in fear, but the Woken seemed to know what was going on. They shouted and cheered and clapped and stamped their feet. Whatever the cascading colors were, they seemed to be celebrating the safe arrival of the colonists, and soon the Gens joined the Woken in hollers and shouts and hugs and kisses.

He had grabbed Lauren and lifted her up. He swirled her around as she laughed and screamed. They celebrated all night.

Lauren. He had to find her.

They'd agreed to meet at the comm module. Using the distant lights leading to the latrine as his guide, he raced towards the meeting point, ignoring the fading protests of the desperate Leader. As he drew closer to the spot, dark, swarming figures of men and women took shape.

The crowd was surging in a blind panic. People were shouting and crying. No one seemed to know what to do or where to go. He went from person to person trying to find Lauren, but she didn't seem to be here. In the chaos, he despaired that he would ever find her. Someone had to organize these people.

He cupped his hands around his mouth. "Everyone, get tools from the stores! We have to find and kill the creatures."

"We've tried," growled a man nearby, lifting a sledgehammer in one hand. "Nothing kills them. Nothing. They're all over the place, and we can't contact the ship. We're dead. All of us. It's only a matter of time."

"We can't give up." There had to be a way. "Come with me back to the barn," he said to the man. "Maybe the creature in there has gone. If it has, everyone can go inside. We can barricade the doors and wait until morning, when the supply shuttle from the ship is due."

"No way. I'm not going near any of those things. I'm staying right here."

"But you're no safer here. One of them could attack any minute."

"I said, I'm not going anywhere." The man lifted his hammer again threateningly, and his eyes glinted in the light from Ethan's lamp. Like the Leader, the man seemed to be barely holding himself together.

Ethan clenched his jaw. It was no use. Their soft lives aboard the *Nova Fortuna* meant they were entirely unprepared to deal with the emergency. And why had no one thought to set a watch while the others slept? They'd behaved like fools.

"Nooo," a voice wailed on the far side of the comm module. "Help him! Please. Somebody help him." The victim's terrible shrieking began, and the man Ethan had been talking to threw down his sledgehammer and, gripping his ears, ran off.

Then, above the shouts, cries and moaning of the crowd came a sound that made his heart leap. It was Lauren's voice, and she was calling his name. He headed toward the sound, pushing others aside as he went. She was calling his name over and over. She seemed close by, though it was hard to navigate in the darkness and the confusion of voices.

"Lauren," he shouted. "Lauren!" There she was.

She'd found Belle, and the two were standing together with their arms entwined. As Lauren saw him, her face broke into a smile of relief and happiness. She started forward.

"No!" a man shouted, backing up fast. He moved so quickly, Lauren didn't have time to get out of his way. He knocked her down, and Belle turned and screamed as Lauren's arm was torn from hers. The man scrambled away as the scaly belly of one of the creatures reared up. Ethan leapt forward, but he was too late. The creature fell on top of Lauren, flattening her to the ground. Its wriggling legs disappeared as it hunkered down. Belle's hands flew to her face and she stumbled backwards, screaming.

The creature covered Lauren almost entirely. Only one of her feet remained visible, kicking. The crowd fled from the scene, scattering like cockroaches exposed to light. He grabbed the creature's hide, desperately trying to lift it up. Agony shot through his hands as the caustic liquid burned his skin. Belle was frozen in horror.

"Move out of the way," commanded a voice, but Ethan barely heard. He felt a kick, and as he turned, light seared his eyes. A woman was standing behind him holding something he had only ever seen in vids. Through his blurring tears he saw she held in each hand dead fronds of the vegetation surrounding the camp, and the fronds were on fire. Blue and yellow crackling flames spitting sparks rose from them.

"Here." The woman held out a burning frond. "You do that side."

He took the burning plant, though the pain from his hand made him gasp. The woman thrust her flaming brand into the creature's back. He ran to the far side and did the same, pushing the fire deep into the tough hide. A great convulsion shook the animal. Its domed form flexed upward and became concave, exposing jerking legs and a writhing underside. Strings of a white substance hung from it.

The fire from the brands set light to the creature's back, and the flames burned golden as they grew higher. The animal squirmed and bucked as if trying to rid itself of the blaze. With a sound like peeling plastic, it pulled away from Lauren and dashed off, twitching and weaving as it went.

Lauren's body was still. He turned his head. The world was swimming around him as he fought to erase the image from his mind. Despite the light from the flames, darkness encroached the edges of his vision.

"I'm so sorry," the woman said.

He had forgotten she was here. She was watching him, flamelight flickering over her dark skin and black eyes. The burning frond she'd given him lay on the ground where he'd unknowingly dropped it.

"Will you help me kill the rest?" she asked.

"I...I..." He swallowed. He couldn't speak.

"Please. I'm very sorry about what happened to your friend, but you have to help me. We have to kill these creatures before they attack again."

He nodded numbly. She was right. If no one did anything, more people would die. Lauren wouldn't want him to stand there and weep over her while others were in danger. "I can help." Wincing, he pulled his shirt over his head and wrapped it around his right hand before retrieving the burning brand. With his left hand he picked up the lamp he'd also dropped and slid it over his forearm.

"Follow me. We'll light some more torches and share them out. Do you know where the Leader is? Are you his assistant or something?"

"I'm just a farmer."

"Really? I thought you must be someone in charge."

"Why would you think that?" He had never been in charge of anything in his life.

"You were the only one with a lamp."

The woman led him to a pile of dead fronds that had fallen from vegetation overhanging the fence. His brand had nearly burned down. They lit more and carried them around the compound. People were attracted by the flames and approached them, their ravaged faces lit with tentative hope.

They handed out the burning brands and went back to light more.

———

The woman was one of the Woken. Even if he hadn't seen her before, he knew that.

It was easy to tell the Woken apart. Their height varied more than the Gens', and their skin tone ranged from a deep, dark brown through tan and yellow tones to pale, pinkish white. He guessed the controlled breeding of Gens had resulted in an evening out of height and skin tone differences usual on Earth. Male Gens were taller than females, but they differed by only a few centimeters from each other, and all Gens' skin was colored light to medium-dark olive.

He might have seen the woman before among the other Woken as they went around in their exclusive groups. He wasn't sure. But his clear memory of her was from when he'd boarded the shuttle that had brought him down to the planet surface.

The incident had stuck in his mind because it was one of the few times that he'd seen Dr Crowley angry. She'd always been kind and patient when he'd asked her endless questions about Earth, and she'd never patronized him over his ignorance. Neither had she subtly punished his curiosity in the way his teachers had. It had been a joy to finally find someone who would answer him seriously and not refer him to a vid or the Manual, both of which only repeated the tedious teachings of his classes.

He'd been taken aback when he'd seen the ire on Dr Crowley's face as he joined her in the line to board the shuttle—Lauren and Belle had gone on ahead. The black-haired woman had been striding away from the doctor, so he'd only seen her from behind, but the stiffness of her back indicated she was also raging.

"Is something wrong?" Ethan asked.

Dr Crowley expelled a short huff of frustration. "You probably don't want to open that can of worms. Some people..." her gaze was on the retreating woman's figure, "some people are just unable to let things go."

"Oh." He would have liked to know more, but Dr. Crowley's stormy face prevented him from pushing her.

"I mean, it's been nearly two centuries. It's time to *move on*."

He nodded sympathetically, though he still had no idea what the doctor was talking about. He didn't think he'd ever seen her in such a passion. Did she have some bad history with the other Woken woman from before the *Nova Fortuna* had left Earth?

He must have been looking puzzled because D. Crowley eyed his expression before giving a short laugh. Her anger drained from her face. Passing a hand across her brow, she shook her head and sighed. "I'm sorry. I shouldn't have let her wind me up so badly. I'm a foolish old woman sometimes. My friend has her reasons for thinking as she does. She can't help being paranoid. I just wish she could understand that we need to look to the future now. The Earth we knew is far away and long ago."

The line to board the shuttle had shuffled forward without them, and the person behind told them to move up.

His skin prickled with excitement at the idea of going down to the surface. The Planet or the New Home was how everyone referred to it. The Manual stated that the world should not have a name until the first settlement was built. Then, the colonists would hold the Naming Ceremony where everyone could put their suggestions forward and vote on a final choice.

Though he had no name for it, His heart raced whenever he imagined what the planet was like. He could hardly imagine how it would feel to breathe a natural atmosphere, to look up into a sky or at a far horizon, and to walk on the ground rather than a starship's deck. The *Nova Fortuna's* circumference and spin created artificial gravity to match that of the new planet, but he was sure that treading its surface would feel very different.

They stepped aboard the shuttle, and his excitement quickly drove thoughts of Dr Crowley's disagreement with the black-haired woman from his mind.

———

Together, he and the Woken woman organized teams to search the compound for the creatures and kill them with fire. Gradually, the tide began to turn, and the colonists began to take control.

As a patch of lightening sky and dimming of the stars signaled the rise of the new sun, the settlers began to slow down their sweeps of the encampment. Some had already stopped entirely and given themselves up to grieving over those who had died.

He and the Woken woman went to the barn. He spread a blanket over Dr Crowley's remains after they'd set alight and driven off the creature still feeding on her.

After covering up Dr Crowley, he sat on a cot. Something inside him broke. He put his head in his hands and bawled like a baby. He could hardly believe he would never speak to the doctor again; that they would never have one of their long conversations about Earth, hope, and the meaning of life ever again; that he would never see the faraway look in her faded blue eyes when she talked of her past.

And in the depths of his grief, he couldn't even begin to think of Lauren.

He became conscious of a hand on his shoulder. The Woken woman was sitting beside him.

"I'm so sorry." Silent tears streamed down her face. "Meredith was a wonderful woman." He realized she was referring to the doctor. He'd never even known her first name.

"She was. She was a good friend too."

The woman nodded. "I wish our last conversation hadn't been an argument."

He swallowed and wiped his face with the shirt still wrapped around his hand. His skin was raw from touching the creature that had killed Lauren. "What was the argument about?"

She glanced at the door of the barn before replying, "Did Meredith ever tell you that powerful anti-science factions on Earth protested the *Nova Fortuna* expedition?"

"Dr Crowley did say a lot of people had turned against things they'd decided weren't natural."

"That was one of the reasons we decided to leave without waiting for the development of a Faster-Than-Light engine. If we'd waited much longer, the public sentiment against the project could have become so strong that the whole thing would be canceled."

"But you made it, right?" Why were these historical facts were still important enough to argue about?

"Yes, we made it. We got away. But..." The woman paused. "Hey, I don't know your name."

"Ethan."

"I'm Cariad. You did some great things tonight, Ethan. When everything was in chaos and everyone else was panicking, you stayed in control. Without your help, more people would have died."

He was about to object to her assessment, but she held up a hand to silence him. "Whatever you think, what I said is true. I think I can trust you. I'm going to tell you something that I want you to keep secret until, and if, it becomes necessary that more people should know." She got up and checked outside the barn before returning to the cot.

"Before we departed Earth, I and some of the other founders suspected that one or more members of the Natural Movement had infiltrated the project and were planning to come with us, either as Gens or in suspended animation. We insisted that a cache of weapons be secreted aboard to fight them if necessary."

His eyebrows rose. "Weapons? But the Mandate says—"

"I know what the Mandate says. *The new world is to be free of the scourge of human conflict.* But we argued that if we were inadvertently bringing along factions opposed to our plan, we had to be able to defend ourselves." Cariad sighed. For a moment the passing of the years she'd spent in a near-death state showed in her features.

"It's an old argument," she went on, "but I believe weapons are a necessary evil. Sadly, most of those who agreed with me didn't survive revival. A few are still suspended. I was the only one around to argue that we should bring the weapons down to the planet surface. That was what I was talking to Meredith about while we were waiting to board the shuttle. I was hoping to persuade her at the last minute. The *Nova Fortuna's* systems are heavily protected against sabotage. We made sure of that. If someone from the Natural Movement had wanted to jeopardize the settlement, the first opportunity would have been tonight."

"The electricity to the fence had been turned off," Ethan said. "And the Leader said the comm module had been sabotaged."

"Exactly."

"But...that's crazy. Whoever did those things would have been committing suicide."

"You have no idea how fanatical the Natural Movement was," Cariad said. "Many of them didn't hesitate to die for their cause."

"But..." His mind was whirring. "Do you think they knew about the creatures?"

"It's possible. They'd had infiltrated most areas of government and the scientific community. Someone could have easily *lost* some data."

"They're coming back," screamed a voice. "They're climbing the fence. Get the fire. We need more fire."

They raced out of the barn. While they'd been talking the sky had brightened. The edge of the rising sun was cresting the waving fronds surrounding the camp. At the now-visible fence, a patch of dark shapes moved.

He ran over to see what was happening. His heart froze. The creatures were climbing over the bodies of their fellows still clinging tenaciously to the electrified wires. Whether some had sacrificed themselves to create a safe path for the others was impossible to tell, but the bridge of corpses was effective. The creatures were swarming across, and beyond the fence, hundreds, perhaps thousands of their squat grayish-brown bodies swarmed among the vegetation.

Cariad caught up to him. The color drained from her stricken face as she turned and said, "I don't think there's anything left to burn."

The pile of dead vegetation that had fallen inside the fence had been almost entirely used up, and the materials they'd brought from the ship wouldn't burn—deliberately so. But without fire, how could they kill the creatures?

The first shriek came. All the horror of the previous night returned. Unless they could find a way to fight off the second wave of predatory organisms, they were all going to die in agony.

Cariad said, "What can we do?"

Slowly, he shook his head. He was out of ideas. The weapons she had mentioned were kilometers above them aboard the ship. But then he recalled his idea the previous night. "If we get everyone inside the barn..."

"...we might last out until the shuttle returns," Cariad finished. "You take that half of the compound." She gestured right.

Another shriek resounded among the increasing screams, shouts, and cries.

He started to run. "Go to the barn," he yelled at the colonists.

Cariad went in the opposite direction.

As he ran and called out , a terrifying thought occurred. What if everyone went to the barn and the creatures got inside too? They would be trapped, served up to the voracious organisms like dinner on a plate. But it was the only thing they could do.

All around, men and women were heeding his instruction and streaming past him on their way to the barn, but shrieks still ripped the air. More people were dying. Everywhere he looked, the creatures' low forms were roving the ground, looking for easy victims. It was only his speed that saved him from being targeted. He just hoped he could keep up his fast pace until he'd swept his half of the compound and returned to the barn. He hoped Cariad could too.

The sun was above the vegetation. They had an hour or longer until the shuttle was due. He wasn't sure they could hold out that long from the sustained attack, nor how they could reach the safety of the shuttle when it finally arrived.

He'd reached the far end of the compound. His throat ached from shouting, and his leg muscles trembled from the exertion of running all night and morning. Exhaustion was making him want to retch.

A few of the creatures were motionless, hunched over on the ground, no doubt digesting the settlers they'd caught. More of them were roaming around, covering the distance between him and the barn. To get to safety, he would have to run the gauntlet.

He set off. Deprived of slower prey in the nearly empty compound, the closest organisms ceased their aimless wandering and turned as he sped past. As they turned, others farther away followed their movement and converged. He dug deep into his depleted reserves and sped up.

He was running for his life.

The barn drew closer quickly, but not quickly enough. The creatures were nearly upon him. One reared up in front of him. He kicked the middle of its scaly belly. As the thing toppled onto its back, its nearest fellows fell upon it, covering it with their bodies and sticky white digestive fluid.

A creature ran across his path. He leapt over it and landed heavily on the other side, almost overbalancing. Somehow, he stayed upright and continued running, through sharp stabs of pain pierced his ankle.

The barn was only fifty meters distant. He only had to make it that far.

He was approaching the side of the structure and creatures were swarming toward him around it. No one else was available for them to chase. Which meant... A wave of horror washed over him. He rounded the side of the barn.

The doors were closed.

He was alone.

The organisms were drawing rapidly closer. He spun around. A hum sounded above him, but he couldn't take his eyes off the creatures surrounding him. They'd killed Dr Crowley and Lauren and now they were were going to kill him too. All his short life aboard the *Nova Fortuna*, all the learning and preparation he'd done had come to this: a lonely, grisly death.

A squat, grayish-brown form made a run at him. He kicked the creature, lifting its edge, spinning it over and onto its back, where others quickly claimed it. His shock and fear were turning to anger, then rage. He would die fighting.

Another creature approached and reared up. He kicked that one too. How long would he last? Dimly, he heard the hum grow louder, but he couldn't pay it any mind. He had maybe another few seconds of life.

A shadow fell on his back, cooling the warmth of the morning sunlight. He turned. A massive creature, around three meters tall, was rearing up. He ran directly at it, his head down, and butted it square in the middle.

But as he turned again, another was already rearing, closer this time. He stepped backward and tripped over the one that he'd just butted, or rather another that had clamped down upon it. Before he could do anything to save himself, he was on the ground. He struggled to rise, but as he put weight on his injured ankle his leg bent beneath him and he fell again.

This was it.

He looked up at a descending mass of scales. His heart seemed to seize along with the rest of his muscles. He held his breath and closed his eyes, waiting for the inevitable agony.

Nothing happened.

He opened his eyes. Where the creature had been was the sky and a faint trail of vapor. The air was filled with fizzing sounds and the smell of burning. A brilliant light flashed. He covered his eyes with his arm. Too late. He was blinded. All he could see was a green afterglow.

He squeezed his eyes shut and futilely shook his head to clear his vision. A deep bass rumbling resounded and the ground vibrated.

The shuttle. The shuttle had arrived. But it was early, and the people aboard it were shooting the creatures with weapons. That didn't make sense. Cariad had said the weapons cache was a secret hardly anyone knew.

The fizzing noise was dying down. An acrid reek choked him, and he coughed and retched. Slowly, his sight was beginning to return. Something dark approached. One of the creatures. He shuffled backward on all fours, his burned palms shooting out bolts of pain.

"Whoa, take it easy," came a man's voice. "I'm not going to hurt you."

He stopped and blinked in the direction of the voice. The dark shape hadn't been a rearing creature. It was a man. Someone had come out of the barn to help him.

But as he squinted up at the figure becoming more defined in his sight, his confusion increased. The man was wearing clothes of a type he'd never seen before. They were nothing like the clothes the colonists wore.

Behind the man was another puzzle. It looked like a shuttle craft, but it was much smaller than the *Nova Fortuna's*. The craft was also sleek and streamlined for speed.

"Can you stand?" asked the man. "There's nothing to be afraid of. We're exterminating the rest of your little infestation."

He nodded, surprise stilling his tongue. The man reached down and grabbed his forearm, carefully avoiding his burnt hand, and pulled him to his feet. When Ethan wobbled on his sore ankle, the man pulled his arm across his shoulder for support.

"Come with me. I'll fix you up. We have medical supplies on board the ship." He began leading him toward the shuttle.

"What..." Ethan croaked. He swallowed and coughed. "What's going on?"

———

The woman was white-faced and shaking as they led her to the center of the compound three days later, but he didn't feel even a twinge of pity. She'd been a nursery worker, of all things. He hadn't known her, and he was glad of it. He couldn't imagine being the friend of someone responsible for so many horrible deaths.

The sun was high and the day was warm. A steady wind stirred the fronds of vegetation around the camp as it had on that first, terrible night.

As she was marched to the spot where she would die before those who had volunteered to bear witness, the woman stumbled. The guards flanking her pulled her up and forced her to walk on. Her sobs rose above the rush of the wind.

Ethan's rescuer sat next to him. He couldn't help but think of the man and his shipmates as people from the future. Arriving at the last minute in humanity's first FTL ship, it seemed that they were almost superhuman. With their state-of-the-art tech and advanced knowledge, they were vastly superior to him, a lowly farmer.

He wished that Lauren and Dr Crowley were alive to meet the newcomers. His head sank low. He didn't think he would ever forgive himself for not preventing the deaths of the two people who were most important to him.

"You don't feel sorry for her, do you?" the man asked, mistaking his glum look.

He shook his head. "So many people died. I wish I'd done more."

The man placed a friendly hand on his shoulder. "You were a hero. You turned on the electricity to the fence, and along with your friend you fought off the first wave of the creatures. You bought some time, long enough for us to arrive."

The man had explained as he was tending Ethan's wounds that archaeologists on Earth had stumbled upon the Natural Movement's plot to sabotage the colony in ancient computer files, but that the FTL Drive hadn't been invented until recently. "I wish we could have made it here sooner, but there was nothing we could do until we had the technology to catch up to you. I'm sorry. We came as soon as we could."

The saboteur was at her execution spot. She'd stopped weeping and was looking around her in a daze. Ethan had heard that even the truth drugs of the people from Earth hadn't made her divulge the names of any co-conspirators. He hoped she really was the only one.

One of the guards raised his weapon. The woman stood still, awaiting her death.

He looked away.

The wind blew.

ETHAN & CARIAD'S STORY CONTINUES IN...

SPACE COLONY ONE
(Universal link)

DAUGHTER OF
DISCORD

The Books of Star Mage Saga

DAUGHTER OF DISCORD

A battle had broken out, and it was up to Carina Lin to stop it.

Scalobites had escaped their enclosure and were driving through hastily assembled kruekin ranks. Sprays of acid arched from kruekins' mouths, but the attackers were barely affected as the scalobites methodically tore their ancient enemies apart.

Surprised and all-but defenseless, the kruekins were suffering heavy losses. Pieces of carapace were scattered across a wide area, along with the remains of articulated limbs, still twitching. Spatters of white blood and green goo festooned the walls.

It was a massacre.

Carina traced the scalobite line back to where they had eaten through their enclosure wall. She stuffed a rag in the gap. It wouldn't hold the insects forever, but it would do for the moment. Returning to the kruekins' station, she scooped up two handfuls of scalobites and carried them away. As she transported them back to their enclosure, they bit her hands with their fierce mandibles, sometimes puncturing her skin. She winced and dumped the creatures in their home before returning for more.

Six times she made the trip. On the seventh turn, only a few scalobites remained. The kruekins were overwhelming the stragglers, shooting jets of acid that scored their shells. Was it kinder to leave the last few scalobites to a quick death, or return them to safety, where they might linger for days? She bit her lip.

She picked out the few who were still moving, grasping their legs between her fingers and thumbs, and carried them over to their enclosure. But when she put them down, their fellows immediately set upon them and ate them. She decided to leave the rest of the ones in the kruekins station to their fate.

Squatting down, she examined the hole the scalobites has gnawed in their enclosure wall.

"Carina!" her grandma called from the front of the shop.

She frowned. She couldn't leave her pets right now. If she did, the scalobites might eat through the rag and escape again.

"Mei Mei!" her grandmother yelled. "Come here."

"In a minute, Nai Nai."

"What's that?" The old woman's voice rose in outrage. "Carina Lin, come here immediately."

She didn't reply, buying just a little more time as she sprayed quick-dry resin over the hole in the scalobites' home.

Within seconds, her grandmother jerked aside the curtain separating the front and back of the shop.

Though the old woman only stood one hundred and forty centimeters tall, she was a formidable sight. Metal pins stuck out of her severe black bun like daggers, and her worn, plain clothes were stiff with starch. Even her flat cloth shoes seemed menacing as Carina watched them, not daring to meet the woman's eyes.

Her thoughtless defiance melted like a snowflake next to a furnace. She jumped to attention, her chin on her chest and her hands at her sides. Though still only a child, she already towered over her father's mother, but she dared not even look down upon the woman's head. She firmly fixed her gaze on her own bare, dirty toes.

"Why are you wasting your time with back here?" her grandmother demanded. "Why aren't you polishing stones like I told you? How do you expect my shop to support us when you fritter away your time with these useless bugs?"

"I'm sorry, Nai Nai."

"Are these insects going to bring us money? Is your apology going to put food on our table?"

"No, Nai Nai."

The old woman clicked her tongue and gestured energetically in the direction of the curtain. "I have too many customers. Come out here and serve them before they tire of waiting and leave."

Carina nodded and followed as her grandmother returned to the shop front.

But as she stepped through the doorway, a high-pitched whine filled the air. She clapped her hands over her ears.

Her grandmother spun around to face her, terror in her face. "Not again!" She grabbed Carina's arm, her fingers digging painfully into her biceps.

The last time the alarm had sounded, less than two years ago, a band of marauders had raided the slum settlement, looting and destroying wherever they went. The place had barely recovered from the attack, and now it was happening again.

Her grandmother was already pulling her into the rear room. "We must get into the hideaway!"

She resisted. "No. I don't want to hide. I want to fight! I want to help with the defense."

"You're too young. Come with me, Mei Mei. Now!"

Nai Nai was deceptively strong for her size, and her grip on Carina's arm was vice-like. She found herself being dragged along, her feet slipping on the worn floorboards.

When they reached the back room, her grandmother released her and pushed aside a rug. Beneath it, a square door was set into the dirt floor. The old woman tugged on the ring at the center of the door.

"Help me, child," she gasped, managing to lift the door only a few centimeters.

Carina hadn't given up her hope of fighting the invaders, but she couldn't leave Nai Nai defenseless. She gripped the door edge and heaved it up.

After the previous marauder attack, when they had luckily been away from town searching for unusual stones in the wilderness, Nai Nai and she had dug a small hole in the back room floor. Empty and dark, it was barely large enough to hold them. She balked at the idea of crouching inside the cramped space for hours, listening to the attack and the marauders looting her grandmother's humble shop over their heads. Besides, if they both went into the hole, who would pull the rug over it to hide the door?

"What are you waiting for?" her grandmother asked. "Get inside, quickly. They'll be here any minute." Then the old woman caught the look in her granddaughter's eye. "Wait. What are you thinking? Don't you dare—"

Not too roughly, Carina pushed the small woman into the hole. Nai Nai tried to stand up, but she pressed down on the woman's bony shoulder, forcing her to crouch.

"How dare you! Come inside here with me, now!"

Using her other hand, Carina lifted the door up and over her grandmother. It closed with a thump, muffling Nai Nai's protests. She quickly dragged the rug over the hatch, but it lifted as her grandmother tried to push up the heavy door. Holding the door down with one foot, Carina stretched and grabbed the scalobite enclosure, drawing it over the rug. The plastiwood box would prevent her grandmother from opening the door easily.

Before she left, however, she hesitated. Should she stay with her grandmother to protect her? But she could fight the attackers best if she wasn't hiding in the shop. She could already hear the whisper of pulse rifle rounds. Though she hated to leave Nai Nai alone, the old woman was very capable of defending herself.

She knelt on the rug and shouted at the floor. "Nai Nai, stay inside and don't make a sound. I'll be back as soon as I can. If you hear them coming, Cast, okay? I'm sorry, I have to go."

She took a bottle of elixir from a table and dropped it down the front of her shirt. Her grandmother always carried hers on a string around her neck.

As she rose to her feet, she heard a faint, *Mei Mei!*

She went into the front of the shop, her jaw set.

Outside, the screaming had begun.

———

All the customers had run away, neglecting even to take the coins lying on the counter or their bags of highly polished pebbles.

Carina went to the curtains separating the shop front from the street and opened them a slit. Outside, all was deserted. Not a soul could be seen in the dusty, dirt road, and the windows of the old, ramshackle, single-story homes were empty. Distant shouting and the sound of pulse fire echoed through the empty space.

She slipped out, but, rather than running down the street in the direction of the fighting, she turned to scale the shop's rough wall, climbing up onto its corrugated roof. Placing her feet carefully to tread only on the roof supports and avoid the flimsy covering, she stepped quickly toward the center of town. As she lightly ran over the rooftops, she retrieved the bottle of elixir from her shirt, lifted it to her lips, and pulled out the stopper with her teeth. She put the stopper in her pocket.

Her Casting skills were not yet on a par with her grandmother's, but she might be able to do the attackers some harm. However, she could not afford to be observed. If anyone from the settlement were to witness what she intended to do, both she and Nai Nai would be at great risk.

No one in the settlement knew she and her grandmother were mages. All her life, Nai Nai had warned her that their neighbors wouldn't understand or tolerate their powers. She had impressed upon Carina that if she let out their secret, she might as well have signed their death warrants. Slavery and/or torture would be the best they could expect.

Suddenly, from somewhere up ahead, came a shriek that froze Carina's heart. She scanned the streets to find the source. She spotted it: a dark, blurred shape was lifting up a woman and carrying her away. The shape of the creature blinked briefly into focus before fading to a blur again.

Hunched. Dark gray. Many-limbed.

It was a Regian.

Her guts twisted, and she thought she might vomit.

The attackers were not regular marauders. The settlement stood little chance of surviving a Regian attack. The aliens could shift in time, a little into the past and the future. It made them hard to see, and it meant they could predict their victims' next moves.

What the creatures did with their victims, no one knew, but none had ever escaped a Regian ship.

Their raids were devastating because they were difficult to hit with pulse rounds. The round had to hit at the exact moment the Regian existed in the present, or it passed through the target. From the flashes of light coming from doors and windows, it was clear the settlement's defenders were doing their best, but they were fighting a losing battle.

Did the same targeting problem apply to a Cast?

She would soon find out.

She ran on, her long legs carrying her from strut to strut where the corrugated roof panels overlapped. More Regians appeared, carrying away victims.

She mulled over which Cast to make. She wasn't confident about Transporting the creatures. They were large, there were too many of them, and they were moving fast. Besides, where would she Transport them to? No matter how far away she put them, they would only come back. Could she Lift them and let them fall?

It would be more prudent to do something she was confident would work.

Cries of pain and anger rose above the general tumult. In a nearby street, a father was in a tug of war with a Regian, each pulling on an arm of a wailing child. The alien solved its problem by letting go of the child and grabbing man *and* child, lifting the struggling humans onto its back. The pair bobbed oddly as they writhed and fought, and the alien momentarily disappeared and reappeared.

Then they were gone.

Indecision immobilized Carina. She had to do something. Anything.

She lifted her elixir canister to her lips and swallowed a mouthful, grimacing at the taste of the bitter, sour liquid. She focused on a Regian and closed her eyes. The first Cast that entered her mind was Split. It might work. It would have to do.

Exactly as her grandmother had taught her, she shut out all other thoughts, sounds, and feelings, and focused on mentally writing the Character. The strokes formed in her mind's eye. They had to be completed perfectly, each stroke performed in the correct order, each line running in the correct direction.

The character was drawn.

She sent out the Cast and opened her eyes.

The Regian she'd targeted was now forcing down the door of a house. At first, nothing seemed to happen to it. She was about to take another sip of elixir and try something else, but then, as the Regian's dark form flickered into focus again, she spotted a small tear in its carapace.

That was something, at least.

Should she move closer, or try a different Cast?

A second later, the Regian's back ripped open.

Like overripe fruit bursting, dusty matter exploded through the opening and fell to the ground around the creature's many limbs. The alien collapsed, and the weird oscillations ceased. Briefly, the creature's lines were defined, then it was gone.

The Cast had worked!

But there were many Regians, and her elixir bottle contained only ten or twelve mouthfuls. Could she Split more than one of them at once? She spied a large patch of darkness moving along a road. Altogether, the patch had to be three or four Regians.

After taking a large swallow of liquid, she closed her eyes once more. The Split Character remained fresh in her mind and was easier to draw the second time around. Her eyes flew open and she watched the dark patch.

Within a few moments, the Regians had erupted through their own backs and disappeared. She'd killed three or four at once.

She quickly checked the reactions of the people of her settlement to what she'd done. It wouldn't do her much good if her secret were discovered, but no one seemed to have noticed her up on the roof or connected her with the dying aliens. Everyone was too busy fighting for their lives.

Time for another Cast. She took a drink of elixir, but before she could close her eyes, she spotted movement in her peripheral vision. To her left, twitching antennae were rising above the roof edge. A Regian had seen her and was climbing up to capture her. It was only two paces away. She wouldn't have time to Cast before it reached her.

She ran to the creature and aimed a kick at its head, but her boot sank into nothingness. A limb flashed up and fastened around her ankle, sending a strange pulsating sensation through her leg.

She pulled away, but the 'off' timing of the creature as it moved through time was not sufficient to allow her to escape. She was dragged inexorably toward the roof edge. She overbalanced and dropped her elixir canister. Liquid spilled out as it hit the iron sheet. Throwing herself backward, she snatched up the container. Fighting the Regian's tug on her leg, she pulled the stopper out of her pocket and shoved it into the canister's neck.

Just as she managed to slip the container into her shirt, the Regian pulled her down and onto its back.

She screamed.

The creature shifted its pincer grip from her leg to her waist and also grabbed her shoulder, tipping her to a horizontal position, facing downward. It felt like knives cutting into her flesh. She had only minutes to free herself or she would be aboard the alien's ship and on her way to whatever fate awaited.

She struggled like a wild thing. Her life was important to her, but it was the thought of her grandmother trapped beneath the shop floor that made her fight her hardest.

Then it came to her. In her terror of the beast, she'd forgotten that she'd only just sipped elixir. She might still be within the limited window of time to Cast.

She ceased fighting.

To create the character in her mind, she needed calm and concentration. It would be hard to achieve the state while being carried to her probable death, but she had to try.

She closed her eyes and breathed in slowly before releasing the breath in a long, soft sigh. Stroke by stroke, the Character formed in her mind, black ink on a gently glowing background of silver, just as her grandmother had taught her.

It was complete.

She Cast.

Below her, a jagged opening formed in the Regian. She sank down. The pincers gripping her disappeared, and the dusty innards of the creature puffed around her as it broke apart. With a thud she hit the ground. What remained of the Regian's carapace crumbled while its legs jerked and twitched.

As she leapt up, the creature faded to nothingness.

She was in the town square, at the center of the attack. All around her, people were running, fleeing their hiding places as they were forced out. Pulse rounds hissed and whispered, occasionally hitting the invaders and scoring their dark shells.

She licked dust from her lips, then spotted two Regians bearing down on her. She bolted, heading for the nearest exit.

The alley was familiar, but it led away from her grandmother's shop. She had to get back to Nai Nai. The townsfolk had put up a valiant fight, and her Casts must have helped, but the Regians were winning. They were spreading out from the settlement's center and down the dirt streets leading to the poorer areas.

They were heading toward Nai Nai's's shop.

She glanced over her shoulder and saw she was no longer pursued. The Regians who had been chasing her must have diverted to slower prey. She grimaced wryly. Her long years of practice at running away from bullies had paid off at last.

Climbing onto the nearest windowsill, she grabbed the overhanging eaves. As she pulled herself up, grunting with effort, her legs swung freely until she could hook a toe on the roof edge. Another minute's struggle and she had returned to her lofty vantage point.

And found that she wasn't alone.

A boy was lying on his stomach on the corrugated metal. At first, she thought he was dead. He was lying entirely still and didn't look up as she climbed next to him. Then she noticed the rapid rise and fall of his ribs.

He was alive, but terrified.

He looked a few years older than her, and as she peered more closely, she recognized him. When she realized who it was, she was tempted to pass him by, but something—maybe the sight of a fellow human being among the chaos and slaughter—made her pause.

"Saul."

The boy's head lifted. His face was drained of color, but his terror-stricken expression faded at the sight of her. "It's *you*. I thought..."

"You thought I was a Regian climbing up to get you?"

"Yes...no." His pale cheeks flushed. He began to get to his feet, though cautiously.

"Why didn't you run?"

"I *didn't* think you were a Regian!"

She made a sound of disgust and moved to go past him. He was standing between her and the next roof, where she needed to go to get back to her grandmother.

He grabbed her. His face was red. "I said, I didn't think you were a Regian."

"Let me go! I don't care what you thought. I don't care if you're embarrassed about hiding up here." She tried to peel his fingers from around her arm.

"I *wasn't* hiding." He grabbed her other arm and drew her close to him.

She was so close, she could see the fine hairs of his pubescent mustache. She cursed to herself. Saul was the leader of one of the settlement's gangs of children. He had a reputation to uphold, and he didn't want her telling anyone about his cowardice. She regretted her unwise words. "I don't have time for this. Let go of me. I promise I won't tell anyone what you were doing, if anyone's still alive after this."

His grip tightened. He drew her so close she could feel his breath, warm and moist on her face. "What do you mean? What was I doing? What wouldn't I want you to tell anyone?"

Her patience was at an end. Unlike in previous encounters with Saul, he didn't have his cronies to back him up in a fight.

She headbutted him. Her forehead hit the bridge of his nose square on, and the cartilage crumpled satisfyingly.

He shrieked in pain and released her to grab his nose, which was leaking streams of blood. "You black-eyed bitch!" He made another grab for her, but she was already past him and leaping the gap between two roofs. As she landed she staggered and slipped, but she was quickly on her feet again and running toward the next gap.

A thump from behind told her that Saul hadn't given up on his revenge. The settlement brat was hard on her tail.

As if she didn't have enough on her plate.

She sped across the rooftops, but she had no time to take her bearings. She thought she was heading toward her grandmother's shop, but she wasn't sure. The sun and their sister planet were nearly overhead, so it was hard for her to get a sense of direction, and though she'd completed her share of rooftop journeys, this part of the settlement was unfamiliar.

Saul was matching her speed, remaining a steady distance of roughly a rooftop away. She was struggling to maintain her pace. Her chest ached and her breathing was deep and rapid. She wanted to shout at him to leave her alone, that they both had more serious problems right now, but she couldn't spare the breath.

Where *was* Nai Nai's shop?

Finally, she saw a landmark she recognized: the decorated gables of the town exchange, where farmers sold their produce to offworld traders. She paused. She'd come too far east, but if she turned at a right angle, she would hit the market within a couple of minutes, then it was a straight, unbroken route back to Nai Nai.

The moment she took to calculate her new route gave Saul the time he needed to catch up. He must have guessed her plan, for he ran to block her intended path.

"Get out of my way," she said between gasps, her chest heaving.

In answer, he spread his arms wide and beckoned with his fingertips. He grinned, cracking the dried blood that had run from his grotesquely swollen nose.

It was no good. She would have to get past him somehow, even if it meant pushing him off the roof. She lowered her shoulder and prepared to take a run at him, but a dark blur rose above the roof edge behind him.

"Saul!" she yelled. "Watch out!"

His grin spread wider, as if he thought she was bluffing, but something in her face must have told him that wasn't the case. He looked behind him. Simultaneously, the Regian fastened a claw around his ankle and jerked him off his feet. He fell forward and was dragged away. He grasped uselessly at the corrugated ridges of the roof.

She leapt to him and snatched at his wrists.

She had him.

She resisted the tug of the Regian, and Saul hung between them.

If only she could take a sip of elixir, she could Cast, but to do that she would have to let go of Saul.

As his terror returned, he suddenly looked much younger than his years. He was inching away from her, and there was nothing she could do about it. He was crying and squirming in her grasp.

"Kick it," she said.

"I can't. It's holding me too tight."

"Pull up your knee. Climb back up here."

Tears flooded his eyes and he shook his head. "I can't. I'm dead. Let go of me. Run! Save yourself."

"No!" She pulled harder, but his skin was slippery with sweat.

He slid closer to the roof edge. Only his shoulders, head, and arms remained visible.

"Let go," he sobbed. "It's too late."

"No." Tears dripped from her chin.

One of Saul's arms slipped from her grasp. She gripped his other arm with two hands, but a tug from the Regian below broke him free.

"Don't tell them I hid, okay?" He disappeared.

She ran forward and looked down. A blurred Regian was carrying Saul away. She drew her canister from her shirt and took a sip of elixir before closing her eyes to make the Cast.

The strokes began to form, but before the Character was complete, they faded. She couldn't stop weeping.

Swallowing her tears, she tried again.

And failed once more.

She opened her eyes.

Saul and the Regian were gone.

Her sobbing broke out afresh. Saul had bullied her on more than one occasion, but he was just a kid. He didn't deserve to die. None of her neighbors did. Why were the Regians attacking them?

She had to get back to her grandmother.

She leapt the large gap between the roofs and teetered on the brink on the other side. Then she was running again. As she sped across the settlement, she saw more and more of the Regians had made their way to its outer reaches. They were searching the houses, sometimes going in the doors, sometimes crawling through the windows.

Hidden children and babies were being found and carried off.

The aliens seemed determined to clear the place of all humans.

———

When she reached the shop, she caught a glimpse of dark blur disappearing through the curtained entrance. "Nai Nai!"

She bounded from the roof down to the dusty street, rolling

onto her back to soften the impact. Before she even fully regained her feet she was speeding toward the entrance, heedless of everything but her destination.

How much time had passed since her last swallow of elixir? It had been so long, the effect must have dissipated. She pulled out the stopper from the canister and, in her haste, accidentally dropped it. She tipped up the too-light container. Only one small mouthful remained. Would it be enough?

She burst into the shop. The front section was a jumbled mess. The Regian had overturned the desk and cabinets full of stones. Sliding on the smooth, shiny pebbles, she fell hard on her behind. The shock jolted the breath from her lungs.

"Nai Nai," she wheezed.

A rustling sound was coming from the back room. She needed to see the Regian for the Cast to work, but if she went in there, it would see her and catch her. She also had very little elixir left. If the Cast didn't work, she wouldn't get a second chance. But if she didn't go in, the alien would find Nai Nai.

She thrust aside the inner curtain. The scalobite enclosure was overturned, the rug lay beneath the opened trapdoor, and her grandmother was staring in terror at the alien towering over her, nearly filling the tiny room.

As Carina watched, it reached in and lifted up Nai Nai's tiny, frail form.

The old woman had seen her. "Leave me, Mei, Mei. Run!"

Carina drank the last of her elixir and squeezed her eyes shut. She would make the Cast. She had to. She wouldn't fail Nai Nai like she'd failed Saul. She would rather die.

"Please, child, go." Her grandmother's words broke her concentration. "My life is nearly over. Forget me. Your father's spirit wants you to live."

Carina felt the looming presence of the Regian. It was coming for her, too.

One stroke of the character formed in her mind.

A hard, articulated limb fastened around her waist.

Another stroke formed.

She was lifted from her feet.

The third stroke appeared.

Her grandmother was crying, a soft, reedy lament.

The fourth and final stroke cut through the rest.

She Cast.

She dared not open her eyes. She couldn't face her grandmother's look of reproach. She hadn't done as she was told.

There was a thud and a cry of pain. Her eyes jolted open. She was in the front of the shop, and she was falling. She hit the floor and scattered stones.

The Regian had faded and died, but Nai Nai was hurt.

Carina crawled over to her grandparent. The old woman's head had struck the counter top when the alien released her. Blood oozed alarmingly from the wound, and her grandmother seemed dazed. Carina wrapped her arms around her thin shoulders and lifted the small woman onto her lap. She took a corner of her shirt and pressed it against the cut, trying to stem the flow of blood. "Nai Nai, I'm so sorry. I'm sorry I disobeyed you. I shouldn't have left you."

The old woman's small, delicate hand sought out Carina's and patted it soothingly. "No, you were right. You killed the Regian. Your mage powers have grown strong. You did the right thing in trying to protect everyone."

She shook her head. "I tried, but it wasn't enough. There are too many of them. I can't kill them all. I have to get you away from here." She was fearful of moving the old woman in her injured state, but their only chance was to try to escape into the wilderness.

"Maybe we don't have to run," Nai Nai said weakly. "Maybe you can save the others."

"How? I have to see the aliens to kill them. It's too hard, and I don't have time. I'll carry you away. I won't ever leave you again, I promise."

"You don't have to see them, not if you're strong enough. I think you can do it, Mei Mei. Take my elixir. Drink it all. When you form the Character, send your mind out. Imagine the settlement. Imagine as many Regians as you can. Don't be afraid. Find your power and unleash it."

Carina blinked away the tears obscuring her sight. The old woman's gaze was steady and full of confidence.

Maybe she really could do it.

She took Nai Nai's canister and downed the elixir in one go. It made her gag, and she struggled to not vomit up the disgusting liquid.

With a final glance at her grandmother's expression, willing her to succeed, she closed her eyes. She drew the Character. She thought of Nai Nai and what the Regians had done. She thought of Saul, and the woman, man, and child she had seen carried away.

A rage arose in her, and with it came a new source of power. Her heart thumped and her breathing sped up. Her anger threatened to consume her, but she didn't allow it. She took hold of her hatred and directed it outward, imagining the settlement and the Regians.

She let her Cast fly, her fury bearing it along.

It was gone.

She collapsed.

When she returned to consciousness, she was lying on top of her grandmother. She lifted herself up, horrified that she had hurt the old woman.

Nai Nai smiled at her faintly. "I think you did it. You killed enough of them to make them leave. Listen."

No more screams or shouts were coming from outside. The hisses of pulse rounds had ceased. The settlement was quiet.

A sudden sense of alarm seized her. Had she hurt her neighbors as well as the Regians? But then she heard voices in their street, calling the names of missing relatives and friends.

"I think maybe I did," she said wonderingly.

"You did a great thing. You killed the Regians and saved us, though no one will ever know. Now, I have a little more to teach you before I d—"

"No!"

"Yes. I am old, Mei Mei. I have done my best, but you must learn to live without me. I am content. You are strong now. You will survive."

"No, Nai Nai," she whispered. She didn't feel strong. She felt young and helpless. She didn't want to be alone, and she couldn't imagine life without her grandmother.

"Don't worry, child. I'm not dying just yet. At least, I don't think so. Help me up. Let's fix this cut, then you can tidy up the shop."

Carina rubbed her sleeve across her face, and then helped her grandmother to her feet.

Escaped scalobites were crawling up the old woman's pants. She brushed them off. The insects had to be all over the shop and probably in the kruekins' station too. It was a shame she hadn't been able to save her pets, but she had more important concerns now.

CARINA'S STORY CONTINUES IN ...

STAR MAGE SAGA

STARBOUND

THE BOOKS OF
SHADOWS OF THE VOID

ONE

Jas Harrington gripped the handlebars of her snow mobile and pressed the throttle. The machine pulled away beneath her, sending up sprays of powder snow on either side. She grinned.

It had snowed the day before. The first snow that year, though winter was almost over. Maybe the last snowfall at low altitude on Earth forever, some said. Over the last few decades, Antarctica had changed almost beyond recognition as raised global temperatures melted its massive ice sheets, calving icebergs as large as countries to melt into the ocean.

At that moment, Jas didn't care what humans had done to their home planet. She didn't feel as though Earth was *her* home anyway. She'd grown up on Mars until she was twelve and already weak-boned from the low gravity. When the paperwork came through from the Martian colonial government, she left the home for cared-for children and traveled to the mother planet to complete her adolescence at a second institution.

After months of aching muscles and headaches, her body had finally adjusted, but the policy of separating the Martian children for better 'integration' meant she'd been lonely. No one had told the Earth children they were supposed to let the newcomers integrate.

Sergei was riding his snowmobile parallel to hers as she powered over the ice, the roar of the engines making speaking impossible. A fellow student from the training college, his black hair streamed out from beneath his hat. Like hers, his eyes were hidden behind dark snow goggles. He waved at her and pointed in the direction they were heading. They had to be nearly at their destination, though she couldn't make it out against the snowy white landscape and bright clouds.

She nodded in reply, and her heart surged. She didn't think she'd ever been this happy.

They were almost upon the igloo before she saw it. A crude lump of slightly dirty white became visible in the landscape. Sergei was already slowing down, and Jas did the same.

As they stopped and she stepped down from her vehicle, she smiled. The igloo was very clumsily put together, as if the builders had been drunk. Roughly cut blocks of ice balanced precariously upon one another, creating a haphazard wall. It looked like it would have fallen down if not for the freezing temperatures holding it together.

"This is it?"

Sergei was taking off his goggles. "How many other igloos do you think there are around here?"

She pulled off her hat and gloves. "But I thought you said it took you and Aaron two whole days to build it?"

"More than two days, if you include cutting the blocks." He removed his gloves. "Do I detect a tone of disbelief? I get it. It's hard to credit that we could construct such a magnificent edifice in such a short time."

"You're right." She tilted her head to take in the detail. "I...can't quite believe it." She couldn't hold in her laughter any longer. She burst into giggles and found she couldn't stop. She bent over, nursing her aching stomach. Pulling off her goggles to wipe her eyes, she finally began to catch her breath. "So *this* is what you meant by your Love Palace?"

Sergei frowned. "You dare to insult my Mansion of Delight? Be careful. You're treading on dangerous ground. I might have to remind you of something pretty important, now that we're out here in the snowy wastes, far from civilization and..." he went to the compartment of his snowmobile, reached inside, and pulled out a small battery-powered heater. "...warmth."

It was unusually cold today, even for Antarctica. Her tears of mirth were already freezing on her cheeks. An icy wind had penetrated her snowsuit as they'd driven over, and she was chilled through. "Oh, come on. I was only kidding. It's a beautiful igloo. You and Aaron have some real talent. Let's go inside and warm the place up."

Sergei slowly shook his head. "I don't think so. I think I'll just go in by myself and get toasty, seeing as my Chateau of Sensation isn't good enough for your refined tastes. You can head on back to your dorm and cuddle up with your roomie instead. Maybe she's more your type." He winked at her.

"Don't be an idiot. Your Love Palace looks great. It really does. I don't know what I was thinking. I can hardly believe it only took you forty-eight hours to put it together. It would have taken me at least...I don't know..." She cast her gaze over the comical building.

Sergei's fake frown began to disappear at her apparent effort at reconciliation, and he raised the heater to hand it over.

She concluded her sentence. "Forty-eight minutes."

He snatched the heater back. She made a lunge for the appliance, but Sergei sidestepped her, and she slipped and stumbled.

Laughing, he ran to the other side of his snowmobile and dangled the heater invitingly. She scrambled to her feet, slipping again twice, and reached across the vehicle. He turned and sped away. She followed, and soon she was right behind him, her long legs carrying her quickly closer. He wasn't running fast, as if he wanted her to catch him. When she was almost there, he skidded and tumbled down. She tripped over him.

The heater skittered across the ground, coming to rest a few meters away. Laughing, they crawled after it, grabbing at each other to slow the other down. Their breath plumed in the frigid air. Both were gasping as they fought to be the first to reach the heater. Jas lunged, and her fingertips brushed the appliance's edge where it lay upside down.

Sergei grasped her waist and dragged her backward, pulling her underneath him on the slippery surface. He tried to climb over her, but she turned on to her back and pulled him down. As they came face to face, they stopped struggling and their chuckles faded. Their warm, condensing breath intermingled.

Sergei's intense blue eyes were very close. She felt herself disappearing into them. His muscles relaxed under her hands as they gazed at each other.

"That's *my* heater," she said softly.

"No, it isn't," he murmured. He leaned down to kiss her.

A few moments later, she wasn't cold any longer. The snow behind her head was melting and soaking her scalp in icy water, but she hardly noticed.

He drew away. "Shall we go inside?"

She reached up and pulled his head down to hers. "In a minute."

For many years, she remembered that day as the happiest of her life.

Two

Four months earlier, Jas had arrived at the McMurdo Sound Training Institute fresh from her Earth children's home. The journey had been long—the meager amount of money she'd received when, at eighteen, she'd 'graduated' her care program hadn't stretched to a shuttle flight to the southern continent. She'd had to travel by old-fashioned airplane, and by the time she'd arrived she was exhausted.

When the autobus drew to a stop outside the two-story college, she was dozing. She only caught a glimpse of the prefab buildings before the bus pulled up. She disembarked, yawning, with the rest of the new students and collected her luggage from the compartment under the bus. Passing through opaque plexiglass doors, she went into the lobby.

The college wasn't much warmer inside than outside. She rubbed her arms as she stood in line waiting to register. The place was poorly lit and dank. It looked as though it hadn't been refurbished in the last thirty years, much like the areas of McMurdo Sound they'd passed through on the bus ride.

She was already regretting her decision to do the security training course, or at least her choice to do it at this remote location. She couldn't remember why she'd picked this college at the end of the world. The thought that she'd be spending the next three years here made her heart sink.

The line shuffled forward and she went along with it. The other students had their heads down, too tired or disinterested to begin making friends just now. Her nose was beginning to drip. She fished in a pocket for a tissue.

Her hand brushed a circle of plastic, and she pulled out the familiar object. It was a picdisc displaying rotating images of the friends she'd left behind when she came to Earth. Like her, the children were olive-skinned and their hair and eyes were reddish-brown. The coloring was common to all Martians—the gene therapy colonists received to help them survive the radiation altered skin and hair pigmentation, and the effects were passed on to their offspring.

A feeling of nostalgia hit, and she remembered what it had been about Antarctica that had appealed. She'd thought its climate and remoteness might be something like Mars, and she'd been right. Gnawing cold, low sunlight, and what seemed to be a grinding, survival nature to everyday life, did make the place like another planet. Antarctica already reminded her of her early childhood in the nearest thing she had to a home.

The line moved forward. Why hadn't they automated the registration process? Did they want to see each student face to face? Others in the line were giving her glances. As always, her height and tell-tale skin and hair color betrayed her origins, attracting curiosity. The attention bothered her, though she'd grown somewhat used to it over the last six years. At least it prevented the necessity of answering questions about where she was from. Such questions always led to the awkward revelation that, as a young baby, she'd been the sole survivor of an infamous colony disaster.

The fact was a conversation killer, and as she had no memory of the incident and didn't even like to think about it, the information was something she preferred to keep quiet.

Another new student was staring at her. The girl's curly brown locks bulged out from under a thick hat she still wore even though they were now inside. She smiled at Jas, and deep dimples appeared on her round cheeks.

Bemused by the girl's friendliness, Jas smiled back, a little half-heartedly.

The girl pointed at the line and rolled her eyes.

Jas wondered if she was making an embarrassing mistake, and that the girl was actually looking at someone behind her. She glanced over her shoulder, but everyone else was engrossed in hand held interfaces, reading, texting, or playing games. She was definitely the object of the strange girl's attention. Hesitantly, she smiled again.

A gap opened up in front of her new acquaintance. Jas gestured at it, and the girl turned and moved up. She was almost at the desk, where three administrators sat. In another moment she was in front of one and giving her details.

Jas took a final look at her old Martian friends before returning the picdisc to her pocket. She pushed her wheeled luggage forward with her toe as the line moved again.

———

Jas's roommate was a long-haired, quiet girl called Aggy. When they met after registration, they said hello and put their things away. Aggy gave monosyllabic responses to Jas's efforts to be friendly. At dinner, she separately and read her interface. Jas contented herself with filling her cold, empty stomach.

Classes started the following day. Combat training, fitness drills, weapons instruction and discipline, target practice, and survival training were compulsory. Battle tactics and leadership skills were options intended for students who wanted to make security a life-long career, rather than use it as a cheap stepping stone to becoming a new world colonist. Working security aboard a colony starship was one way to avoid paying the fare, which cost many their life savings and more.

Other options included extraterrestrial life forms and zero and high gravity combat. Jas was taking all these and the career options.

Though she wasn't eager to lead, she knew she would be bored if base-level security work turned out to be repetitive and undemanding.

After the first day, she flopped into an armchair in the shared living room of her dorm, physically tired but not exhausted. Though the training had been challenging, she'd exercised regularly for as long as she could remember—a mandatory aspect of Martian life to help alleviate the effects of low gravity—and her height gave her an advantage in hand-to-hand combat that made things easier.

She had half an hour to kill before dinner, and she wasn't sure what to do. She didn't want to go to the room she shared with Aggy. Her roommate was in a long-distance relationship, and maintaining it took up every spare moment she had. Whenever Jas saw her, she was having intense conversations with her far-away boyfriend, and at Jas's appearance she would drop her voice to a whisper, sometimes harsh, sometimes loving.

A door to another bedroom opened, and the girl who had stared at Jas in the registration line came in. She'd finally taken off her hat. A near-Afro of brown curls framed her head. Her dimples reappeared. "Hey, are you in room 239?"

"Yeah, that's right."

"I was wondering if it was empty. I didn't see you or your roomie at the dorm get-together last night."

"I didn't know there was one."

"Really? I put a note under everyone's door."

Had Aggy picked up the note and not told her about it? "I didn't see it."

"And you didn't hear us?"

"I'd had a long flight, and I sleep pretty sound."

The girl held out her hand. "Tamara."

"Jas."

They shook, and Tamara sat down. "Sorry for staring at you in the line. It was a little rude of me. I was interested to see a Martian in real life."

"That's okay," Jas replied, tensing as she prepared for the inevitable personal questions.

But Tamara went on, "I'm studying colonial adaptation biology. You know, adaptive gene therapies and physiological and metabolic responses to extraterrestrial environments." Jas must have looked wary because she laughed and added, "Don't worry, I won't treat you like a test subject. I was just interested to meet you, that's all."

Jas relaxed a little. "I'm doing security training."

"Deep space program?"

"That's right."

"Extraterrestrials?"

"Yeah."

"Sweet. I'll wanna hear all about it. Hey, have you eaten yet?"

"No, it's too early." Jas winced a little as her words gave away that she had to eat in the cafeteria, revealing she was a scholarship student.

"It's never too early for my chili and rice. It's a secret family recipe. I invited some of the other girls, and you're welcome too."

"Thanks, I'd love to."

"How about your roomie?"

"I think she might have other plans."

THREE

Jas's opponent hit the mat with a thump, his eyes wide. He lay there in shock, his exceptionally hairy arms and legs splayed out. At nearly the same height as her and a minimum of fifteen kilos heavier, he'd taken his victory in their sparring for granted. Over-confidence was a mistake only inexperienced fighters made. Her years of practice fighting bullies at her Earth children's home meant she was far from inexperienced.

After a month of hand-to-hand combat training, she had sparred with all of her classmates, and the result had been the same every time. Each of them ended up on the mat at her feet. After she'd worked her way through half the class, some didn't even try to fight. They threw half-hearted punches and slow kicks, as if only passing time while waiting for the inevitable conclusion.

"Get up," their instructor shouted at the defeated student. The young man got to his feet, but the instructor's eyes were on Jas. His name was Trankle, and he looked annoyed, though she had no idea why.

From his attitude and demeanor, it was obvious that Trankle was ex-military. He was bull-necked and strong-jawed, and his stance was awkward due to over-large muscles in his arms and legs. She had attracted more and more of the man's attention as the class went on.

She guessed it was something to do with her beating everyone, but what was she supposed to do? Lose so that the others could feel good?

A movement to her side caught her eye, and she raised her arm just in time to parry a blow from her defeated opponent. Her forearm smashed into his, and the blow went wide, just missing the side of her head. Instead of leaving the mat, he'd tried to sucker punch her, only he hadn't gotten quite out of her range of vision.

Years of play yard fights and sneaky attacks from bullies had honed her reactions to muscle reflexes. Without thinking, she swung round with a fist, hitting the student square on the side of his face. His head snapped around, and he staggered backward, dazed.

"Hey," Trankle shouted. In a couple of strides, he was at her side and wrenching her arm behind her back, almost lifting her from her feet. She gasped in pain and tried to twist free.

"Aww, come on, man," said a student. "He deserved it." Others mumbled vague protests, while some looked quietly pleased.

She was sorely tempted to fight back, but not only did she think she wasn't a match for the heavily muscled, highly trained brute, she didn't want to get kicked out of the class. Attacking a member of staff had to be an expelling offense, no matter the provocation. The instructor forced her across the room, the bristle of his chin against her neck.

"Think you can take everyone?" he breathed in her ear. "Kratting Martian scum. Should have stayed where you belong on your filthy colony planet."

He twisted her arm so hard, she cried out. It felt like he was going to rip it from its socket. Once they were at the side of the room, where the other students sat to watch the sparring, he relaxed his hold and pushed her down.

There was no space for her. The students shuffled to get out of the way but they weren't fast enough. The whole thing had taken only a couple of seconds. She landed on them, to many exclamations and protests. It was a few moments before everyone could move along and settle into new positions. A couple of friendly students patted her back while Trankle returned to the mat.

Her shoulder hurt badly, and the instructor had humiliated her in front of the rest of the class. She'd done nothing except try her hardest. Wasn't that what they were supposed to do? Tears pricked her eyes and she blinked them away, determined not to let her hurt show.

The hairy student who'd tried to punch her sauntered by on his way back to his spot in the audience. He looked down his nose with a sneer on his face, but she noticed with satisfaction that his eye was already turning purple. He would have a shiner by tomorrow that he'd have to explain somehow. She smiled grimly.

———

Tamara was sympathetic. She'd made her chili and rice again. Jas couldn't get enough of it, especially after a long day's training and studying. Tamara loved to cook. She said it relaxed her. She'd gotten into the habit of cooking nearly every day for both of them, diplomatically avoiding all Jas's protests without drawing attention to her lack of creds.

Spooning a heap of chili from a pan onto the rice in Jas's bowl, Tamara said, "What a misborn. I can't believe it. Didn't any of the other students say anything? Are you going to report him?"

"A few of the others stood up for me, but not so loud that he had to take notice." Jas picked up her fork and dug into her meal. She chewed and swallowed a mouthful, then added, shaking her head, "I'm not going to say anything. He didn't leave a mark on me, and neither did that asshole who tried to punch me. It'd be hard to prove I didn't start it."

When Tamara opened her mouth to interrupt, Jas went on, "Believe me, I saw enough of this kind of thing at the children's home. Sure, some of the others might stick up for me and tell the truth about what happened, but some won't. Some'll lie because getting beat by a girl hurt their pride. And who's most likely to be believed? A low-income scholarship student or a faculty member?"

She shrugged. "I don't want to make trouble. I only get one shot at free college. If they throw me out, I won't get another scholarship. I'd have to take out a loan and start over somewhere else next year. I don't know what I'd do for creds between now and then. I'm okay. Don't worry. When you grow up like I did, you get used to this kind of thing."

Tamara pulled out a chair and sat down to eat. "It doesn't seem right to let him get away with it."

"He didn't hurt me that much." Jas sighed. "I don't know why he hates Martians, but he does, and he isn't the first bigot I've met. I don't know why some people hate us. Looking different's a crime to them, I guess. I'll do what I've always done—keep my head down. I'll lose a few fights. That'll take his attention off me."

Tamara tutted and dumped a generous dollop of sour cream onto her food. "Hey, how about we have a party to cheer you up? We can invite some people from the other dorms. From the men's dorms." She raised her eyebrows and grinned.

"Oh, I don't know. It's been kind of a long day."

The truth was, she wasn't good at parties. It wasn't that she didn't like to make friends, but at parties she always got the feeling that everyone else was following rules she didn't understand. The idea of inviting guys over also didn't appeal. Her few forays into the world of romantic relationships—furtive behind the backs of the carers at the children's home—had been awkward and embarrassing. She wasn't good at flirting or anything like that.

"Come on. It'll be fun," Tamara said. "Don't you want to get to know some more people? Or do you want to be a hermit like Aggy? By the way, I heard her arguing with her boyfriend before you came back. Real humdinger it was. Loud enough that I could hear what she was saying through the door. Are you sure you want to spend the evening eavesdropping on her relationship problems?"

Jas groaned and put down her fork. She knew more about Aggy's relationship than she or her boyfriend did. The couple had two settings: blissfully in love or hating each other's guts, and nothing in between. She'd rather fight Hairy-ass again than listen to another episode of the drama that was Aggy's love life. It was also Friday evening and she had no reason to get up early. "Okay, a party it is."

"Sweet. Let me call some people." Tamara took out her interface and began swiping it with her fingertips while simultaneously forking chili and rice into her mouth with her other hand.

In the space of a month, Tamara seemed to have gotten to know everyone in college. She was constantly receiving messages and disappearing for social engagements. Jas didn't know how she fit it all in along with her studies. Her friend was one of those 'hub' people, effortlessly making connections left, right, and center. She hailed from what remained of New Orleans. Jas had wondered if her skills were due to the necessity of making good friends quickly when faced with repeated natural disasters.

Tamara looked up from her screen, her curls bobbing. "All done. People will start arriving about nine. Do you want to give me a hand cleaning the place up? I've ordered drinks and snacks. They should get here in half an hour."

"Sure." Would she navigate this party better than all the others? She got up and took the dishes to the compactor. It was nearly full, so she set it to crush and sent the waste down the chute.

She started tidying the kitchen and putting away Tamara's ingredients packets. In truth, there was little to do. Knowing well the habits of college students, the administration had installed sanobots, which cleaned up the dirt and the debris of everyday life. Jas wasn't sure how they worked, and it had taken her a while to get used to the idea of machines too small to see constantly crawling over every inanimate object in the place. At the children's home, the children had done the cleaning the old-fashioned way.

A loud ping-ping-ping sounded from outside the window. A light was shining in from the midwinter Antarctic darkness. It was the time of year when the sun was little more than a brief glow at the horizon.

Tamara's order had arrived. Jas opened the window and took the boxes from the sling on the underside of the drone, shivering in the downdraft from the spinning rotors. As soon as it was empty, the drone sped away into the night, its solitary light quickly lost among the many of McMurdo Sound. She put down the boxes and quickly shut the window.

Tamara appeared from her room. She'd changed and tamed her curls into cascading waves. She spotted the boxes at Jas's feet. "Thanks. I'll start setting things out. You go get ready."

"It's okay. I'm not getting changed. I'll help you."

"It's a party, Jas. Don't you want to put a dress on or something?"

"I don't have a dress, and anyway, I'm more comfortable in pants."

"You can't wear the clothes you've been wearing all day. You *must* have something else you can put on. Go and find something." Tamara pointed at the door.

Jas held up her hands. "Okay, okay."

Inside her room, Aggy was fast asleep, her face streaked with tears. Her most recent fight with her boyfriend had left its mark. Jas didn't doubt that tomorrow Aggy would be back to loudly whispered professions of deepest love.

She went to her closet and took out her only remotely fashionable outfit. As she was changing, the sound of voices alerted her to the fact that guests had begun to arrive. She went to the door and rested her hand on the door knob, hesitating. Maybe now that Aggy was asleep she could have a quiet night in? But if she didn't go to the party, Tamara would notice and come get her. She opened the door.

FOUR

The party had been going for a couple of hours, and things were really warming up. People were drinking and the dancing had started. Jas noticed pills changing hands with little effort at subterfuge. The drugs were certainly hyping up the atmosphere. Illegal drug abuse carried the threat of expulsion, but Jas wasn't much interested anyway. She yawned. She'd chatted with a few people, but she was feeling a little bored and tired.

The music had woken up Aggy about half an hour ago, and she'd appeared from the shared room looking irate and haggard, but her complaints had been ignored. When she gave up, she'd signaled her disapproval by slamming the door.

Tamara was passing through the throng with a plate of snacks. She spotted Jas in the corner and headed over. Dancers' hands reached in to grab the snacks. She had a few left by the time she reached Jas. "Can I interest you in some peanut cheese flakes?"

Jas looked down at the palm-sized crackers. Peanuts and cheese? Was that a Southern thing? "No, thanks. Actually, I'm kinda tired. I might—"

"Aw, you're going to bed so soon? I guessed you might not be enjoying yourself. I thought a party would cheer you up."

"I know, and I appreciate it. I'm just not a—"

A couple had arrived late. Another guest opened the door to the man and woman. The man was tall with shoulder-length black hair, and the woman he had linked arms with was slim with ashy brown hair cut above her ears. Jas had paused in her conversation with Tamara because something seemed familiar about the man. She peered at him, trying to pin down where it was she'd seen him before.

He was scanning the room while his girlfriend talked to the student who had opened the door. He was idly watching the dancing and chatting party-goers. His gaze found Jas. Their eyes met, and deep inside her, something clicked. The man looked startled.

Even at the distance across the room, Jas saw that his eyes were a deep, rare blue. But it wasn't the color of his eyes that affected her. The sense of recognition she felt was profound. She was also sure that, in fact, she'd never seen him before.

"Jas?" Tamara asked. "Are you okay?"

Jas looked at her friend wordlessly. Tamara turned to find out what she'd been looking at. By then, the blue-eyed man's girlfriend had noticed his preoccupation and was questioning him. She looked annoyed.

"Oh, Sergei and Bree have arrived," said Tamara. "Do you know them?"

"I don't think so."

"I'll introduce you. Let's go over."

Panic fluttered in her stomach. "No, it's fine. I think I'll just—"

"It'll only take a minute. You never know, you might have something in common. Come on. I want you to enjoy yourself." Tamara took her hand and pulled her toward the couple, weaving through the dancers.

Sergei's eyes flicked to her again and again as Tamara led her over, though his head was facing his girlfriend.

"Sergei arrived late. He only started college a couple of weeks ago," Tamara shouted as they passed a speaker thumping out bass notes. "He transferred from another college. Someone was saying he *had* to transfer, like it was either that or drop out. Bree didn't waste any time snagging him, and they seem pretty good together. I'm surprised you haven't met him. I thought he was studying security too."

Her heart was racing. She also felt sick, but it was a pleasant kind of sickness. She'd never felt that way before. She hoped she would make it through the impending encounter without embarrassing herself.

She and Tamara arrived at the doorway where the couple were still standing. Students were now crushed into the room and it wasn't easy to move. Bree's attention had been diverted by twins in identical party dresses. Sergei was smiling, ready to greet them. Once more, he and Jas locked eyes. She was light-headed.

"Sergei, this is..." Tamara paused as she noticed the look passing between them. "Oh my."

Bree noticed Jas and Tamara and extracted herself from her conversation with the twins. Her hand was still on her boyfriend's arm. She frowned and gave him a little shake, breaking his distraction. "Hi, Tamara. Good to see you again," she said between her teeth.

"Hi Bree," Tamara replied, a little ruefully. "This is Jas. I don't know if you've met."

Sergei held out his hand, and Jas took it. His skin was warm and dry and a little hard, as if he did some kind of manual work. "Hi."

"Hi," Jas replied, feeling like she was greeting an old friend she hadn't seen in a long while.

The five of them started up a conversation about college stuff. It turned out that Sergei was also studying security, but he was taking the domestic option, focusing on anti-theft, including cyber security. She was surprised. It was mainly desk work, with maybe some high-level guard duty thrown in. His hands had told her he was physically active.

Bree was a language specialist studying extraterrestrial communication methods. She hadn't been slow to cotton on to the fact that something was going on between her boyfriend and the tall Martian. Her clear annoyance caused the conversation to sputter to a close, and after an awkward pause, Tamara and Jas withdrew.

They sat down on a sofa behind dancers occupying the middle of the room. Jas drew in her long legs to avoid tripping them, while Tamara curled up next to her, tucking her legs beneath herself. She leaned toward Jas's ear to be heard above the music. "What was *that* about?"

"What?" Jas irritated even herself with her disingenuous reply.

Sergei and Bree were passing through the dancers on their way to the side table holding snacks and drinks. Every time Sergei's eyes flicked toward her, Jas registered the look inside, like a gong chiming or cymbals clashing.

"Don't play the innocent," Tamara said. " You know what I mean. You and Sergei. I've never seen a look like that before. I didn't believe it ever really happened."

"What do you mean?" Jas tore her eyes from the black-haired figure looking back at her.

Tamara tutted. "I'm not going to spell it out for you. But are you glad we threw this party now or what?"

"I guess so." Jas smiled sheepishly, though she didn't know what she felt so happy about. Sergei was already with someone, and she hardly had time for her studies, let alone a relationship. What was more, she was planning on flying off to the stars as soon as she graduated. And yet... She glanced up and saw a pair of blue eyes.

Gong. Clash.

She'd never known anything like this either.

Five

Jas didn't see Sergei for a few days. She spent the weekend witnessing the breakdown of Aggy's long-distance relationship. Her roommate was alternately furious and pleading with her absent boyfriend. Though the woman was irritating as hell, Jas couldn't help but feel sorry for her as her plans for the future slowly unraveled.

Jas avoided their shared room as much as possible by studying in the library and going for long walks around town. By Sunday evening, Aggy's many long vidmail conversations finally came to an end, and Jas returned from a walk to find her lying silently on her bed, staring at the blank screen of her interface. "It's over."

Jas wasn't sure of the best thing to say or do. She tried to offer some words of friendship and comfort. When that didn't work, she attempted to distract Aggy from her misery by suggesting they do something together. This offer was met with a scornful glance. Aggy cradled her silent interface in her arms like it was a sick baby and turned onto her side, presenting Jas with her back.

By the time Jas returned from class on Monday evening, Aggy had gone, for good. Her side of the closet and her desk and shelves were empty. The mattress on her bed was bare. If it hadn't been for her interface in the middle of the floor, its screen shattered, she might never have been here.

Jas sighed with relief and threw herself on her bed. She put her arm over her eyes. With luck, it would be too late in the semester for the administration to assign another student to the room, and she would have it to herself. She would look forward to being alone each morning and night.

There was a tap at the door. Her heart sank. Had Aggy returned? But she had never bothered to knock. Jas called out for her visitor to come in. A black-haired head with blue eyes appeared around the door edge.

Clash. Gong.

"Hi," Jas tried to say, but her throat had suddenly turned dry. She sat up.

Sergei smiled at her croak. She swallowed and tried to look nonchalant.

"I was passing, and I wanted to say hello. Tamara said you'd just gotten back."

"Oh, yeah, that's right."

"It...er...it turns out we're classmates for a few classes. I just found out you're studying security too. You have a leadership skills class in the morning?"

He'd been asking around about her? "I do. You're taking that class too?"

"Yeah."

"What's it like? I started late this semester after I transferred from another college. I had to take whatever spare places they had."

"I know. It's good. I mean, the leadership option is good."

Sergei smiled again. "Great. I'll see you tomorrow then." He turned to leave.

"How's..." She had only one thing on her mind, but she didn't want to say it. She knew how it would look. But she couldn't help herself. "How's Bree?"

There was that smile again—a knowing smile. Sergei was a little cocky. "Oh, we split up. It wasn't really working out."

"I'm sorry."

Sergei's eyebrows lifted. *No, you aren't.*

No, I'm not.

They both laughed a little.

"I'll see you tomorrow," Jas said.

As he closed the door, she lay down and covered her eyes with her arm again. Beneath it, her mouth was curved into a grin.

———

Sergei sat behind her in the leadership class the next day, which Jas found deeply distracting. She constantly wanted to turn around to look at him, and she felt his gaze on her back like a spot of warm syrup, sweet and tempting. Whenever she did turn around, he was always watching. He would wink at her.

In spite of her pleasant diversion, she tried her best to concentrate. In an unpredictable world, her studies had always been the one steady rock she could cling to. She wasn't a natural student—excessive energy made sitting still and paying attention hard—but her grades were above average, and she planned on keeping them that way.

"In any organization involved in security, there's always a strict hierarchy," the professor, Clements, was saying. "Whether it's one of the armed forces, the police, or a private company's security division, someone at the top gives orders to those directly below them, and so on down the chain to the bottom of the pyramid."

In front of each student was an interface. The screens lit up, and a diagram like a family tree appeared. It was the chain of command in the space navy—a complex list of ranks and related insignia.

Clements continued, "Effectiveness and discipline are built on the foundation of obedience. For the efficient functioning of any group involved in security operations, it's *vital* that each member obeys the commands of those above. They don't have to know why, and sometimes the command might seem odd or even nonsensical. It doesn't matter. In an operating situation, there's no time for discussions, explanations, or justifications. Obedience should be the first response.

"This doesn't only apply to those at the bottom. Compliance is necessary right up the hierarchy. Today, we're looking at how a leader's behavior and attitude affects the likelihood of obedience in those below him or her." She picked up a laser pointer.

A hand went up.

Clements glanced at her seating plan. "Mr Archer?"

The hand's owner, a scruffy young man in a thick jumper, said, "But what if we're told to do something against our conscience? Like, I don't know, kill a kid?"

"Good question. We'll be looking at ethics toward the end of the class, but to give a brief answer, providing the order is lawful, you must obey. However, in the extremely rare event that an order is unlawful, you are legally required to disobey."

Another hand was raised. Before the lecturer had time to check whose it was, a female student said, "How do we tell what's lawful and what isn't? I mean, it isn't like we go through law school."

"Basically it comes down to this," Clements replied, putting down her laser pointer and folding her hands. "If a person of ordinary sense and understanding would judge the order illegal, then you must disobey. To take Mr Archer's example, it's hard to think of a case where it would be lawful to kill a child. But you must judge each situation according to its context."

The spot of syrup on Jas's back was growing warmer, but she resisted the urge to look around. Something was bothering her about what Clements was saying. Hers was the third hand to be raised that morning. She waited for Clements to find her name. "Ms Harrington?"

"I wanted to ask, what if you're on the ground during a maneuver and you're ordered to do something that doesn't make sense? I mean, what if you think what they're telling you is wrong? If you don't trust their judgment?" She was thinking of Trankle. She'd hate to be serving under him. He'd probably send her on a suicide mission.

Clements snorted a short laugh. "You don't get to make that call about your superiors. Compliance should always be your first response. There's no room for personality clashes in security. It's dangerous. You'll have to accept that you're not going to get along with everyone you work with."

"I understand, but not everyone we work with is going to be good at their job."

"Ms Harrington, I know what you mean, but you're muddying the waters here. You have to trust the system that put your superior in his or her position. We can quibble all day about what ifs. As I've been saying for the last five minutes, unquestioning obedience is the bedrock of a successful security operation. From the top down, everyone has to follow orders."

The professor's answer left Jas uncomfortable. Though she hadn't been badly behaved at the children's home, the chaotic nature of the place had left her with a lack of faith in authority. She also wasn't sure she could trust her life to someone like Trankle.

SIX

After class, Sergei asked if she wanted to come out with him and some friends to a bar in town that Friday evening. She agreed, a little too fast, her stomach fluttering. For the remainder of the week, anticipation of the casual date made her feel like she was walking through molasses. Lectures and seminars dragged even more than usual, and in fitness and combat training, she found it hard to concentrate.

It wasn't until Thursday she saw Sergei again. It turned out that he was also in her weapons class.

They were learning the basics of firepower worked, especially the latest powered weapons. It was supposed to improve their skills in handling them. A range of disarmed examples were stored in the classroom: old-fashioned guns, rifles that fired rounds, and the newer 'laser' guns. They were *called* laser guns, but the pulses they emitted were based on the phenomenon of ball lightning. Laser guns emitted short bursts of energy that could shock a living organism's nerves enough to stun it or, when the weapons were set to full power, burn through skin, tissue, and bone.

Firing the laser guns was very different from shooting with bullets. As Jas discovered during target practice, they didn't produce any recoil, nor any sound apart from a faint fizz. Their range was shorter than projectile weapons', but the strongest wind had no effect on the trajectory. The laser guns were armed with pre-charged power units, and when the energy ran out, they were as useful as an empty pistol.

The students were assigned to groups and given a weapon to take apart and reassemble to understand how it worked. Jas and Sergei were assigned to the same group. As they started, she realized where Sergei's firm skin on his hands might have come from. He picked up the laser gun and examined it at eye level, clearly fascinated. He ignored everyone as if he'd forgotten they were here.

On the table was an open case of tiny screwdrivers. He ran his fingers through it and took one out. In a few seconds, he carefully removed the casing, revealing a complex system of wires and coils. He bent his head over the weapon, the screwdriver poised in his hand, and closely studied the interior.

She folded her arms and looked on, bemused. Another student in the group coughed. Sergei looked up and seemed to remember the others. "Ha, sorry." He pushed the opened weapon to the center of the table and leaned back. Jas caught his eye. He looked a little embarrassed. "Interesting, huh?"

"Yeah." She peered into the mysterious inner workings of the gun. "I guess so."

———

It was finally Friday evening. Classes were over for the week, and though she had a mountain of homework to do over the weekend, she could afford to take few hours to relax and enjoy herself. Sje was getting ready to go out. She had to meet Sergei at the front of the college in ten minutes. She'd showered and was trying to decide what to wear. The only clothes she had that were suitable for a bar were the ones she'd worn at the party. She felt a little silly, and poor, to wear the same outfit again. But her height meant that she couldn't borrow anyone else's clothes. Sighing, she began to get dressed.

She was tingling all over in terrified excitement. It seemed inevitable that something would happen. Probably something good. She hadn't spent much time examining her feelings for Sergei—introspection usually led her down roads she didn't want to travel. She couldn't explain what had happened when their gazes had met his in that clichéd way *across a crowded room*. She also couldn't deny the experience, and from his behavior, she didn't think he could either.

Tonight would be interesting to say the least.

She went to Tamara's room. Her friend opened her door at Jas's knock. "You're going now? You look nice."

It was a white lie, and Jas knew it, but she appreciated it all the same. She'd grown to like Tamara a lot in their short time in the dorm. "Yeah. You sure you don't want to come?"

"You know I'd like to, but I really have too much work to do. We started a whole new section today, on life on high-gravity planets, and I don't know anything about it. We didn't cover the subject at school. I have to go right back to the basics. That's as well as everything else. And we have a test in two weeks." Tamara's normally cheerful face was looking strained and tired.

"If you're asleep when I get back, I'll see you in the morning."

"If you get back to your room," Tamara said, and her dimples appeared.

Jas laughed as a flush crept up her face.

———

The night was bitterly cold. Just going from the door of the college to the autocab awaiting her made Jas appreciate the scant warmth of the building's central heating. Two male students were in the vehicle as well as Sergei. From their behavior she guessed they were a couple. Sergei introduced everyone, and they set off through the brightly lit darkness to the town center.

Alcohol was supposedly banned on campus, but she had seen many inebriated students. Beer and liquor were easy to purchase in town. At eighteen, she could legally drink in Antarctica, but she hadn't up to that point. She wasn't against it, she just hadn't sought it out. She supposed tonight would be her first time.

She'd also never been in a bar, she suddenly realized when, after a twenty-minute drive, the cab pulled up outside *Rashid's Tavern* in downtown McMurdo Sound. The exterior had been cracked and warped by time and the weather. Beneath the wide signage were two windows and a door. The plexiglass windows were divided into small rectangles, separated by lines of brick.

She hesitated while the others went directly to the door. Sergei paused, holding it and looking back at her. "Something wrong?"

She was wondering why the bar's owner—Rashid—thought it was necessary to have such heavily protected windows. Did they get broken often?

People inside were shouting to Sergei angrily to close the door. "Come on in."

She hurried inside, faint prickles running up her spine.

SEVEN

It was early evening, but the bar was nearly full. Sergei's friends had found a tall table, and they waved them over. All the bar stools were taken, so they stood around the table. Sergei's friend, Aaron, offered to buy the first round. He went over to the bar and attracted the bartender's attention. As the woman turned around, Jas was startled by her face.

The bartender had either had extensive surgery or she wasn't human. Her skin was patterned yellow and brown, and where her mouth and nose should have been was a prehensile snout with whiskers on either side. She nodded as she took Aaron's order. When she moved down the bar to make the drinks, he turned back to them with raised eyebrows, as if to say, *Did you see?*

"Is that Rashid, do you think?" Jas asked.

"Rashid? Who's Rashid?"

"The bar owner. Didn't you see the sign? It said Rashid's Tavern."

"Did it? Krat. The autocab's brought us to the wrong place. Terry, you told it where to go. What did you say?"

"I gave it the address you told me."

"I don't think you did," Sergei said. "Maybe you misheard me. Come to think of it, this doesn't look much like a student bar."

Jas had been wondering about that too. While waiting for Aaron to bring their drinks, she'd been looking around at the crowd. They definitely weren't students. They were older, and they didn't look the types to be interested in education. Their faces were roughened and red from cold exposure, and they wore clothes representing fashions of several decades, including many items that were timeless, such as thick, shapeless coats and hats. Judging by the behavior of some, they'd been drinking for several hours already.

No one dressed up to go out to this bar.

As Jas was looking, a man turned to meet her gaze. Gray-blond stubble coated his chin and cheeks and grew not much longer on his head. A tattoo of an anarchist symbol ran up the side of his face. The man leered as he looked Jas in the eyes, revealing weirdly decorated perfectly square teeth. She turned away uneasily.

"Checking out the local action?" Sergei asked.

She laughed. "No."

"Sure you don't see anyone you like?" His face was mock serious.

She took another look around the room at the crowd of locals. She was beginning to understand McMurdo Sound. It was where people came when they wanted to escape something, whether it was the law, a relationship, family, or social conventions. Her spine was still tingling strangely. "Do you think maybe we should go somewhere else?"

Aaron arrived, his large hands wrapped around four glasses of beer that he deposited on the table. Sergei passed them around, picked up his own and took a sip. "Do you really want to leave? It's cold outside, and it's going to be hard to get a cab now the evening rush is on. Let's stay here a while. Seems friendly enough."

Aaron asked, "Did you get a look at the bartender? Where do you think she's from?"

"How would we know?" Terry asked. "She could be from anywhere."

"I mean what planet," Aaron replied. "She isn't human. Couldn't you tell from her face?"

"She could easily be human. Doesn't matter what she looks like," said Terry. "You can get all kinds of things done these days. Between surgery and gene therapy, you can look like a woolly mammoth if you want."

"No," replied Aaron, "she's definitely alien—if she is a she. Did you get a look at her hands? I'm using the word loosely."

As Aaron and Terry continued their discussion about the origins of the bartender, Sergei moved a little closer to Jas. If he'd been anyone else, he would have been a little too close for her preferences, but she found herself welcoming the proximity.

She sipped her beer. It tasted bitter but not unpleasant. She wondered when she would start to feel the effects of the alcohol. "You like weapons, then?" She raised her voice to compete with the increasing hum of conversation in the bar.

"What makes you think that?"

"You seemed very interested the other day in class."

"Oh, right. I guess I was, but not because it was a weapon. I like taking things apart to find out how they work. That's all." He undid his coat. The place was getting warmer. "So you're in the deep space program?"

"That's right."

He shook his head slightly. "Doesn't the idea of starjumping freak you out? But you must have already made at least one jump from Mars."

"I did, but just the one. It was okay." She tensed, wondering if he would move the conversation on to her background, but he didn't.

"Doesn't it scare you just a little bit? I mean, I don't think they even know exactly how starjumps work, do they?"

"Hmm...from what I understand, they know the math, they just don't know where the starship actually goes while it's in a jump state."

"I'd like to see other planets, but I don't know that I could make the trip, you know?"

"I guess I know what you mean, but it is a tested technology. People are starjumping all over the galaxy these days. Maybe if you could take apart a starship engine and look inside?"

Sergei laughed. "Maybe." He took a swig of beer.

More people were arriving, blasts of icy wind accompanying them whenever the door to the bar opened. Music started playing from speakers, and Sergei and Jas had to draw even closer to hear each other speak. They talked about their classes and professors, life at college, and other students.

She found herself telling Sergei about her background. She told him about her first memories of life in the Valles Marineris Institute for Cared-For Children—how one day she'd asked why other children lived with their parents, and how the care worker had told her abruptly that both her parents had died years ago. She also told him about the bureaucratic hiccup that had resulted in her being sent to Earth almost too late for her body to adapt to the higher gravity. She even told him of the difficulty of life at the new children's home, and how she'd been bullied over her height and origins.

He listened gravely as her story poured out. She didn't know why she was telling him about her life, except that it felt right. He didn't comment much, seeming to sense her need to just get it all out. She was grateful. As her story wound down and finished at the time she left for college, he put his hand on her shoulder. He was looking at her so intently, she wondered if he was about to kiss her.

To break the tension, she asked, "How about you? How did you end up here?"

He put down his glass. "Well, I can't compete with you in the interesting childhood stakes."

As he went to speak, Aaron folded his arms and leaned on the opposite side of the table, causing it to rock. Their glasses fell over, and beer splashed everywhere.

"Krat," Sergei exclaimed.

A woman with her back to them turned round as beer splashed down her legs. "What the hell?" She was with a man, and they were both locals, judging from their weather-beaten looks and oddly cut hair. The man peered over to see what had happened. A sly look passed between him and the woman.

"Hey, you're gonna pay to get her pants cleaned," he growled.

"What?" Terry said. "It's only beer. It'll wash out."

"You think I wash my clothes myself?" the woman asked. "Who the hell does that these days? I pay for all my cleaning, and these are genuine imitation sealskin. They cost me a fortune."

"Look, man," said Aaron, "I'm sorry, but we're students. We're not rolling in creds." Aaron's words only caused the man and woman to scowl more deeply. "I didn't mean to mess up your pants. How about if I wipe them down with something wet? That should get most of it off. It isn't like this beer's strong."

The man and woman were clearly taking advantage and trying to scam Aaron out of some money. But it was going to be hard to avoid giving them something. The man grabbed the front of Aaron's coat.

"Get his credchip, Marl. I got a reader here somewhere." She felt inside large pockets in her jacket.

Sergei gripped Marl's arm. "Let go of my friend."

"Hey." Jas lifted her hands. "It's okay. I'll pay. Look, here's my chip." She held out her wrist.

Around them, the chatter in the bar quietened. The bar's patrons had noticed the dispute and were watching. The bartender was on an interface talking to someone.

"No, Jas," Sergei said. "Don't pay them a cred. It's only a little beer. They're out of line."

Aaron looked down disbelievingly at the hand grasping his coat.

Marl shifted his gaze from Aaron's face to Sergei's hand on his arm. Jas knew what was about to happen, even if Sergei was oblivious. He had less than a second. She could either say something to try to cool the situation, or stop Marl from punching him. She didn't have time for both. She made her decision.

As Marl released his grip on Aaron, she picked up one of the fallen beer glasses. As he drew back his fist, she got ready to throw. Marl's punch was about to land on Sergei's surprised face when the glass hit Marl on his forehead. It didn't stop the blow from falling, but it lessened its impact.

Sergei fell back, and Marl's attention was diverted to a new enemy—Jas. His lip lifted in a snarl. But the students had worse problems. At a bar for locals, when it came to a dispute there could be no doubt about whose side the patrons would take. They began to murmur angrily. Terry had realized the danger of their situation too. "Let's go," he shouted, and began pulling Aaron toward the door.

A punch landed on the back of Jas's head, and the table loomed up as she fell forward. She caught herself before she hit it and turned dizzily to face her attacker, but all she could see was Sergei's back as he jumped on her assailant.

It was a fight they could never win, and if they didn't get out soon, they might never get out. She grabbed Sergei and pulled him off the man who had punched her. Blows and kicks began to rain down on both of them. Aaron and Terry seemed to have made some progress toward the door, and holding Sergei back as best she could, Jas edged over in their direction.

A particularly hard kick landed on her right shin, and she cried out. Sergei had calmed down a little, but he became inflamed again and struck out at a local. "Stop it!" she yelled. "We've got to get out."

Somehow, they all managed to make it to the door and out into the street. As soon as they were outside, they ran. Jas and Sergei went one way, Aaron and Terry another. A few streets away, Jas and Sergei drew to a halt. The locals had given up their pursuit.

Sergei began to laugh.

Jas couldn't understand why. "What's so funny? We could have been killed back there. We were lucky to get away."

He controlled his guffaws. "You're right. I'm sorry. It was kind of fun, though, wasn't it? How's your head?"

She recalled the punch and put her hand to the back of her scalp. A painful lump was forming. "I'm okay. How's your eye?"

He touched his face where Marl had punched him. "I don't know. Can you take a look?"

She brought her face close to his to assess the damage in the dim streetlight. It was only when she was centimeters from him that she realized his ploy. He was gazing into her eyes. It was her turn to chuckle, a little nervously. She drew back. A silence stretched out, thin and tight as a drum skin.

Tension knotted her stomach. "It's weird, isn't it? This...feeling we have." Had she just made a fool of herself? She'd thought he was experiencing the same strange attraction as she was. What if he wasn't? Had she misinterpreted the looks that had passed between them? Was she just another girl to him?

"It is weird," Sergei said. "When I saw you at Tamara's party, it was like..." He paused. "It was like I'd known you all my life, only I hadn't met you, until then." His eyes were black in the darkness.

She nodded. Neither said anything. They had stopped in a short alleyway, where the illumination from the street lights barely reached. The winter cold was biting her face.

What would happen next?

Was this how it was for other people? From what she'd seen of romantic relationships, she didn't think so. On the other hand, friends had told her about meeting *the one*. Was there something she was supposed to say? *Was* there anything to say? As with many things, there seemed to be rules to the situation that she didn't understand.

Sergei touched her upper arm and stepped closer.

She said, "Is this the part where we—"

He kissed her.

EIGHT

The buzz about the bar fight between students and locals—which apparently had been started by a female student throwing a beer glass—died down after a while. The bar didn't have CCTV, so no one could prove who had been the instigator. However, verbal descriptions pointed fingers strongly at the only Martian on campus.

Jas's combat training instructor didn't need anything like firm evidence to support his opinion on the subject. His prejudice against her increased to the extent that he virtually ignored her in class and routinely 'forgot' to include her in sparring sessions. This was doubly annoying: combat skills would be essential in her job, and hand-to-hand fighting was about the only thing that she naturally learned quickly. Everything else she had to work for.

Meanwhile, all the other students except for Tamara had started to keep their distance. People she thought had been her friends began to pretend they didn't see her in the corridors between classes. If Tamara and Sergei were busy, she ate lunch alone. She seemed to have gained the reputation of being aggressive from the combat class too, which didn't help.

She didn't know what to do about it, or even if she should do something. Maybe she didn't need friends who believed in gossip rather than finding out the truth. Tamara told her that she put straight anyone who talked about Jas within her earshot, but everyone knew they were friends and probably concluded that Tamara's judgment was clouded. Jas didn't think there was any point in defending herself. Anything she said would seem like an excuse or justification.

Her growing relationship with Sergei was the saving grace of the whole situation. As far as she could without slipping too far behind with her work, she spent every spare moment with him. After a couple of blissful weeks of having her room to themselves, another late transfer arrived and was allocated the empty place.

Sergei also shared, so they couldn't be alone in his room without inconveniencing his roomie. He solved the problem by persuading Aaron to help him build something vaguely resembling an igloo a little way out of town. It was a chilly setting for love trysts, and they couldn't run a heater too long without the walls melting and ice-water pooling on the floor, but she didn't care. Wherever they were, being with him was enough, and he seemed to feel the same about her.

Yet she wasn't so blindly in love that she couldn't see they were very different. Sergei didn't work as hard or pay as much attention to his studies as she did. He wasn't the stereotypical 'bad boy', but he didn't care about his grades, or even if he would make it to graduation. He often missed class because he was working on something. In fact, one of advantage of the igloo was that wires, transistors, silicon chips and other paraphernalia weren't strewn around the place. In the igloo, she didn't suddenly become aware that a part from a motherboard was sticking in her back.

Sergei avoided her hints at questions about why he'd transferred from his previous college, but she had a strong suspicion it had something to do with flunking out. She didn't press him for an answer. She didn't really care. He was a good, kind person, and he didn't have any addictions or vices, unless he hid them very well.

The only thing that niggled was the fact that, if they both continued along their current paths, it would be hard for them to be together. She was studying to work in security on a starship, he was studying to...well, he had no particular ambition, if the truth was told. But whatever it was he did, it would never be aboard a starship. He had a deep dislike of the idea of traveling in space. Airplanes, he could handle, he'd said. Maybe even shuttles, though given the choice he'd rather not travel by them. But he seemed to have an actual phobia of deep space travel. The idea of disappearing from the physical universe, even for the few seconds that most starjumps took, sent chills down his spine.

It wouldn't be fair to expect him to wait the months or years a mission took, only to see her for a few weeks before she left again. As she could find no solution to this problem, she pushed it to the back of her mind and concentrated on enjoying the time they had together. Decisions about their long-term future could wait. Maybe she would be content with an Earth-based job.

———

She was a little late for her zero-g combat training class. When she arrived, she was surprised to find no one had changed into their swimwear. Though starship gravity drives could create gravitational forces, no one had invented a machine that could turn gravity off. The usual zero-g fighting practice consisted of underwater training. The students used rebreathers and propeled themselves from the swimming pool walls and each others. No actual swimming was allowed. In space or a gaseous atmosphere it wouldn't work. The instructor—a man called Elba—had explained that water wasn't much of a substitute for no gravity, but it was the best they could do.

She bypassed the changing rooms and went to the only remaining seats at the top of the tiered benches bordering the swimming pool. As she sat down, she realized the instructor was going over a scheduled zero-g exercise in space. Her shoulders sagged. The trip was taking place over the next weekend, and all she knew was that it cost a lot—far more than she could afford. She hoped it didn't count as a large percentage of their final grade.

"And I have a little surprise for you all," said the instructor. "Normally, this class would visit an orbiting space station for the training weekend. We would be training in micro-g rather than zero-g. But I have a friend who runs an interplanetary import/export company, and it just so happens that this weekend she has a special consignment to Mars."

Elba paused for effect, scanning the students' faces. "She's agreed to let us all travel on her ship at a discounted price that matches the usual fee. We'll complete a starjump and train in real zero-g for a whole day."

The students hollered and clapped, except for Jas. A trip to Mars would be nice. The thought of returning for a visit crossed her mind fairly often. But it wasn't possible. Still, she would have a whole weekend with Sergei.

Elba went over the details of the trip and what the students had to bring. Then he took questions. He spent the remainder of the class explaining the combat techniques they would be practicing, and what differences the students could expect when sparring in zero-g.

Class finished a little early. She put her bag over her shoulder, ready to leave. She had to wait for most of the students to file out before she could make her way down the stairs between the benches. As she went past Elba, he stopped her. "Could I speak to you for a moment, Ms Harrington?" He waited until the last student had departed, then said, "Can I ask, is something wrong? You looked a little down in class today. Aren't you excited about our trip?"

"It does sound exciting, and I hope you all have a great time, but I can't come."

"Is there a problem? Do you have something planned for the weekend? If so, I'm afraid it'll have to wait. The real-life zero-g training isn't optional. It counts toward your final assessment."

"Yeah, I thought it might." She sighed. "You see, I'm a scholarship student. I don't have the creds to—"

"Is that all? Then there's no problem. You need to read your entitlements document properly. Any mandatory class materials, equipment, and other expenses—including class trips—are covered by your scholarship. It would be a little silly if they weren't, wouldn't it? What's the point of awarding a scholarship if the student can't complete a whole class and graduate?"

"It's all paid for?"

"Everything's covered. *Everything.* You don't have to worry about it."

"You mean, I get a trip to Mars for free?"

The man's face fell a little. "I'm sorry, but we won't be landing on Mars. There isn't time, and if there were, Mars has far too many visitation controls. We wouldn't be able to arrange visas and health checks. But you will get to experience a starjump and real zero-g. That's something, isn't it?"

A tiny flicker of hope that had flared up in her sputtered out. She'd gone from expecting to miss out on a trip, to anticipating a visit to her birth planet, and then to the lesser delight of a space trip, within less than a minute. "Yeah, it's something."

NINE

She was with Sergei. They were on the sofa in her dorm living room, and Tamara was in the kitchen cooking dinner. She was leaning on her boyfriend, resting her head on his shoulder and stretching an arm around his waist. He was wearing a thick sweater that felt soft and comfortable against her face. His arm was draped over her shoulders.

He was telling her about something broken that he'd been trying to repair. She had forgotten what it was. She was content to listen to the sound of his voice and feel the slight vibration of his throat and chest as he spoke.

She'd spent the afternoon doing her fitness training, first on the all-weather track and then on the machines in the fitness center. Her muscles ached pleasantly. She wondered if he would give her a massage later. Slowly, her eyes began to close.

A kiss on the top of her head woke her up.

"Am I that boring to listen to?" Sergei asked. "You were snoring."

She sat up. "Sorry. But you fixed it, right?"

"Yeah, I fixed it." He smiled and held out his arm, inviting her to snuggle up again.

She returned to her position, but immediately sat up again. "Hey, I just remembered. We had weapons today. You skipped class."

"Yeah, I had to—"

"Again."

"Yeah, but—"

"You're going to fail if you don't attend. You'll get kicked out of school. Then how will we be together?"

"Don't worry," he replied, pulling her in for a kiss. "I'll get a job as a custodian."

There was a cough. Tamara had appeared from the kitchen carrying two plates. She put them down as Jas and Sergei drew apart. She'd made avocado-boat starters. Where had she found avocados in Antarctica?

Tamara sat down in an armchair across from the sofa. She rested her elbows on her knees and her chin in her hands as she gazed at the couple. "You two are so cute." She sighed. "Come on. Eat up. The main course is almost ready." She returned to the kitchen.

Jas passed Sergei a plate. "I'm leaving early tomorrow for the spaceport."

"Huh? Oh, I forgot. Your Mars trip. That's tomorrow, is it? How long will you be gone for?"

"Only two days."

"Two days to Mars and back. How long did the first mission take? Two years?"

"Something like that." She wondered how long it had taken to get to Mars when her parents emigrated there. Had they been among the original settlers, or had they been part of the global warming rush? She'd been born on Valles Mariniers Five, scene of the worst colony disaster in the history of humankind's expansion into space. A massive explosion—possibly originating in the oxygen storage tanks—had devastated the base. Only those at the periphery had survived the initial blast, and then only for the few seconds it took the fireball to reach them.

She had never researched the disaster. A care worker at the Martian children's home had once offered to show her the records of the couples who had died, but she hadn't wanted to speculate about which of the twenty or so might have been her parents. She'd never been able to see the point.

"Are you sure you'll be okay doing this starjump?" Sergei asked. "Is your instructor's friend legit? Is her ship safe?"

She put down her fork and touched the side of his face. His concern was heart-warming, though she knew it was also borne out of his distrust of space travel. "I'll be fine. In fact, though I'll miss you, I'm looking forward to it. Don't worry. I'll be back before you know it."

———

The *Alexandria IV* was a mid-range, multi-purpose utility vessel of the type often purchased by space entrepreneurs just starting out. The ship's design didn't define a specific business strategy, allowing the flexibility to alter direction if the first venture failed. It had a hold generous enough for a substantial shipment, the crew's quarters, and twenty modest passenger berths.

It was also a ship for spacefarers who never settled on one thing. They spent their lives roaming the stars, picking up a group of colonists here, a shipment there, taking whatever work they could find wherever they could find it, eking out a living.

Jas saw the appeal of such a life as she arrived from the McMurdo Sound Spaceport. The white-streaked, brilliant blue globe that was Earth slowly rotated to one side, and through the shuttle windows on the other side of the passenger cabin sat the *Alexandria IV,* its long snout. The snout was mostly engine, that much she knew. Star-jump tech was bulky.

After docking with the other vessel, the students filed through the opening linking the shuttle and the starship, Elba bringing up the rear. A small, wiry woman met them in the narrow, bare-metal passageway. She greeted them and Elba when she appeared, and directed the students to follow her, explaining the layout of the ship as they went.

Jas was immediately taken back to the first and only starjump she'd ever experienced, when traveling to Earth at the age of twelve. She'd been alone and lonely. Her Martian friends had either already left for Earth a year or two before her, or they'd still been too young to make the trip. Aside from that, she couldn't remember much of what had happened.

"Here are your cabins," the ship's owner announced they drew close to a set of ten doors, five on each side. "You can figure out which ones you're taking later—they're all doubles, so you'll have to share. Before you enter your cabins, I'm going to take you to the jump suite. You need to know where you'll have to be in around four hours, when we've maneuvered far enough away from Earth and built up energy for the jump. Please make sure you aren't tardy. Time's money."

"Don't worry," said Elba. "They won't be late." He was in the lead now, walking alongside his friend. He shot a look over his shoulder to impress the instruction on his students.

The jump suite was only just large enough for the twenty-five jumpseats it held. The smell of the foam and plastic reclined seats made Jas a little nauseous. Open safety harnesses hung down from them. Memories of her first jump returned at the sight. She recalled the crew members finding her a spare adult seat as the child-sized one had been too small.

"Isn't there a window?" one of Jas's male classmates asked. "I wanted to look outside as we jumped."

"No windows on starships, son, and you wouldn't see anything if there were," replied the owner. "You'd only notice the stars had changed position."

"So it really is like falling asleep and waking up?" another student asked.

"It's more like falling down a well, then being suddenly thrust to the surface again. You'll float for thirty seconds or so as the gravity comes back online. There are sick bags in the slots on your seats. If anyone feels like they're going to throw up, hold the bag around your mouth, okay? I'm sure you can all imagine what it's like when someone upchucks in zero-g. If you can't, I don't want you finding out aboard my ship. I take it you can all remember the way here from the cabins? We jump at eleven hundred sharp. Meanwhile, you can make use of the passenger lounge and the cafeteria, but you're not to enter any crew areas. They're clearly signed."

"Are we doing the training when we arrive?" the male classmate asked Elba.

"We'll be training in the cargo bay, so we'll have to wait for the Mars shuttle to collect the shipment. Then we'll move out of orbit and turn off the gravity for a few hours."

At eleven hundred, Jas was strapped into a jumpseat, listening to the countdown. The ship's owner had explained that the seats weren't to protect them from violent movements of the ship, but from any accidents that might occur.

She briefly wondered what kind of accidents were possible, but there was no time to ask. Maybe Sergei was right about space travel. The trip seemed like a lot of work for just a few hours' training, and she wouldn't even be able to go to Mars.

The owner, Elba and three crew members with the coloring and build of Martians were also strapped into jumpseats. A vibration began building, in her seat and in the air. The jump suite walls also seemed to subtly shaking. The movement penetrated her skin, her teeth, and her bones. Over the speaker came the pilot's voice. "Four, three, two, one..."

She fell.

TEN

It was hard to believe that, after several hours of building energy, the engines released it all in a split second, catapulting the *Alexandria IV* tens of millions of kilometers across space. Was catapulting the right word? It was more like the ship and everyone and everything in it had disappeared out of existence for a millisecond, only to reappear in an entirely different place. She had a sense of climbing or clawing her way back to the physical universe—to life.

The experience had left her more shaken than she'd thought it would. She didn't recall feeling so disoriented the first time around. She wasn't the only one affected. A couple of students had made use of the sick bags. After the artificial gravity had started up, everyone but the owner and crew crowded into the cafeteria for a warm drink to settle their stomachs.

She was squashed between the petite classmate she was sharing a cabin with and the male student who had been asking the questions about starjumps. No one was saying much. As she recovered a little, she decided that starjumping wasn't too bad, and she wouldn't mind doing it more regularly.

A woman in a flightsuit arrived. Her eyes searched the students crowded at the tables, and when she saw Jas, she beckoned her with a finger. The others watched as Jas got up and made her way over to the woman. She had to be the pilot as she hadn't been in the jump suite during the jump. She lacked the Martian coloring of the other crew members, so Jas assumed she was from Earth. She followed the woman out of the cafeteria.

"They said we had a Martian student aboard," the pilot remarked when they were out of earshot of the other students.

"I guess I'm not difficult to spot."

"Do you get back to Mars often?"

"I haven't been since I was twelve."

The pilot nodded, though Jas had a suspicion that the woman was asking questions she already knew the answers to, out of politeness. Jas's scholarship student background was hardly a secret.

"We don't often have passengers, you know," the pilot went on as Jas accompanied her, wondering where they were going. "Owens usually runs shipments. The regular transports get most of the passenger traffic. She can't compete on price. And when we do have passengers, it's usually a bad idea to invite them to the flight deck. You never know when someone's going to accidentally flip a switch or touch a screen."

"You're taking me to the flight deck?"

"Where did you think we were going? Here we are." The pilot put the flat of her hand to a panel, and a door slid open.

Jas could see another good reason for not inviting passengers to that part of the ship: the place was tiny. Two seats took up nearly all the available space. In front of and above the seats were interface screens, switches, and buttons. That was it. That was all there was room for. Jas wasn't even sure how the pilot got into her seat.

She still didn't know why she was here.

"Can you squeeze in okay?" the pilot asked her as she made a deft maneuver that somehow landed her in her seat. Jas's movements were far less graceful as she clambered and twisted her way into a sitting position, almost elbowing the pilot in the head. Apparently, she was about to get a lesson in flying a starship, though she had no idea why.

The pilot reached forward, but stopped midway to a screen and turned to Jas. "You do know why I've brought you here, don't you?"

"Umm...not exactly."

The pilot laughed. "Sorry for not explaining. I thought it was obvious. You'd like to see Mars, right? It's okay if you'd rather not."

"No, I'd love to." Jas realized the truth of the words as they left her mouth. She did want to see her home planet, desperately. "But I thought there were no windows on starships?"

"There aren't, but pilots can get a visual if we need one." She held a finger over the largest interface, directly in front of both seats. "Ready?"

Jas gripped her arm rests. She nodded.

The pilot swiped the screen, and an image of a red planet appeared. The *Alexandria IV* was in orbit. The curved, deep red Martian surface spread from horizon to horizon. The pilot explained how they'd arrived from their starjump some distance away, then navigated into orbit to await the cargo shuttle's arrival, but Jas only barely took in her words. The image of Mars was sinking into her mind.

"Where's Valles Marineris? Can we see it from here?" she blurted.

"Is that where you grew up? It's on the other side of the planet at the moment. It should be coming around in half an hour or so, if you want to wait."

"Yes, yes, I do." Jas rested her elbows just below the screen, taking care to avoid touching anything else. She scanned the rust-red image, and as she looked more closely, she began to notice patches of dark red and gray that had to be the settlements. They were set in squares, rectangles, and spreading starbursts.

She remembered the blue-green, cloud-swirled surface of Earth she'd seen from the shuttle. Mars was dry and barren, and it didn't resemble anything like her memory of it. She recalled the camaraderie and warmth of the children's home among her friends. Though they were all orphaned or abandoned or removed from their parents due to abuse, they'd found a kind of family with each other. Dysfunctional and sometimes unpredictable to be sure, but a family nonetheless. The image she saw before her seemed hardly capable of supporting the pulsing life and energy of humanity.

After a little while, the pilot pointed out that Valles Marineris was coming into view. To Jas's eye, it looked the same as the rest of the surface. She could hardly believe those lines running out from the valley bottom were once the scene of the disaster that had claimed her parents' lives, or that she had been a tiny baby there. Had her mother or her father put her in the safety capsule? Why hadn't they gotten in with her? She wished she could meet them and tell them she'd made it.

A keen yearning grew in her heart. She wanted to travel to new planets. For years, she'd entertained the idea of a career in deep space —something interesting and challenging to do with her life. But seeing the dusty expanse of alien soil slowly revolving had turned her idea into much more. Space travel wasn't something she was choosing to do, it was something she *had* to do.

Her heart sank. Space travel also meant a life without Sergei. He would never come with her.

"What do you think of Mars?" asked the pilot.

"I think I've seen enough. Thanks." She awkwardly climbed out of her seat and left to go to her cabin.

The room was empty. Her classmate was probably in the cafeteria with the others. She lay down on the bottom bunk, curled on her side, wondering what she was going to say to Sergei when she got back to campus.

ELEVEN

The cloud of her decision hung over Jas throughout the Mars trip, and when she got back to McMurdo Sound, Sergei could tell immediately that something was wrong. She didn't waste any time in telling him. It wasn't fair to allow things to continue as they were when their relationship had no future.

She didn't cry easily, but the tears were soon pouring down her face as she explained what she'd realized when she'd seen Mars. She was being torn in two. She didn't think she'd ever love someone again like she loved this man, but neither could she be happy while Earthbound.

As she went on, Sergei looked down and swallowed. Her explanation drew to a close, and he looked up with a forced smile. "It's okay. I'll just learn to like space travel."

She put a hand to his face. "No, you won't."

He shrugged. "People change. Maybe you won't feel the same way in a couple of years. Maybe I'll get over my fear. I could try hypnosis. Or drugs."

They laughed, sadly.

"No drugs," Jas said.

"But we'll stay together for now?"

She nodded and wiped her eyes. "For now."

Her studies continued, and soon it was time for her weekly hand-to-hand combat session with Trankle. She had avoided confrontation with him as much as she could, especially since the bar incident. Whenever he criticized her for a mistake she hadn't made, or when he passed over her when picking students for sparring, she gritted her teeth and let it go.

The session had started out like the rest. She'd stayed at the back and avoided the man's gaze. But it wasn't enough. Maybe her depression over a future without Sergei was showing on her face, or maybe Trankle took her morose expression personally. During his explanation that the class was to be about techniques for defeating a larger opponent, he stopped twice to stare at her. The other students also looked at her curiously, as if to figure out what was bothering the instructor.

"Don't be intimidated by size," Trankle said after his second pause. He addressed all the students but then fixed Jas with a glare. "It doesn't matter how big the other guy or girl is, you've got advantages. Speed, agility, and—if you've learned anything in this class—technique. If you have time, play the long game. Wear your opponent out. Some heavier types slack off on their cardio-vascular. Got no stamina. It goes without saying, but avoid grappling. Duck in, and hit the vulnerable spots, hard. Throat, diaphragm, solar plexus, groin, kidneys. If your opponent doesn't go down on your first attack, back up and wait for the next opening."

He paused again and threw Jas another look.

"Harrington," he barked. "What's your problem?"

She was startled. "What?" She'd been following what he was saying. Not closely, but she'd been listening.

"Think you know better, huh? Get over here."

The students shuffled aside as she made her way to the front. Tension rose in the room. All the students knew Trankle's antipathy toward her.

"There." The instructor pointed at the mat. She went over and stood where he'd pointed, her muscles taut. An uncomfortable prickling began running up and down her spine.

"These techniques are useful for women fighting men," Trankle went on. "Ninety-nine times out of a hundred, the guy's gonna be bigger and stronger. But with the right moves, a woman *can* incapacitate a man. Harrington here's the biggest woman among you. By far," he added. A few of the students snickered, though many looked grave and embarrassed. "If any girl among you stands a chance of taking me out, it's her. Wanna try it, Harrington? I'm guessing you do."

He joined her on the mat and got ready to fight, bending and spreading his arms and legs. He fixed his narrow eyes on her, as if to say, *Now's your chance, bitch.*

Her arms hung limply at her sides. The whole situation was ridiculous. The teaching method Trankle had used up until now was to demonstrate a technique first, then ask the students to practice it. He was expecting her to use techniques he hadn't taught.

She debated pointing this out, but Trankle's lips were thin, and his bull neck was rigid. He looked really mad. He was only going to get madder if she questioned his methodology. She would have to do as he said and try to fight him.

She was thankful for her protective sparring gear. A head and face guard and body shield were the only advantages she had over this burly, expert fighter. He didn't deign to put on safety gear.

She began to circle the mat, and Trankle turned to follow. "Not bad, Harrington. So you *did* think you had something to learn from this class." He lunged and grabbed, but she hopped backward, out of his reach. She quickly sidestepped to the other side of the mat. Trankle spun around and lunged again, but she repeated the same avoidance maneuver.

"Gonna try and tire me out, huh?" said Trankle "Sad for you, we don't have time for that." He stopped moving and straightened up. Beckoning with his fingertips, he said, "Attack me."

She was also still. She looked into Trankle's hate-filled eyes. The watching students were silent and unmoving, holding a collective breath.

"C'mon," the instructor said. "What are you scared of? You're wearing your safety gear. I can't hurt you." He moved his hands to his hips. "Look at me. Get a lucky hit, and you could do me a lot of damage. C'mon, Harrington. I know you want to."

Still she hung back. What did he want? To beat her. That was what he wanted. He wanted to defeat her, to hurt the filthy Martian. He knew she'd been pulling punches and throwing her matches. He wanted to show her she had something to be scared of. Her gaze flicked to the watching students. Some were looking on sympathetically. Did they realize Trankle's intentions too? But there was nothing any of them could do to help. They had to obey him as much as she did.

"Harrington," the instructor barked, making her jump. "I gave you an order. Or do you only fight people weaker than you?"

Anger flared up, and without thinking, she rushed in and kicked upward, trying to reach the man's head. He deftly caught her ankle one-handed. Grabbing her foot with the other hand, he twisted her leg cruelly around. Her body followed. She cried out in pain, and suddenly she was face downward on the mat, her knee and hip agonized.

The students gasped.

She remained motionless, waiting for the pain in her leg to dissipate. Her face smarted where it had slid along the mat.

"Get up, Harrington," Trankle said. "Quit faking. I didn't hurt you that bad."

Wincing, she stood, wobbling. She limped to the back of the audience, the students parting silently to let her through.

"Harrington provided us with a great example of what *not* to do," said Trankle. "Now we're gonna look at some *effective* ways you can beat a stronger opponent."

———

"Wow, tough class today?" Sergei asked when he met her for dinner in the cafeteria. He was referring to the bright red abrasion on her face from its encounter with the training mat. He put down his tray and sat opposite.

"Tough instructor." She went on to explain what had happened.

"What an asshole. Did you report him?"

"No point. I can't prove he was doing anything other than a normal training exercise."

"Jas, you can't let him treat you like that. Some of the other students will back you up. They saw what happened."

She sighed. "It's okay. I can deal with it."

"For krat's sake, listen to yourself. The misborn assaulted you. You have to do something about it. You can't go through the rest of your life letting people push you around. You're in security. What are you going to do if you get attacked by aliens? Run away? Tell the people you're supposed to be protecting that you couldn't prove the aliens were attacking?"

"Hey," she replied defensively. "Of course I won't. I'll do my job. This is different."

"Not from where I'm sitting, it isn't."

Her lips thinned to a line. "I don't have a choice. I can't make waves. I can't afford to get kicked out of school. If I don't get through this, I'm not going to get another chance. I'm not like you. I can't just drift from college to college because I'm too lazy to do the work."

Sergei put down his fork and sat back, staring at her.

She closed her eyes. "Sorry. I didn't mean that the way it sounded."

He shook his head and resumed eating, silently.

She reached out and took his hand. "I went over this with Tamara months ago. There really isn't anything I can do. I just have to suck it up and hope he doesn't teach any of my classes next year."

"You mean this has been going on for a while?"

"A little. Off and on."

He looked at her gravely.

"Don't look at me like that. You don't get it. You're from Earth. You aren't different from everyone else. You don't stand out wherever you go. People aren't constantly asking about your background. They don't treat you differently. You're accepted for who you are. It isn't like that for me. To everyone else, I'm not Jas, I'm The Martian. Maybe the administration would believe me. I don't know. But I get too much attention as it is. I don't want any more."

"Jas, most people don't give a krat where you're from. This isn't the children's home. Most people aren't like your instructor. You don't have to put up with his behavior."

She recalled being jumped in the stairwell by the children's home kids, having things thrown at her in class while the teacher's back was turned, and being the victim of subtle ostracizing. "I know you think what you're saying is true, but you don't get it, and you never will. So let's just not talk about it, huh?"

He looked hurt, but he didn't press the issue. They tried to talk about other things, but their conversation was dry and forced. Ever since she'd told him of her passion to travel the stars a distance had been developing between them, and it broke her heart.

TWELVE

It was early summer, and the Great Antarctic Melt had begun. Every year, more and more of the deep layers of ice covering and surrounding the continent were lost to the sea. In the past, massive icebergs had calved, shrinking and altering the shoreline, which in turn hastened the decimation of penguins and other species whose breeding strategies were dependent upon the landscape's stability. Freed of the weight of the ice, the landmass was rising to a higher elevation.

One element of Jas's leadership skills class was regular excursions, when the students would conduct staged battles. Each team would try to defeat the others in order to reach a target. The teams had leaders, and the rest of them had to obey his or her orders. Afterward, they would analyze their leader's strategies as well as the reasons for their success or failure.

Everyone had taken their turn at playing the leader except for Jas and two others. The instructor had informed the class that they had one more opportunity for an excursion. Soon, the Melt would make it impossible to travel over the ice.

When the final excursion the year arrived, Clements assigned leadership roles. Jas was to be one of the leaders. They weren't allowed to choose their own teams. In real life, only rarely would they be able to choose who they would have working under them.

As they prepared to set out to the battle site, Clements called out the team members. Sergei wasn't on Jas's team. She was sadly relieved. He went over to his leader while the four students she was to command approached her.

A transport took them a few kilometers away, into the bare, windy landscape. Dusk was quickly falling. The vehicle stopped around four hundred meters from the ocean, where huge ice blocks provided places for the students to hide. The blocks not only provided cover as the teams staged their battle, they also offered variability in the routes to the target. The leaders were supposed to figure this into their strategies. The class had been at this place before, and by the time they alighted the transport Jas had already figured out the best route to the prize.

She waited at the back of the line of students retrieving their packs from the underbelly of the vehicle. Their equipment consisted of suits of light-sensitive material in team colors and true laser guns. A beam of light from the weapons would register on the suits if it hit. They also had helmets with comms.

Most of her team had retrieved their packs, and they were waiting for her on the other side of the vehicle. She couldn't see Sergei. Looking round, she noticed he was right behind her. The students in front of her took their packs and left, and then it was just the two of them. He touched her back, and a familiar warmth and sweet ache radiated through her, dispelling the uncomfortable prickles that had been tickling her spine.

He leaned in for a brief kiss. "I love you," he murmured as he drew back. She stood there in surprise while he took his pack and left, casting a smile at her over his shoulder.

Her mind spun. He had never said those words to her. Why had he chosen here and now to tell her that?

She was slow getting her pack and joining the rest of her team. They had only minutes before the exercise began. Her team was looking at her expectantly. A short distance away on the uneven ground, Sergei stood with his group, toeing a shard of broken ice that was quickly melting to slush. The darkness was deepening by the minute.

She cleared her throat. "Okay, over there." She pointed to an outcrop far from their goal. She received some distrustful looks, but her team jogged over as she'd ordered. Clements was standing to one side, whistle in hand, checking the time.

They put on their light-sensitive suits. If a laser beam hit them, their suits would vibrate and sound an alarm. If they were hit in a vital part of the body, a 'death' alarm would sound, and they had to cease firing and stay where they were. A hit in a less-vulnerable spot would trigger a 'wound' alarm. After three wounds, they had to act as though dead. The suits recorded if any student disobeyed the rules.

Behind the outcrop, Jas drew the team together and explained her plan.

"But we're the furthest away," one of them complained. "The others will get there minutes before us."

"No, they won't. They're going to be fighting it out between them. If we stay at the back for a while, the others will take each other out along the way. They won't be firing at us. We can pick them off from behind. We'll stay out of sight. They're going to think it's the other side who's firing, and they'll shoot at them, not us. When we've taken out the opposition as best we can, Richard can do his stuff."

Her team's expressions changed at her explanation.

"Okay," one said. "Let's do it."

The whistle blew, and the teams began to move. Almost immediately, an alarm sounded. Someone had tried to make a quick dash for the prize. The alarm was a high-pitched burst of sound. They'd been fatally hit. The 'dead' student sat down disconsolately. More students appeared briefly among the ice blocks. Another alarm sounded, and another. Wound alarms.

"Milas, go left," Jas said into her mic. She'd caught sight of another team's member who had figured out her strategy. The student was doubling back to sneak up on them from behind. Milas hadn't seen the approaching student. He was running for cover, but he wouldn't make it. She lifted her gun to her shoulder to take aim. The high-pitched alarm sounded again, and the attacking student threw down his gun in anger. Someone had shot him. Jas glanced around to find Milas' savior. Sergei was behind her, pretending to blow smoke from the muzzle of his weapon.

What was he doing? He wasn't even on her team. "Why'd you do that?"

"You don't always have to play by the rules, Jas."

She was vaguely annoyed. It was only a game, but if everyone messed around, no one would learn anything. She turned away, then immediately felt guilty. This was the man who loved her, and she loved him. She looked back to give him a smile, but he'd gone.

The other two teams were down to two people each. Milas' head popped out from around a chunk of ice. He shot and took out another student. Everyone was only fifty meters or so from the prize.

"Final stage," Jas said into her mic.

Richard started his run. He was the fastest of all of them. Jas knew where one of the other team members was, and she was waiting. As the woman peeped out, she shot her. A death alarm sounded, and the woman stood up. Richard was still running. A wound alarm rang out. Was he hit? Where was his assailant? Milas and another student rolled into view, throwing punches.

Another wound alarm. Someone was shooting at Richard. She desperately scanned the ice blocks in the deep twilight. Who was still left to shoot? Jas saw her. It was the smallest student, curled into a ball behind a small ice boulder that didn't look large enough to hide anyone.

Richard was almost at the target. The small student raised her weapon to take another shot, and Jas fired. As Richard put his hand on the prize, two alarms sounded. Death alarms. Jas had hit the student square in the back. There was no doubt that she was dead. But had she managed to kill Richard before he'd gotten to the prize?

Everyone who was hiding revealed themselves, and the dead

students stood up. Clements would tell them the outcome and give a brief breakdown of events. They would complete a more thorough analysis the next morning.

As Jas was going over to join the others, a faint rumble seemed to come from nowhere. She paused, confused, and looked up. Was there storm on the way? The sky was starry and clear. The rumble grew louder. Vibration ran up her legs. The sound was coming from the ground.

The instructor was shouting, ordering them to run to the transport. Jas froze for a moment, wondering what was going on. The vibration got stronger, rocking her and almost throwing her off her feet. Then she understood. The ice they were standing on was breaking free of the land. They were on a newly calving, massive iceberg.

She sprinted for the vehicle, joining the other students speeding across the ice, slipping and stumbling in their haste. The driver had started the engine by the time they arrived. The students piled in. The instructor climbed aboard last, made a quick survey of the dark, empty landscape, and told the driver to go.

Most of the students hadn't had time to take seats. They were thrown backward into a jumble of bodies as the transport flew from the scene.

She was crushed against a window at the back. Behind them, a fissure yawned blackly in the shimmering surface. It quickly grew, exposing sheer walls of fresh ice. Her mouth fell open. The area where they'd just been standing was moving. It was crumbling, shifting. Millions of tons of ice was drifting, slipping away, out to sea. Huge waves rose up in the fissure and smashed down. A tidal wave of sea water rushed toward them, catching up to them even though the transport was tearing away from the scene. Her heart rose into her mouth.

The water seemed to rear up and reach out to the vehicle, but when it crashed down, it fell short. Only its feeble fingertips scrabbled at the transport's sleds.

Most of the other students had gotten into their seats while the scene was playing out, oblivious to what had just happened. When Jas was unpinned from the window, she saw Clements looking back, white-faced.

She found an empty seat and sat down, washed over with relief at their narrow escape. She took off her helmet and unzipped her suit. Her pulse began to slow, but something niggled at her. Something was wrong.

A terrible dread clutched her. She whipped around in her seat, looking for a face among the students in front and behind.

Sergei.

Where was Sergei?

Thirteen

Jas was in a starjump. She was nowhere. She didn't exist. She lay on her bed, unmoving. At times, Tamara came to her, talked to her, fed her. In between her friend's visits, sights and sounds entered her consciousness. The movements of her roommate, shadows that fell as she blocked the light. Noises from outside. Wind, and the hum of drones passing. Daylight filled the room, then darkness. Light, dark. How many times?

She was in a pit. She was at the bottom of a well, underwater. Somewhere above her, life carried on as normal, but she couldn't reach it. She couldn't climb out. Or was it that she didn't want to?

Murmuring in her room. "How long?" asked a voice. "It's been too long."

The college medic came. He checked her over, took her pulse, listened to her breathing, looked into her eyes, tested her reflexes. He asked her questions, but it was like he was speaking through wool. She heard the words, but as soon as she thought she understood, the meaning would slip away like threads of silk in the wind.

He left.

Pills arrived in Tamara's hands. She pushed Jas up, put them in her mouth, and made her drink water. She slept.

As she woke, she heard her roommate say, "She doesn't even cry. It's weird."

Jas opened her eyes. Tamara was here. Jas moved, and her friend noticed. "Jas, you're awake," she said, coming over and squatting down. "How are you feeling?"

Her jaw muscles were strangely weak. "Groggy," she mumbled.

Tamara exhaled and touched her head. "That's the first thing you've said in days."

She thought this information was probably significant, but she didn't know why.

"Becca and I were thinking it would be a good idea if we swapped rooms for the rest of the semester. I'll look after you until you're feeling better."

Was she sick? That had to be it. She had to be sick.

"Is that okay?" Tamara asked.

She forced her neck down, giving a slight nod.

———

It was weeks before she could mention the accident, and then she couldn't say his name. One evening, as Tamara was doing her homework and Jas was looking sightlessly out of the window, she said, "What happened after?"

"Hmm?" Tamara said absently. When Jas didn't reply, she looked up. She registered what Jas had said, and her face crumpled in sorrow. "I'm so sorry. After...after it happened, as soon as it was safe, you all went back to look for him. The police sent out a search party. They had boats out and helis. Everyone looked for days. Don't you remember?"

She shook her head. "All I remember is..." The last thing she recalled was the tendrils of seawater slipping from the tracks of the transport, and the dark, frozen landscape retreating. That, and the figure of a man pretending to blow smoke from a gun.

Then he was gone.

———

The next day, she got up and checked her interface for today's classes. Battle tactics, weapons, survival, hand-to-hand. She went to take a shower, but Tamara was in the bathroom. She waited outside until her friend came out, toweling her hair.

"You're up already?" Tamara asked. "Do you want some breakfast? I could make us both some. I still have time."

"I don't want any breakfast."

"You've got to eat. You're wasting away to nothing."

"I'm fine," Jas said as she closed the door.

When she came out and started to get her things ready, Tamara asked, "You're going to class?"

"I've gotten really behind. How much have I missed? I don't know. It's been weeks."

"You don't have to. The college said you can repeat this semester on health grounds." Tamara looked alarmed. When Jas didn't stop putting things in her bag, Tamara went over to her friend.

"Jas," she said, gently taking her bag from her. "Honestly, you don't have to go to class. It's okay."

Jas took her bag back. "I *do* have to go to class. I do." She finished packing her bag. Then she put on her coat and hat and went out. She walked quickly. She was almost running. Something was inside her—something squirming like a damned soul trying to escape hell. If she could keep moving, if she could maintain focus, maybe she could prevent it from emerging and overwhelming her.

Gazes were upon her at her first class, but she barely noticed. Dealing with the attention being a poor Martian had brought was nothing compared to what she carried around now and forever. She listened carefully and made extensive notes. A test was coming up next week. The final for that class. Had so much time passed? She could hardly believe it. She would have to catch up on the work. It would be hard, but she could do it. The same with the other subjects. She wouldn't skip the semester. She would graduate on schedule, and then she would leave on the first starship that would take her. If she left Antarctica far behind, maybe that would quiet the thing that writhed.

The morning flew by. Over lunch, she fixated on her interface, hungrily devouring the information, but not her food. In the afternoon, she was a silent member of survival training while the rest of the class discussed gathering water from the air in a desert.

Then came hand-to-hand combat. As usual, she stood at the back, but she was the tallest person in the group. There was no way that Trankle could fail to notice her return. The first thing he said when he came into the training room was, "So Ms Martian's here. Welcome back. Glad you're over your *illness*. Feeling better?"

She didn't answer. She fixed her gaze on him.

He lifted his lip scornfully, turned to the other students and clapped his hands. "Last session of the year. Most of you have done pretty well. Some not so well. Today, we sort the wheat from the chaff. You know the drill. Five minutes per pair, on the mat, anything legal goes. Got it? Who's first?"

Two students went to the mat. Trankle took out an interface and stood to the side. He nodded, and the students began to fight. Jas followed their motions, their blows and holds. They were pretty evenly matched. Had Trankle paired them up himself according to their fitness and ability? Who was her partner?

Trankle blew a whistle. The five minutes were up. He waved the students off and made notes on his interface. Another pair took their place. They too began to fight. A third pair replaced them, and a fourth. The process was efficient. Trankle gave no indication whether a student had passed or failed.

Finally, all the students had fought. Only Jas was left. The class was an odd number and there was no one to partner her. The students were standing around, waiting to be dismissed. The final pair to fight were panting.

Trankle completed his notes, smiled to himself, closed the interface, and put it down in a corner. He returned to the center, folded his arms, and rocked on his heels, a small smile still playing around his lips. "Looks like there's no one left to fight with our Martian.

Shame, but it doesn't really matter. You've missed so many classes, Harrington, you've already failed."

"Huh No. I only have to pass the test. It doesn't matter how much I've missed. I have a health exemption."

Trankle shook his head. "My class, my rules. And I don't accept health exemptions."

He was lying. "I want to fight."

"I've just told you, you can't. The course is over. Class dismissed."

She didn't move. "I want to fight."

"Give her a chance," a student said. "I'll fight again. I'll fight you, Jas."

"Yeah, give her a chance," a few more students echoed.

Trankle snorted. "You just don't know when to give up, do you, Harrington? Right. So you want to fight? You can fight me. Come on. Let's do it." He backed up until he was on the training mat.

She didn't hesitate. The thing inside drove her. She ran at her tormentor, taking him by surprise. At the last second, she jumped and kicked him in the stomach. Trankle tried to block her foot, but she was too fast. Her heel sank into his abdomen, and if the man hadn't been well-muscled, that would have been the end of the fight.

He doubled over and staggered back, his face red and contorted. She raised her foot again to deliver a kick to his head, but he just managed to catch her calf before the blow connected. They struggled for a moment, Trankle still bent over, one arm over his stomach and the other hand gripping her leg. She hopped and tugged, trying to free her foot.

The instructor regained a little breath and immediately expended it in a cry of rage. This galvanized her. Instead of trying to get away from him, she hopped closer. With her height advantage, she easily brought down a fist on the back of his skull. He fell forward, his grip on her ankle broken. He hadn't even reached the mat before she kicked his head, snapping it to the side. With a dull thunk and a loud exhale, he hit the floor.

She drew back her leg to kick him again, but hands were

restraining her, pulling her away. When she stopped struggling, the hands let go. She was vaguely aware of pain radiating from her foot. She stared at the unconscious Trankle, hardly knowing what she'd done.

For the moment at least, the thing inside her was quiet.

———

The year was over. Tamara was packing, getting ready to catch the autobus that would take her to the spaceport. "Jas, my offer still stands. Why won't you come home with me for the long vacation? My dad really won't mind."

She shook her head. "I'll miss your cooking, but I'll be fine right here. I found a place in town to stay while I catch up on my studies."

"But you passed everything. Why do you need to study?"

"I *scraped* all my passes. If I don't catch up on what I missed, I'm only going to find everything harder next year."

"But what if you run out of creds? Are you sure you have enough?"

"I'll find a job. It's tourist season. There has to be some casual work around. I'll be okay."

"But..." Tamara sighed. "I'm not going to persuade you, am I?"

"I'm going to be fine. I promise. Now I don't have the inquiry into my fight with Trankle hanging over me, I just want to concentrate and work."

"That was sweet how all the students said it was a fair fight, wasn't it?"

She chuckled. "I bet he'll wear his safety gear next time he decides to do some sparring."

"Huh, yeah. Well, keep in touch, right?" Tamara zipped up her case and gave Jas a hug.

When she had gone, Jas started her own packing. She didn't have many things, so it didn't take her long. When she'd finished, she took a final look at the room. She recalled Aggy's sullen face as she'd argued with her boyfriend on her interface, and Becca, who Jas hadn't gotten to know very well. Last, she remembered kind, loyal Tamara, who had cared for her when she was at her lowest.

Someone else had also spent many nights in her room, but she skirted around the memory. She wasn't ready to go there yet.

In another two years, she would be saying goodbye to the McMurdo Sound Training Institute for the last time. At that thought, she climbed onto her bare mattress to look up into the sky. A whole galaxy was open to her. She wondered where she would go and what she would find there.

JAS'S STORY CONTINUES IN ...

THE GALATHEA CHRONICLES

CARRIE HATCHETT'S CHRISTMAS

THE BOOKS OF CARRIE HATCHETT, SPACE ADVENTURER

Book 1: *Mission Improbable*
Book 2: *Passage to Paradise*
Book 3: *Transgalactic Antics*
Book 4: *Wrong Side of Time*
Book 5: *Carrie's Calamity*

CARRIE HATCHETT'S CHRISTMAS IS A SUPPLEMENTARY STORY

Santa's Grotto

Ms. Emily Wainwright stood holding the hand of a little girl in a queue that snaked from the entrance of Selfridges and down Oxford Street, London. Snow had begun to fall, the first that season, and though it was only four in the afternoon, the street lights began to wink on, supplementing the rainbow hues of Christmas lights, bright in the approaching late afternoon dusk. The child shivered a little. Emily looked down and smiled and held her hand tighter.

The little girl wasn't her daughter. Ms. Wainwright worked in a children's home, and the child lived at the home, the most recent of a long string of residences she had lived in since she was born. In Emily's experience, the girl's history was familiar. Babies, especially foundling babies such as the girl had been, were usually easy to place with loving adoptive parents, providing they fitted within the spectrum of what society considered normal. Sadly, the little girl's appearance didn't fall in that category, and no one returned to see her after their first visit.

Emily Wainwright had a big heart, but for some reason she'd never found anyone to share it with, and she'd formed an attachment to the child that she knew was unprofessional. Little Beth Lam wouldn't have been a burden to her. Named after Lambeth, the

London borough in which she'd been found as a newborn, she was a pleasure to be around, and though no doctor had been able to diagnose the cause of her physical oddities, all had concluded that she was otherwise normal in every way. Except that for the last few months Beth had failed to gain any weight, and each day grew paler and more tired.

"Will I see Santa soon?" asked the child, turning her peculiar eyes up at her guardian.

"Yes, Beth," replied Emily, "not much longer now. We're near the doors, and when we get inside we'll be warmer."

"I'm so excited," said Beth, jumping on the tips of her toes.

The temperature was falling as fast as the snow, now that the winter sun had set, but, as was typical for the child, she didn't complain. Emily's own hands were numb, and with her small frame, the little girl must have been chilled. She wore the cheap secondhand clothes all the looked-after children wore. The hood of her thin parka was pulled down over her head to keep her warm as well as hide her deformities from the gaze of curious Christmas shoppers.

A group of carollers were singing to the accompaniment of hand-bells to entertain the waiting customers. People towards the front of the queue began to move through Selfridges' wide doorway and into the department store. Those waiting ahead of the woman and child closed the gap and the pair followed, until at last they were inside and basking in the cranked-up heat of oil-fed furnaces.

Beth gasped aloud, causing the family waiting in front to turn around. A boy stared at her, saying, "Urghh...what's wrong with that girl, Mummy?" His mother tugged on his hand, turning him to face forward. "Don't be rude," she hissed.

A shadow of pain flickered over Beth's face, but the little girl had grown used to taunts and comments, and she had learned to ignore them. "It's beautiful," she said, referring to Santa's Grotto, which occupied a full third of Selfridge's ground floor.

Indeed it was beautiful. Even Emily, who had been coming to Santa's Grotto at Selfridges for as long as she could remember, was impressed. Her mother had brought her every Christmas when she was growing up, until she was really much too big. Later, she had brought nephews, nieces and now looked-after children who often had no parents to bring them. But in all those Christmases she had never seen a display more magical.

Rocky walls stretched from floor to ceiling, their realistic crags dusted with snow that looked freshly fallen, sparkling faintly in the shop's blazing overhead lights. A path wove from Selfridges' front door to the secretive entrance to the grotto, bordered by holly, mistletoe, ivy and pine that scented the air with a resinous odour. Animal figures appeared to gambol through the green growth: foxes, hares, weasels in their winter coats; and birds perched in the branches: snowy owls, red-breasted robins, and speckled thrushes. All seemed to have frozen to stillness only a second earlier. Blue-white snow encrusted the path and forest scene, and Emily and Beth crunched it with their footsteps as they followed the diminishing queue slowly disappearing through the grotto entrance.

"Will I sit on Santa's lap?" asked Beth.

"Of course you will."

"And can I ask for a present? Whatever I want?"

Emily's heart ached. She knew too well what gift most of the looked-after children asked Santa for: something even he wasn't able to provide.

"You can ask for whatever you want," replied Emily, "but Santa might not be able to give it to you."

"Not even if I've been very good?"

"Not even if you've been very, very good, Beth." Emily turned her head to one side and ran a finger under an eye before turning back to the girl wearing a bright smile. "But he'll give you a present, and would you like a mince pie to eat on the way home?"

"Oh, yes please," exclaimed the child.

Another set of people entered the grotto, and the queue shuffled forward several steps. Emily and Beth were among the trees now. They were hung with gorgeous baubles, shining in iridescent hues. Beth pulled on Emily's hand as she leaned close to gaze at her reflection in a shiny surface.

A cry came from with the grotto. It was a deep voice, a man's voice, shouting in alarm. The hum of conversation in the queue abruptly stopped, and the people looked around as if to check that others had heard the same thing. Another cry, louder, sounded, followed by the shouts of more voices. Looks of puzzlement in the queue turned to alarm, and some members edged away from the grotto entrance.

"Ms. Wainwright," said Beth, looking up at her guardian for reassurance. "What was that?"

But Emily had no reassurance to give. "Perhaps we'd better come back tomo—"

A bang shook the grotto, vibrating the floor beneath Emily and Beth's feet. The queue melted and people began to run for the doors. The rest of Selfridges' customers also began rapidly leaving. Emily scooped Beth up into her arms and tried to fight her way through the stampede, struggling to keep her feet.

"Please," she gasped as a large man pushed roughly past, almost causing her to drop the child. Woman and girl were carried through Selfridges' doors and into the street, where Emily had no choice but to follow in the direction of the crowd as she was swept along. At a Tube entrance, however, she took her chance to escape. She stepped to one side out of the flow of the throng into the lee of the Underground entry wall.

Setting Beth on her feet, Emily peered out from their place of safety and back towards Selfridges. She'd heard nothing but the noise of the crowd since the bang. Shoppers continued to flood from the department store's doors, but no smoke or fire was to be seen, and no one seemed injured. Sirens wailed up Oxford Street, and in the distance the lights of emergency service vehicles flashed.

Wary of stepping out into the mad rush with a small child, Emily waited a few more moments, watching the crowd and hoping for a gap in the foot traffic, and this was how she got such a good view of the cause of the disturbance, though she didn't know it at the time.

The first thing she saw of them were the points of their green felt hats, low down among the shoulders of the escaping shoppers. A sparkling scarlet feather waved to the side of each green point as the elves approached. The frontrunner confirmed Emily's suspicion that the hats belonged to Santa's elves. He—it appeared to be a he, though Emily found it hard to be sure, as the elves looked quite androgynous—he was wearing a bright green tunic that matched his hat, bright green leggings, a silver belt and pointed silver boots. The rest of the elves appeared behind their leader, dodging and weaving through Selfridge's advancing customers like long-distance runners making their way to the front of a race.

Emily had only a few seconds' close-up view of the faces of Santa's short, plump helpers as they passed by, but what she saw made her gasp.

A Surprise Visitor

Carrie Hatchett was in her kitchen, smoothing the top of a freshly made cake. The sound of thumping came from somewhere in the region of her feet. Her dog, Rogue's, tail was repeatedly hitting the floor as he looked up at her hopefully, drooling.

"Sorry, you've got to wait until Christmas." Carrie scanned the recipe instructions. It was the first time she'd made a dogfood cake and she didn't want to get anything wrong. She'd followed the instructions exactly right up to the last sentence on the page, *Mold the mixture into a shape of your choice*. She'd made a large bone.

Carrie wiped a hand on her apron and flicked over the page, but the new page showed a new recipe, a wild bird food mixture. What was she supposed to do with her finished masterpiece? Put it in the oven? Leave it to set in the fridge? She looked from Rogue to the cake and back to the dog. He ate anything she put in front of him and whatever else he managed to get his sloppy jaws around, whether it was cooked, uncooked, or three days old and smelly. She put the cake in the fridge.

Carrie paused a moment at the opened fridge door and took stock of the rest of the goodies chilling inside.

It was Christmas Eve, and her festive preparations were nearly complete. It was going to be a quiet Christmas this year. Her family had gone abroad, and she had been unable to join them. Being the owner of a call centre meant precious little free time, especially during the festive season when the phones were ringing off their hooks with inquiries about presents. Luckily her best friend, Dave, was also at a loose end, and he was going to join her for Christmas dinner. So far, she had Brussels sprouts, carrots, broccoli, potatoes, nut roast, stuffing, a cheese platter and crackers, crisps, olives, fruit, brandy snaps, gingerbread, shortbread, plum pudding, a Yule log, mince pies and double cream. She wondered if that would be enough.

Her cat, Toodles' present was already made, though she'd had to wrap it in two plastic bags and lock it in a cupboard to prevent the scent of catnip from driving the animal wild.

Yes, it would be a nice, quiet Christmas for the four of them. Carrie had even managed to explain the importance of the Christmas holidays to her alien employers for her second job, which was with the Transgalactic Council. She'd been promised three days free of assignments in her role as Transgalactic Intercultural Community Crisis Liaison Officer. Travelling across the galaxy and meeting aliens was fun, but everyone needed a break now and then.

Carrie closed the fridge door, stood upright and cocked an ear. Dave had popped over to lend a hand with the preparations, but he'd gone to the bathroom and had been away a suspiciously long time. Her friend was a lovely man who was also a Liaison Officer, but he happened to have kleptomaniac tendencies. She was never quite at ease when she didn't have her eyes on him.

Rogue gave a loud bark, causing Carrie to jump. He looked at her expectantly.

"I've told you, you can't have any cake until Christmas."

Rogue gave another bark, ran to the kitchen door, lolloped back to Carrie, and looked up, wagging his tail.

"What is it?"

Her dog gently took her sleeve in his mouth and tugged her towards the door.

"Carrie, someone's calling on your translator," Dave shouted down.

"Oh, that's what you could hear," said Carrie to her dog. "Clever boy." She climbed her stairs. "Why are they contacting me now?" she asked Dave, who was waiting on the upstairs landing. "We're supposed to be getting some time off."

Her friend shrugged. "Better answer it. It sounds like someone you'd like to hear from."

"You were gone a long time," Carrie said over her shoulder as she went into her bedroom. She caught Dave's glare while she fished her translator out of her Transgalactic Intercultural Community Crisis Liaison Officer toolkit.

The voice she heard was familiar. "Liaison Officer Hatchett, please—"

"Gavin?" Carrie asked. Surely it couldn't be...?

"Yes, Carrie, it is I."

"Gavin," exclaimed Carrie, "this is brilliant. Have they given you your old job back? Are you my manager again?"

"No, no," replied Gavin, "I have not returned to my former employment as a Transgalactic Council Manager. This is a one-off assignment and somewhat of an emergency. The Council contacted me because I am their only expert in Slevih. It is an obscure language, and I learned it on a whim, never expecting to have an opportunity to use it. It is fascinating. The language has thirty-two tenses, one of which is based on the orientation of the speaker and listeners, and another that conjugates according to whether the speaker or speakers have ever observed the action described."

"Gavin, what are you talking about?"

"Oh, haha, I do apologise. I became a little engrossed in my subject matter. Perhaps it would be better if I came there and explained in person?"

Dave was standing in the doorway. As Gavin's offer his eyebrows rose and he waved his arms as he backed away.

"Come here? To my house? Are you allowed to come to Earth?" asked Carrie.

"Not ordinarily, but the Transgalactic Council have allowed an exception. In this case it is unavoidable. I will open a gateway and be there in a moment."

"Say no," called Dave from the landing. "Say he can't come. He won't fit in your bedroom anyway. And he's got jaws. Massive jaws."

"Don't be silly," Carrie said as a green mist formed in midair and began to swirl into a spiral. "It's Christmas, and Gavin's our friend. What better time is there for him to come over? And you know he's lovely. I can't believe you're still scared of him."

"Scared? Who said I was scared?" asked Dave. "Anyway, I'm going downstairs. I'm feeling a bit...hungry. Have you got any biscuits?"

The swirling green mist widened until it reached floor to ceiling, and a large, spindly, insectoid leg appeared through it.

"No, I haven't got any biscuits," said Carrie as Dave descended and disappeared. "You ate the last lot I had, and I haven't had a chance to buy any more." She stepped back to make room for her former manager as he arrived. "Hello, Gavin."

The massive alien's one hundred compound eyes turned to Carrie, and his razor-sharp inner jaws protruded, dripping saliva that steamed and hissed as it hit Carrie's carpet. She would have to give the carpet another clean tomorrow, but it was no trouble when it meant seeing the creature who had first introduced her to exciting galactic adventures.

"Hello, Carrie, my dear."

The alien's large frame squeezed Carrie into a corner. "It's lovely to see you again, Gavin, but what are you doing here?"

"As I was explaining, I have been brought in because the Council has no one else who can speak Slevih. It is so rare the translators have not been programmed with the language."

"And why...?"

"Oh yes, of course, you have not yet been informed. For the first time in millenia, Slevs have been sighted. They are an ancient, evil race, and they appear to be invading Earth."

"What?" exclaimed Carrie. "What are we waiting for? Let's go."

"Do you not think you might require a little more information?"

Carrie flushed a little. "Shall we go downstairs?"

ELF INVASION

"I'll make us some tea," said Dave, leaving for the kitchen as Gavin followed Carrie downstairs and into the living room.

"I don't want any tea," said Carrie. "Come here. You need to hear this. We've got a job to do, and Gavin's come to help us."

Dave stood with his back to the living room wall and his arms folded while the alien hulked in the centre of the room, blocking the sunlight from the windows and casting everything into shadow. Carrie turned on the light. Gavin's bronze carapace gleamed.

"Run us through it," said Carrie to the giant insect.

He sank down, the joints of his ten pairs of legs rising above his head and abdomen. "The Slevs are a mysterious species who have roamed the galaxy since time immemorial, or at least we believe so. Tales of creatures resembling them exist in the ancient history of many cultures across the reach of space. The tales speak of abductions and other evil acts, usually referred to as forms of magic, though of course the Slevs were no doubt using advanced technologies that the locals did not understand at that point in their development. Slevs have never to anyone's knowledge applied to join the Galactic Unity, nor availed themselves of transgalactic gateways, preferring instead to spend years crawling the galaxy in their starships.

"And now they have arrived here on Earth, instilling terror and panic. Why they have come, no one knows. Their behaviour indicates their motives are malevolent. Perhaps they have decided to give up their nomadic lifestyle and settle in one place. Your planet has many attractive features, despite the depredations of humans."

"Can't the Unity just round them up and force them to leave?" asked Dave.

"That is the problem. We cannot make them leave because we cannot find them. That is where you and Carrie come in. We need your help to locate the invaders."

"How do you know they're here?" asked Carrie.

"There was an initial sighting in London a week ago, but since then they seem to have disappeared without trace."

"Aliens running around London and no one can find them? What do they look like?" Dave asked.

"They are a little shorter than the average human," replied Gavin, "though otherwise their physical structure is similar. They carry a green, pointed, odour sensing organ on their heads, which has a red protuberance rather like the feather of an Earth bird. Their skin is a medley of green and silver and resembles human clothing. Their ears differ markedly from humans, however, in that they are fleshy and pointed and rise above their heads. It is this characteristic that clearly sets them apart. I am surprised we have not had more notifications of sightings from members of the general public."

Carrie and Dave were looking at each other. "Elves," they said simultaneously.

"No, Slevs," said Gavin.

Carrie turned to the alien. "They look like Santa's elves. It's Christmas, and people are dressing up as elves everywhere. That's why no one's spotting them."

"Humans dress up as Slevs? Why would they do that?"

"They aren't dressing up as...look, never mind. If these Slevs look like elves, Dave and I know what we're looking for. You said there's been one sighting. Where was it?"

"It was in an establishment adjacent to a highway in your country's capital. I believe the highway goes by the name of Oxford Street."

"We have to find aliens that look like elves on Oxford Street at Christmas?" said Dave. "We've got our work cut out for us."

"We must start in the area they were most recently spotted," said Gavin, "and work our way outward. The local police have been enlisted to help with the assignment, and there are two members of the public who got a close look and might be able to identify them again."

"Hold on," said Carrie, "what do you mean *we*? You aren't going to join us, are you?"

"You'll give everyone the fright of their lives if you step outside Carrie's door," added Dave.

"I will simply engage my invisibility function. It requires a little effort but it is not arduous."

"You can turn invisible?" exclaimed Carrie. "How come you never told me?"

"I do not recall that you ever enquired."

Carrie didn't know what to say to this.

"So, you're going to come with us? Just like that?" asked Dave.

"No, like this," said Gavin, fading before their eyes until he was nothing more than a shimmer like heat haze above asphalt on a hot summer's day.

———

Travelling in a nearly empty first class carriage was the only way to squeeze Gavin's considerable bulk aboard a train and avoid awkward encounters with passengers coming up against his hard, chitinous exoskeleton. Even so, Carrie was sure the buffet cart assistant suspected something when she hit an unexpected invisible barrier while wheeling the cart through the carriage. The puff of chocolate scent that Carrie smelled—Gavin's *Ouch* in his mother language of pheromones—didn't help. She clutched her Transgalactic Intercultural Community Crisis Liaison Officer toolkit tighter. You never knew when you might need some specialised alien technology to make a quick getaway.

As soon as they arrived in London, they went to Scotland Yard, where advance notice had been given of their arrival, as they were ushered immediately into the office of the Commissioner of the Police of the Metropolis. The woman showed no surprise when Gavin uncloaked. Certain key people in relevant positions on all of Earth's nations were aware of the Transgalactic Council and the watch it kept over planets that supported life.

Tall and thin, with short gray hair that still bore a few strands of its original auburn, the Commissioner turned a little paler at the sight of him, however.

"Thank you for coming," she said, gesturing to two seats. Carrie and Dave sat down and Gavin crouched. "We appreciate the aid of the Transgalactic Council in this matter of global security. I'll be brief because in truth we, unfortunately, have very little to tell you. The...Slevs, I believe they're called?...were spotted last Thursday evening at Selfridges' Santa's Grotto, where they caused a disturbance that could have resulted in serious injury to the public."

Carrie gasped. "I remember now. I saw it on the news. But the report said a spotlight had burst, and the shoppers thought it was a bomb going off, so they stampeded out of the shop."

The Commissioner smiled wryly. "Not quite. There's only so much we can reveal to the press, you understand. No, as far as we can ascertain from interviewing the staff, parents and children present, the Slevs were in the grotto helping Santa give out his presents, when one of them removed a child's hat for some reason. This angered the boy, and he tried to remove the alien's hat in return, only to find it was soft, fleshy and warm, and appeared to be part of the Slev's head.

"The child began crying and saying that the elf's hat was alive. To calm his fears, Santa went to remove another elf's hat, but shouted in alarm when he couldn't. At that moment the Slevs seem to have decided to make a run for it, because there was a bang and the lights in the grotto went out, causing mass panic."

"Right, I see," said Carrie. "Can we speak to Santa and the boy?"

The Commissioner sighed. "The boy's parents refuse to allow him to be interviewed again, and Santa has developed amnesia over the incident. He says he has no idea what we're talking about, and repeats the story about the spotlight exploding that he's read in the paper. We've tried playing him the recording of his initial statement, but he insists the voice isn't his. Even hypnotism hasn't worked."

"Damn," said Dave, "we're on our own then. They might have given us some tips on what to look for. I mean, apart from green hats and pointy ears."

"It's easy," said Carrie, "we just have to find elves who aren't really elves. At Christmas."

The landline on the Commissioner's desk rang. The woman picked up the phone, and her eyes widened as she listened. "There's been another sighting. At Shaftesbury Avenue this time. The Slevs have been assaulting children in the audience of a pantomime."

"Oh no," Carrie exclaimed, jumping from her seat. "That's terrible. Let's get over there."

OH YES IT IS

Chaos reigned at the panto by the time Carrie, Dave and Gavin arrived. The insectoid alien was invisible once more to avoid causing even more panic. The show had been stopped and the stage curtains drawn for an impromptu intermission as the theatre management tried to calm things down then start the show again once the Slevs had been found and evicted, but parents were already forming a queue at the ticket office and asking for their money back. Some were simply walking out.

"Thank goodness you're here," breathed the heavily made up, large-bosomed theatre manager, who was trying to persuade families to return to their seats. She spoke to the police officer who accompanied Carrie and Dave, but he quickly indicated that they were the ones to speak to.

"Tell us what happened," said Carrie.

"I'm Mrs. Beaumont," said the manager, shaking their hands before gesticulating wildly and continuing, "It was pandemonium. Strange elves suddenly appeared and ran into the audience. They must have been hiding in the theatre because no one saw them come in. They started grabbing at the children. At first everyone thought it was all part of the show, but soon there were tears and screams. Parents were shouting and fighting the elves off. The actors abandoned their roles and went to help. I heard the commotion from my office. There were punches thrown from both sides, I believe, then the elves ran away, but they didn't leave. They're still here somewhere in the theatre." The woman placed her hands together as if in prayer. "Could you please get them out before they do something else? I can't afford to give the money back for the tickets. The theatre's on its last legs. The bad publicity from this alone could put us under."

"We'll do our best, of course," said Dave. "Could you tell us what they look like?"

"I never saw them close up, but you could ask one of the actors. I'm sure they can give a good description."

"Right," said Carrie, "can you show us backstage?" They followed Mrs. Beaumont through the crowd, leaving the police officer to help calm the situation in the lobby. Gavin cut a swathe with his invisible bulk, leaving some very puzzled mothers, fathers and children behind him.

As they made their way from the public areas to the quieter, colder, plainer stairways and corridors at the rear of the theatre, Carrie heard Gavin mumbling, and she caught whiffs of a strange odour.

In the green room they found both halves of the pantomime horse sipping on tumblers of what looked like whisky. The actor in the back half was still in costume, his legs in large horses' legs suspended on braces over his shoulders. The actor in the front half had taken off his horse's head. It lay on the floor beside him. The men's hands were trembling, slopping their drinks. The actor playing the pantomime dame was with them, wearing an outrageously wide-skirted dress and a huge wig with ringlets. He was looking anxiously through the door that led to the wings.

"Lionel, Lawrence, what are you doing back here?" asked the manager the second they entered the room. "It's Act Two. You should be on stage."

"I can't get them to move an inch," said the dame, his thick stage make-up infused with an angry flush. "They should have been out there five minutes ago. Everyone's been improvising, waiting for them to come on. They can't keep it up much longer."

"We're not going out there," said the back half of the horse. "What if those elves come back?"

"They're horrible, horrible," exclaimed the front half. "Their eyes, their ears, their hats. It isn't a costume, it's them." He shivered and took a swallow of whisky, which made him cough.

"Never mind that now," hissed the dame. "You've got to get on stage. You're going to put us all out of a job. I can see people getting up. They're going to walk out again, then the show really will be over, for all of us."

"Oh dear, oh dear," murmured Gavin.

"What was that? Who spoke?" asked the back half of the horse. "It wasn't you, or you." He pointed at Dave and Carrie. "It came from over there." His eyes searched the half of the room where Gavin stood, only a faint bending of the light indicating his presence.

Carrie said, "There's nothing—"

"He's right," said the front half, his eyes wide. "There's something in here with us. I heard it too."

Mrs. Beaumont's mouth was open.

"Oh dear, I do apologise," Gavin said, before blinking into solid reality.

Both halves of the pantomime horse shrieked, dropped their glasses and flew from the room, bowling over the theatre manager, who stood frozen in rigid terror. Being knocked to the floor seemed to break her trance. She squeaked and backed out of the room on all fours. The sound of her running footsteps echoed from the corridor. Only the pantomime dame seemed to retain a modicum of composure, though his previously angry flush had faded to chalky white.

"I knew it was a bad idea for him to come along," said Dave.

"I am very sorry," said Gavin. "This is most unexpected."

"I thought you said it didn't take a lot of effort to stay invisible," said Carrie.

"Under normal circumstances, that is true. But—oh dear, this is very embarrassing—it is that time of the century. I lost track of my cycle. I am...I am...about to moult."

"What?" Dave's voice rose to a nervous pitch. "You're going to shed your skin? Here? Now?"

"Not quite this moment, but in a little while. Until I have moulted, I cannot make myself invisible."

From the stage came the sound of an actor saying loudly, "No, there are no horses for sale around here. None at all." Into the silence that followed the line came disgruntled muttering from the audience. "None *at all*," repeated the actor, shouting.

"You," exclaimed the dame, pointing at Gavin. "Could you go on stage and pretend to be a horse, just for five minutes?"

"A horse? What is a horse?"

"It's an Earth animal," said Carrie, "and no, he can't, sorry. We have to find the Slevs. They must be hiding here somewhere."

"Please," said the dame. "The actors are dying out there, and the poor children will be so disappointed if we stop the show. He only has to go out and walk up and down the back of the stage for a minute or two. I'll tell him what to do and signal when he can come off. Please help us. It's Christmas. We need our wages."

"But he doesn't look anything like a horse," said Dave. "He'll terrify the entire audience, let alone the actors."

"Oh, it won't matter, as long as we have something out there. We can pretend he's adding a space age theme to the panto. Might even get a laugh." The dame had a crazy look in his eye.

"I am happy to help," said Gavin. "I would not like the human children to be sad."

"Great," said the dame as a third *none at all* sounded from the stage, with a note of desperation. "Step through here."

Carrie and Dave looked at each other in disbelief as Gavin squeezed through the green room door, followed closely by the dame. A moment later Gavin's appearance on the stage was marked by the noisy audience drawing an audible breath. The actor repeated, "None at all," but this time his tone was puzzled and questioning.

A silence followed. Carrie anticipated the sound of hundreds of parents and children stampeding out of the theatre. Then a small child's voice shrieked, "He's behind you."

"Behind me?" said the actor with relief. "Oh no, he isn't."

"Oh yes, he is," replied the children in a deafening roar.

"Let me have a look," the actor said. Gavin must not have followed the dame's instruction to hide himself quickly, because the actor gave a short yell before somehow managing to master himself.

"Oh no, he isn't," he said again, shakily.

"Oh yes, he is," insisted the children, giggling with glee.

After a few more moments of back and forth between the actor and audience, the horse's part was over, and Gavin returned backstage.

"Thank goodness that's over," said Carrie. "Now let's find these Slevs."

"I am afraid I cannot accompany you," said Gavin. "I am about to...ahem. I need to find somewhere private."

As he spoke, the theatre manager reappeared. Her hand was across her eyes, and she averted her head from Gavin's position in the room. "Could you...could you two come out here, please? I have some bad news."

Leaving Gavin in the green room, Carrie and Dave joined the manager in the hallway.

"Something appalling has happened," she said. "Apparently, the elves took one of the children."

HIDDEN SECRETS

Emily Wainwright waited in the theatre manager's office, pacing to and fro and checking the time. She wondered why it was taking so long for the police to come. Didn't they take child kidnappings seriously?

Relief flooded her as the door opened. They were here at last. But instead of an officer from the Met, the theatre manager had returned with two people in civilian clothing. The woman was short and a little chubby. She wore her hair in a ponytail. The young man was tall, dark-haired and handsome. He was stylishly dressed. Both of them looked too young to be detectives.

"Are you the police?" Emily asked. "Please, you have to find her. You have to find Beth. She's just a little girl. She'll be terrified. And she isn't well. I shouldn't have brought her here. Oh, why did I bring her?"

"We aren't the police, but they've been informed. We're here to help," said the woman. "I'm Carrie, and this is Dave."

"But, if you aren't the police...?" asked Emily.

"It's difficult to explain," said Carrie, "but we're kind of specialists in this, and the police are searching for the missing child too. Let's sit down. Tell us everything that happened. Are you her mother?"

Emily took out a tissue from her handbag as her tears welled up. Beth's abduction had been so sudden. Now the reality that she was really gone was beginning to hit. The man, Dave, guided her to a seat as her knees gave way. She wept a little before swallowing the lump in her throat and wiping her eyes and nose. She needed to stay strong for Beth's sake. She needed to help these people get her back.

"I'm not her mother. I work in a children's home. I brought Beth to see the panto with some much older looked-after children—oh my goodness, I forgot about them," she exclaimed.

"It's all right," said Mrs. Beaumont, "your colleague is with them. They're fine. They're watching the rest of the panto."

Emily relaxed a little. "We were watching the first act when those awful elves came running up. The children laughed at first, thinking it was all part of the show. But then the elves turned rough. They were grabbing the children's faces and pulling off their hoods and hats. The children started crying and the parents began to push the elves away. No one knew what was going on. Then when the actors left the stage and started fighting the elves, we realised something was very wrong. I'd suspected it of course, because the elves looked the same as the ones I saw at Selfridges, and the same as...well, never mind that, but I knew I had to get our children away from them as quickly as possible."

"Wait a minute," said Carrie. "You were at Selfridges too? When the...er...the spotlight burst?"

"No light burst when I was there," said Emily. "I don't know why the newspapers said that. It was those elves. I saw them plain as day as they were running away."

"You were in both places, though?" said Carrie.

"What happened next?" asked Dave.

"Oh, I'll never forgive myself," said Emily, bursting into fresh tears. "I grabbed Beth—she was the littlest of the children—and told the rest to follow me. I didn't want them to get involved in that nonsense. But I got confused. I went down the wrong aisle. I thought I was leading them to the exit, but we ran right into some of the elves. I tripped over someone's bag and dropped Beth. Then, because the children were following so quickly they all tumbled over me. By the time I managed to get to my feet, the elves must have taken Beth. I couldn't see her among the children. I turned round and thought I spotted some of the elves running down some steps marked 'private'. I tried to follow, but by then aisles were filling with people who wanted to leave. I got to the stairs, but I must have been mistaken because they led to a dead end.

"I couldn't find any theatre staff for a while. After I finally told them what had happened, they looked everywhere. No one can find her. Those awful elves must have taken her. Poor Beth. I'm so sorry."

"No one in the ticket office has seen any elves leave the theatre," said Mrs. Beaumont, "and the stage manager hasn't seen anyone backstage who shouldn't be, so they can't have got out the exit at the rear of the theatre. I'm sure they must be hiding somewhere."

Carrie put a hand on Emily's shoulder. "It isn't your fault. Don't worry, we'll do everything we can to find her. I'm sure we can get her back. Can you show us where you think the elves went?"

Emily nodded and forced herself to her feet. Mrs. Beaumont led the way downstairs. As they reached the ground floor, there was the sound of arguing. The show was over and uniformed police were manning the doors. No one was allowed to leave.

"Oh dear," said the theatre manager. "The audience won't be very happy about this. I'll have to ask the actors to keep them entertained. Mrs. Wainwright, could you excuse me for a few moments? Can you guide our friends to the stairs in question?"

"Yes, I remember where they are very clearly."

The manager left them, and Emily led Carrie and Dave into the theatre, pushing through the people crowded at the exits. When she reached the spot where she had fallen, she stopped. "It was those stairs over there. But I don't think there's much point. It's a dead end, and the theatre staff have searched that area. They said there's nothing there."

"It won't hurt to look again," said Dave. "Carrie and I can sometimes spot things other people can't."

With a heavy heart, Emily went to the stairs. They were dusty and rarely used, leading down into a door in shadow. The tracks of the recent passage of feet were visible on the treads. Gripping the rickety iron railing, Emily descended and went through the ancient fire door.

Beyond was a short corridor with two doors on either side and a blank wall at the end. Both doors were open. Inside the rooms were piles of old, red velvet stage curtains, grimy props and costumes. Painted scenery leaned against the walls. There was no sight nor sound of the elves or little Beth.

"They came down here, but then where did they go I wonder?" said Carrie, looking around.

"Is there anything else you can tell us?" asked Dave. "Anything at all?"

Emily bit her lip. There was one thing she'd noticed, but it seemed ridiculous. She decided to tell them anyway, but at that moment the door to the stairway opened and the theatre manager appeared.

"This is where they took the girl?" Mrs. Beaumont asked.

"This is where I saw them run to," replied Emily. "If Beth was with them, this is where they brought her."

A frown creased the manager's forehead.

"Maybe they hid here for a while and left, and no one noticed," said Carrie.

"Maybe," said Mrs. Beaumont, "and maybe not."

"They must have," said Carrie. "Unless..." She turned to Dave.

"Gavin said they don't use gateways," said her friend.

"Then they must have gone back into the theatre," Carrie said.

"I think I should show you something," Mrs. Beaumont said. She went into the dead-end corridor. "This theatre is more than three hundred years old," she continued. "It was built at a time when acting was not a respectable profession. Many actors had questionable past lives. Lives that sometimes caught up with them, and when they did, it was helpful if the actors could make a quick getaway." She was at the end of the corridor. She crouched down and ran her fingers along the old, bare floorboards. "I don't tell anyone about this, you understand. Too much temptation for silly pranks from the actors and staff." With the heel of her hand, she pushed quickly down on a section of the floor, and three sides of a square trapdoor popped up. She lifted up the door. Emily peered over the woman's shoulder and into the hole. A rusty ladder led down into darkness.

Behind them, the fire door to the audience area opened. Emily turned in time to see it close by itself, without anything apparently coming through. She squeaked and clutched Mrs. Beaumont. "What was that?"

A look passed between Carrie and Dave and the theatre manager.

Mrs. Beaumont said, "Theatres are strange places, Ms. Wainwright. Please try not to be alarmed. We must concentrate on finding little Beth."

Elf Encounter

Carrie stepped from the bottom of the ladder onto a damp earth floor. She fished in her toolkit and took out a torch. Above her, Dave began to climb down. As the beam from her torch penetrated the shadows, it revealed an ancient tunnel lined with bricks.

While she waited for her friend to descend, unformed ideas niggled at Carrie. Ideas about the Slevs, and something the woman, Emily, had said.

Dave jumped the last few rungs of the ladder. "You two probably shouldn't come with us," he called up. "I'm not sure it's safe."

"I want to come," said Emily. "I have to help. How could I live with myself if I didn't?"

"I'm coming too," added Mrs Beaumont. "It's my theatre. I feel responsible."

Both women climbed down, then they all set off. From behind came the faint pings of something invisible also descending the ladder. Gavin was wise to remain silent and invisible, thought Carrie.

The tunnel must have been built at the same time as or not long after the building of the theatre. The bricks were very old, uneven and a mixture of colours. They were cracked, and the mortar between them had all but disappeared. Steady rivulets of water had worn channels in some areas, and the floor was muddy.

"You said you knew about the existence of the tunnel. Do you know where it leads?" Carrie asked the theatre manager.

"I don't, I'm afraid. I never dared come down here myself. I only know about it because my predecessor showed it to me."

And yet the Slevs had known it was there. Did they have some way of detecting hidden tunnels, or had they been there before, wondered Carrie. "We're so stupid," she said to Dave.

"Speak for yourself."

"I mean about the Slevs. It's been staring us in the face all this time. They look like elves because they *are* elves. Slevs, elves, they're practically the same words. It's like Gavin was saying, stories of Slevs appear in cultures across the galaxy. The Slevs must have visited Earth before, and that's how they knew about the tunnel."

"What do you mean, they visited Earth before?" asked Emily. "Are you telling me the elves are aliens? I thought they were little men in costume."

Carrie sighed. "I shouldn't have mentioned it in front of you, but, yes, the creatures who might have taken Beth are aliens."

"Oh no," exclaimed Emily. "I was hoping that this might be just a silly prank. Aliens? What are they going to do to little Beth? This is all my fault." She began to weep.

"Of course it isn't your fault," said Carrie kindly. "You aren't responsible for any of this. How could you be?"

"I shouldn't have brought her here, not after what happened in Selfridges. She isn't well, but like a fool I thought a trip to the panto might do her good. And it's Christmas. I didn't want her to be away from the other children. It didn't seem right for her to be left out.

"I should have left her safely at home. Poor Beth. She's such a funny, lively, loving little girl, but I knew she would struggle to find a forever home. It's hard enough finding foster parents to take her occasionally, just because she looks a little different. I should have adopted her myself."

Emily had hit one of the things that had been niggling at Carrie. Slevs had appeared at both places where Beth had been. They'd been examining the children, looking at their faces, lifting up their hats. And Beth looked different from other children. Was she being targeted because of how she looked? Carrie grabbed Dave's arm to share her idea, but a peal of laughter sounded from up ahead. High, maniacal, elvish—or Slevih—laughter. With a glance at her friend, Carrie pushed her torch into Emily's hand and raced forward towards the sound.

"Carrie, hold on," called Dave. The beam from his torch jiggled on the ancient tunnel bricks as he ran to catch up.

She'd expected to encounter the Slevs around the next bend, but darkness stretched out before her, deeper than her light could penetrate. The tunnel must have echoed the Slevs' voices from farther away than they'd seemed to be. As they ran on, Carrie worried briefly about Emily and Mrs. Beaumont, who were now far behind, then she recalled that Gavin was with them.

The laughter sounded again, much closer. Ahead of them, light glowed. Light that shone from the wet bricks, shimmering and dancing. There were the Slevs. A group of the creatures sat in the tunnel as if waiting for them. They leapt to their feet at the sight of Carrie and Dave, and began jumping up and down and waving.

It was the first time Carrie had seen the aliens. Her mind filled with thoughts of the captive little girl, and she bore down on them. They were indeed the very image of Santa's elves, looking as though they'd stepped out of a fairy tale. From the long ears that reached up the sides of the green sensory organs on their heads, which looked remarkably like hats, to their silver boots. Rushing towards them, Carrie's resolve wavered for a moment. These creatures didn't look evil. They didn't look the type to abduct children. They even had rosy cheeks, just like Santa. But their eyes, there was something weird about their eyes.

The Slevs were chattering loudly and gesticulating, but of course Carrie couldn't understand what they were saying. It didn't matter anyway. She had only one objective: to get little Beth back safe and sound.

"Carrie," gasped Dave from just behind her, "do you think we should—"

She ran at the Slevs, screaming like a banshee. The aliens took one look at her and tried to flee, but in their panic they bumped into each other and ended up in a heap on the floor.

"Carrie," shouted Dave.

"What?" she snapped. This wasn't the time for a conversation. A Slev had got to his feet and was running away. She bounded after him.

"Wait a minute," said Dave. "Look at them. They aren't putting up a fight."

Carrie stopped and turned back. Behind her were Dave and the dazed Slevs she had terrified. The aliens were getting to their feet and rubbing their bumps and bruises. They began chattering and laughing again. They seemed to have found the experience of being frightened very funny.

She walked back to the group. "What's going on?"

"I'm not sure," replied Dave, "but I think we might have the wrong idea about the Slevs."

"Hello? Hello? Are you there?" Emily asked from somewhere down the tunnel.

"We're right ahead of you," said Carrie. "Just keep walking."

In a few moments, Emily and Mrs. Beaumont appeared.

"There they are," exclaimed Emily when she saw the waiting Slevs. "They're the ones that took Beth. Where did you take her? Give her back!"

A Slev went to Emily and knelt down. He touched one ear then the other to the wet tunnel floor before standing and taking the woman's hand and pulling her forward. Carrie finally got a close look at the creatures' eyes. They were entirely black, with no white showing.

"He wants me to go with him," said Emily.

"I think we should do what he says," Carrie said.

The tunnel air was clammy with moisture, and as the group went a little farther along, the reason for the humidity and the dancing reflected beams on the ceiling became apparent. They arrived at a waterway; an underground river, and floating on its surface was a metallic green, torpedo-shaped vessel. A Slev starship.

Farewell

"I believe it will be necessary for me to become visible again," whispered Gavin's voice in Carrie's ear as the Slevs led them aboard their ship.

"You mean so you can translate?" asked Carrie.

"Indeed."

"I think you're right. Hey, everyone," she called out. "We've brought a friend with us. He's been invisible up until now, but he needs to uncloak. You might think he looks quite frightening, but there's no need to be alarmed."

Mrs. Beaumont clamped her hands over her eyes and peeked between her fingers as Gavin appeared. At the sight of the moulted alien insect, her hands fell away from her face and her mouth gaped. The new Gavin was spectacular. His carapace was transformed from bronze to brilliant gold. He'd grown half a metre in every direction, and on his back he now bore two sets of glistening wings.

"Gavin, you're beautiful," Carrie exclaimed. The Slevs were on their knees, touching their ears to the ground. Emily stood transfixed.

Even Dave seemed to have lost his customary unease over Gavin's appearance. "Nice one, mate."

But the insectoid alien was too busy speaking Slevih to pay attention to these compliments. The Slevs leapt to their feet and walked backwards into their ship, scooping their arms downward and towards themselves, indicating that the rest follow.

"Is it safe?" asked Mrs. Beaumont.

"It is quite safe, I believe," answered Gavin. "The Slevs have been apologising profusely ever since they saw you, only you did not understand."

Carrie winced.

They passed into a wide, hollow space filled with Slevs busily chattering. A child's shout sounded above the hubbub, and a little girl wearing a parka ran out from among them and into Emily's arms. She hugged the woman and buried her face in her belly.

"Beth, you're safe," exclaimed Emily. "You're safe, thank goodness. Are you all right? Did the elves hurt you?"

"Oh no," said Beth. "We've been playing games. And they gave me something to drink. I feel so much better. I don't feel tired anymore."

The little girl looked up at Emily, and her hair fell back from her face. Carrie breathed in sharply. Her eyes. They were completely black.

"And look, Emily, look," the child continued. "They look like me." She pulled down her parka hood. Two pointed ears stuck up and a small green point swelled from the top of her head.

"They do," said Emily. "They do look like you. I couldn't admit it to myself for so long, but it's true. And now I think I know why they're here." She burst into tears.

The Slevs crowded around Emily and Beth, chattering and patting the pair. The Slevs' appearance on Earth, their examination of children, their abduction of Beth, it was all beginning to make sense, but Carrie wanted to check with Gavin. The golden insectoid alien was deep in conversation with a Slev.

"It's amazing, isn't it," said Dave. "They must have flown their starship right under London. Are we in a sewer? It seems too big."

"If I'm right," said Mrs. Beaumont, "it's The Fleet, an underground river. It used to flow on the surface before it got too polluted and was built over. The tunnel from the theatre must lead to its banks, where the actors could make a quick getaway if their creditors were after them. There are many miles of underground rivers and sewers under London, connected in a huge network."

"The perfect hiding place," said Dave. "The Slevs would have access to the whole city from here."

"Ahem," said Gavin, joining them. "Would one of you mind helping me converse with the woman whom I believe is named Emily?"

"I'll help," said Carrie, though she wondered whether Emily would want to hear what Gavin had to say.

Emily and Beth were surrounded by cheery Slevs. They parted to let Gavin and Carrie through. Emily had calmed down but looked very sad. Beth appeared joyful, however, and was bouncing happily from Slev to Slev, poking their round tummies, pulling their ears and giggling.

"Emily," said Carrie, "Gavin has something he has to explain to you."

The woman turned mournful eyes to the insectoid alien. The Slev who had been speaking to Gavin returned to his side, chattering at a clip.

"The Chief Slev, first of all, would like to offer his deepest apologies for alarming you by snatching Beth and running away with her," said Gavin. "He explains that they were desperate. They had to find their child and treat her before she became seriously ill."

"*Their* child?" asked Carrie.

"I am translating correctly, I believe."

Emily nodded. "Beth has been ill these last few months. The doctors couldn't figure out what was wrong with her." She paused before turning to the Slev at Gavin's side. "She...she isn't human, is she?"

"Correct," said Gavin. "Beth is a Slev."

"That's obvious, but how did she get to Earth?" asked Carrie.

"It is most interesting," said Gavin. "The Chief has explained that the Slev reproduce through spores that they spread among the stars. When a spore happens to drift to a planet and encounter favourable conditions, a Slev grows. The Slevs travel the galaxy gathering their children before they reach adolescence, which is when their green sensory organ begins to grow. At this age, the child requires a special compound to fuel its development, otherwise it fades and eventually dies. Time was running out for little Beth, and the Slevs were anxious to find her before it was too late.

"They could tell Beth's approximate position, but they could not make the final identification until they could see her close up. They are very sorry for frightening the children of Earth.

"The Slevs sense the locations of their developing children through an extremely interesting method..." Gavin spoke at some length, but Carrie's mind was on other things. "And so, when—"

"Could you tell him I'm very sorry for frightening some of his people?" asked Carrie.

"Tut, tut," said Gavin. "What did you do? I heard Dave shouting."

"Hey, you aren't my manager anymore."

"Hmpf." A whiff of almond oil was an added signal of Gavin's displeasure. "If I might continue—"

"They want to take her, don't they?" asked Emily. Her lower lip trembled.

"It is not a matter of *want*, so much as *must*. Beth requires regular doses of the compound if she is to survive and grow normally, and the Slevs cannot stay here to supply her with it. They have other planets to visit, other children to collect. In fact, they must leave soon. They were only waiting so that they could explain to you."

"What?" asked little Beth. "I have to leave Emily? I won't do it. I'm not going." The little girl stamped her foot, folded her arms, and pouted.

The Slevs seemed to understand the meaning of her words, for their happy faces fell. The Chief began chattering again.

"He says he would like to thank you for caring for Beth so well that she does not wish to leave you. Usually Slev children are spurned by the natives of the planets on which they grow, due to their physical differences. But you have cared for her like a...a...I believe he is saying, mother."

At this Emily lost her composure. Woman and child held each other tightly. But finally Emily's tears subsided and she broke the embrace. "Is there really no other way?"

"I am afraid not," said Gavin.

"I don't want to go with them," said Beth. "I want to stay here. I won't leave. I won't."

"But you must," said Emily, "if you're going to get better." She turned to Gavin. "Will I ever see her again?"

Gavin chattered with the Slev. "He says yes, of course. They pass by this region of space quite regularly."

"No," shouted Beth, "I'm not leaving Emily. I want to go home. I want to go home right now." She began to sob hysterically.

Carrie was sure it was contravening some galactic law or other, but she was going to say it anyway. "Can't she...can't Emily go with them?"

"Yes," exclaimed Beth. "You can come too. You can come with us, Emily. Oh please, please say you'll come."

Emily looked down at the teary-faced child and around at the starship and its strange occupants. "Go with you? I...I..."

"I am afraid humans are prohibited from leaving Earth without the permission of the Transgalactic Council. According to regulation—"

"But, Gavin," said Carrie, "aren't you forgetting something? You don't work for the Transgalactic Council."

Gavin's transparent wings fluttered. "Yes, Carrie, you are quite right."

CHRISTMAS FEAST

Christmas dinner was held in Carrie's living room that year. It was the only room where Gavin could fit. Carrie and Dave moved the sofa set out and the dining table and chairs in before Carrie laid out the Christmas feast. Luckily, there was still room for the Christmas tree.

A nut roast took pride of place in the centre. Carrie had shaped it to look vaguely like a large bird so that Dave wouldn't feel he was missing out on a traditional turkey too much. Serving dishes of vegetables, Yorkshire pudding, stuffing and gravy steamed around the nut roast, and at the periphery Carrie had placed three sets of plates and cutlery. She wondered if Gavin used plates and knives and forks.

Rogue and Toodles had eaten the last of their Advent calendar treats and received their presents. Rogue's had disappeared almost too fast to see, but Toodles was still drooling over hers in a doped-up stupor. Carrie had also given Dave the shaving toiletries she'd bought him. She'd felt a twinge of disappointment when he hadn't given her anything in return, but she didn't say anything. Some people were just forgetful. She didn't have a present for Gavin, but then she hadn't been expecting him.

Carrie wondered where her guests had got to. The insectoid alien had turned invisible and popped out to stretch his legs, and Dave had been upstairs for ages. What was he doing up there?

The front door opened and closed, letting in an icy breath of wind, and Gavin became visible again in the hallway.

"Great, you're just in time," said Carrie. "Come in and...squat down." She squeezed past the alien and went to the bottom of the stairs. "Dave, dinner's ready. Come and eat before it gets cold."

"Just a minute...whoops," came Dave's voice.

"What are you doing?"

"Come back here," exclaimed Dave.

A creature swept down Carrie's stairs. A large, pale brown, furry creature with translucent bat wings. It landed on the bannister rail and groomed itself. Its head was like a lemur's, with large, liquid chocolate eyes and wide furry ears.

"I wanted to give you it myself," said Dave as he came down. "Happy Christmas."

"What...what is it?" asked Carrie.

"I am a he, not an it," said the animal.

"Amazing, isn't he?" Dave said. "I'd like you to meet Flux."

"He is amazing, but, Dave, you really shouldn't give pets as presents."

"Hmpf," exclaimed Flux. "I'm certainly not a pet. You can think of me as a visitor. I expect to stay one or two Earth years, providing your accommodation is satisfactory."

"Wh...what..." Carrie stared at her friend, her eyebrows raised. "That's what you were doing upstairs all that time yesterday and today. You were..."

"Yeah." Dave looked a little sheepish. "When I came over to help out, I realised I hadn't got you anything for Christmas. I didn't wantcom to make it obvious by rushing out to the shops, so I went somewhere else."

"You went by transgalactic gateway to another planet? But you can't do that without a good reason. It isn't allowed."

"You're right, but, well, you helped, actually. You'd done such a good job of explaining the importance of Christmas to the Council,

I got special permission. I persuaded Flux here to come and stay for a while. I thought you'd like another pet."

"I am not a pet," exclaimed Flux again.

"Sorry." Dave whispered in Carrie's ear. "He's actually on the run. Long story."

Carrie's mouth opened and closed twice. She shook her head. "Thanks, I think. Shall we go and eat? Come on, Flux."

When they were all seated at the table, they pulled their Christmas crackers, put on paper hats and read out terrible jokes before tucking into the feast.

"How do you think Emily and Beth will get on living with the Slevs on their starship?" Carrie asked Gavin as she piled roast potatoes on her plate.

"The child will adjust quickly, I imagine. She is young and her brain is as yet unformed, and of course she is a Slev. The human female may take much longer to become accustomed to her new life. But she was extremely attached to the child. I believe the option she chose was the wiser alternative."

Carrie looked from the shiny golden alien, to her bestie, Dave, and Rogue, who was begging with his eyes, and Toodles, who was blissfully high on catnip, to her new friend Flux, who was perched on a chair back, nibbling a Brussels sprout. Yes, Emily and Beth would be fine, because they were with the people they loved.

READ CARRIE'S STORY IN CARRIE HATCHETT, SPACE ADVENTURER

UPSHOT

MISSING

ONE

The slim silver rocket sat on its pad, silent and still. It was a miniature of the old models humankind had used to travel to the Moon and then Mars long ago. Four fins protruded at the base below the oxidizer and fuel sections, surmounted by the nose cone. The rocket was unmanned, though it did contain something that had once been a living human. Within the cone was a box that held the ashes from a cremation.

The rocket had no particular destination. Its trajectory had been set only to avoid encounters with numerous orbiting satellites and the gravity wells of the Sun and the Solar Systems' planets and moons. The small vessel would fly on for eternity, journeying through the black, perhaps grazing other star systems or passing through the tails of comets, speeding into and out of nebulae, until in the end the deceased's remains would leave the Milky Way and enter the wider universe, millennia after his existence—perhaps the existence of humanity itself—was long forgotten.

Taylan sighed and shivered, though the evening was not cold. Funerals always made her uneasy. She'd seen too much death. She was also sick of listening to the endless speeches. Dusk approached, and everyone and his brother seemed to want to tell their anecdotes. She hoped the current speaker was the last.

"Do you want my jacket?" Wright asked.

"No, thanks. I'm fine."

The speaker was winding down, thank the stars.

Kayla gave a loud sniff. Taylan pulled her close.

The speaker stepped from the podium. There was a pause. The crowd shuffled their feet and murmured. Was the countdown finally about to commence? But another figure appeared, walking up to give a speech. It was Hans Jonte, former Prime Minister of the Britannic Isles. She inwardly groaned. How typical of him to want to have his say and be the last to speak. The man loved the limelight, or perhaps he was only addicted to momentous events. If anything of public importance was happening he had to be in the thick of it.

"Lorcan Ua Talman," he began, sweeping the assembled mourners with his gaze. He focused briefly on Taylan before moving on. "The name conjures memories and images for everyone, does it not? Is there a single person on this planet who has not been impacted by his lifetime of work? Talman touched all of us, and though in his early years the effects were not always positive, I think we can all agree that his later actions more than made up for previous transgressions. He died one of the greatest and most well-loved figures of our time."

Kayla sniffed again. Ever since the news had come of Lorcan's death from a sudden, massive stroke, she'd been wrapped in sorrow.

It wasn't only Talman's passing affecting her. While they'd been away aboard the *Defiant*, twenty-one years had passed on Earth. Kayla's old school friends had moved on with their lives. The adult women and men had little in common with a fifteen year old. When she'd tried to reconnect they'd been standoffish. Then Lorcan had died, and her remaining tie with the world she'd left behind had been severed.

Wright said softly in Taylan's ear, "We can leave straight after the ceremony. No need to stick around for the debriefing."

He was referring to the post-launch reception.

"Maybe," she replied. "We'll see."

If Kayla's mood didn't improve perhaps leaving as soon as

possible would be best, though it would have been nice to trade reminiscences with friends. Taylan had spotted some familiar faces in the crowd, and it already felt like ages since the *Defiant* had touched down, though it had only been a few months.

Jonte's speech was uncharacteristically brief. After he finished, there was a shift in the atmosphere. The select crowd of mourners, standing and seated, silently focused on the rocket through the protective barrier.

The countdown began. The fuel ignited and flames roared from the vessel's base, vibrating the structure with propelling force. The gantry decoupled as the countdown reached zero, and the rocket rose smoothly into the air. Fighting gravity, it became a brilliant lozenge and then a speck of light, lost among the emerging stars.

It was over.

He was gone.

Lorcan Ua Talman had finally achieved his long-anticipated departure from Earth. With his passing, it seemed that one era was finished and a new one begun.

———

Kayla elected to not go home immediately after the launch, saying, "Uncle Lorcan said sometimes life is very hard but you mustn't let it get to you. You have to push through and try your best, every day."

The reception room was already filling by the time they reached it. Dignitaries had been allocated seats at the main table for a formal dinner, while less important attendees could sit at random tables and help themselves to a buffet spread. Taylan, Wright, and Kayla belonged to the latter category.

A live band played background music and a large screen overhanging the hall displayed scrolling images of Talman at all stages of his life, from a babe in his mother's arms to a dignified, imposing figure with his signature flaming red hair, and then a sprightly old man. Most touching were the pictures of him with his wife and children. It was in those photos he looked happiest. Sadly, they had all died in a sink hole tragedy in Antarctica.

"Who's hungry?" Wright asked. "Kayla, do you want to come with me to get something to eat? Do you want anything, Taylan?"

"Not really. You two go ahead." She smiled wanly as he and her daughter headed for the buffet. Even in the most dire straights Wright never lost his appetite, nor his capacity for comatose-like sleep for that matter, though lately his nights had been the most disturbed she'd ever known them.

"Hey," said a voice. "I thought I might see you here."

"Iolani," Taylan responded warmly, hugging the small woman. "How have you been?" She hadn't seen Iolani since they'd disembarked the *Defiant*. They'd become good friends on the long voyage.

Iolani grimaced. "Not so good, if I'm honest. How about you?"

"Why? What's wrong?" Taylan didn't want to go over her own problems. It would only make her feel worse.

"Ugh, just the usual, I guess. It's hard to adjust after being away so long, right?"

"Right. It's like coming back to an alien planet."

The world had changed during their voyage. It was almost unrecognizable. The new understanding of physics gifted to humanity by a mysterious alien species had transformed everything: the environment, day-to-day life, human existence, in fact. The best way Taylan had found to sum it up was that everything was simply *better*. Pollution had been entirely eradicated, and not only pollution of the air, soil, and water—noise pollution had gone as well. Road vehicles whispered so quietly they would have been dangerous if it weren't for their capacity for instant emergency stops. Genetic screening of embryos and early diagnosis of psychological issues, and intervention and support for deprived families meant anti-social behavior had all but disappeared. Work was now optional because humanity could feed, house, and care for everyone regardless of their contribution. While in the past this would have led to addiction to drugs and escapist entertainment, now education focused on teaching children how to optimize their lives to be productive and satisfying.

It was as near as you could get to a perfect society.

Yet Taylan was miserable. So was Kayla and, though he never stated it, so was Wright.

Iolani looked about to speak but then appeared to change her mind.

To fill the slightly awkward silence, Taylan asked, "Where are you living now?"

"I went back to Suriname. No free accommodation on the *Bres* anymore." Iolani flashed a grin.

"Were you sad you missed out on creating the habitats for Lorcan's fleet?"

"Oh, no. I expected it would have left by the time we got back. I gave the eco-engineers detailed instructions and advice. The biomes will operate well enough. The rainforest environment on the *Defiant* was a successful test run."

"It was beautiful."

"Thanks. I loved it. Reminded me of home. You and TJ should..." Her words tailed away.

"We should what?"

"Never mind. Here's the man himself."

Wright had returned with Kayla, bearing full plates.

Iolani and Wright exchanged pecks on cheeks.

"How have you been?" He took a bite from a chicken drumstick.

She shrugged. "Oh, you know. How come you aren't in uniform? Don't you have to wear it for occasions like this?"

"It's optional, but, anyway, I resigned. My discharge papers arrived the other day."

"You left the Royal Marines?!"

He gave a nervous chuckle. "Is it such a big surprise?" Shooting Taylan a glance, he went on, "It was always the plan once the *Defiant's* mission was over. I served for eighteen years, or a lot longer if you count time as it passed here. Unfortunately, the pensions department doesn't. But I think I did my part."

"Oh, absolutely," said Iolani. "No one could say you didn't do more than enough. I'm just finding it hard to wrap my head around you becoming a civilian. What are you going to do?"

"Haven't decided yet."

"Mam!"

Taylan had stolen a chip from Kayla's plate. "It's *one* chip."

"Get your own."

Taylan rolled her eyes. "Shall we find somewhere to sit down? I'm going to need a drink to get through this." More people had begun to arrive and the crowd was growing thicker and noisier.

"Sure," said Iolani. "I heard the wine is vintage. I want to try some. Lorcan didn't spare any expense for his send-off, did he? Kekoa is here somewhere. You look for a table and I'll find her. We can go over old times."

———

Several drinks later, Iolani was flushed and everyone was relaxed and chatty. Kayla had left the table to add her memories of Talman to the store of recordings being created.

Kekoa nudged Iolani in the ribs. "You should tell them about the time Lorcan kidnapped you."

"He what?!" exclaimed Taylan, sitting up. "Are you kidding?"

"Now's not the moment," said Iolani. "Not at his funeral, for star's sake. Besides, he reformed. We should remember him for the good he did."

Wright put down his glass and leaned forward, resting his elbows on the table. "He *kidnapped* you?"

"I'm sorry," said Taylan. "I'm all for not speaking ill of the dead, but you can't mention something like that and not follow through."

"Yeah," said Wright. "Don't leave us hanging."

Iolani tutted and frowned at her partner. "You shouldn't have said anything."

"Well, I did. I'll tell them if you like, though I only remember it from my end of events. I don't think you've ever explained exactly what happened to you."

"That's because I didn't want to go over it. But now you've brought it up..." She proceeded to tell them a bizarre tale about Talman visiting her at her mountain research station, the two of them getting into an argument, and Talman subsequently trapping and drugging her before taking her with him back to the *Bres*.

Kekoa interjected, "You can imagine how the rest of us felt when we realized what he'd done. But no one dared say anything. He was so scary back then. It wasn't even about simply losing our jobs. He could and did ruin people's lives."

"Sounds like he changed a lot," Taylan commented. "He was always generous and kind to me and the kids."

"He was generous in death too," said Kekoa. "Iolani and I will never have to work again, and I'm guessing you two are the same?"

Taylan and Wright nodded. Taylan said, "Kayla is set up for life too, though I haven't told her yet."

"He was a complicated man," said Iolani. "Do you know his heart isn't among the ashes? He had it buried next to his wife and children's graves in Antarctica."

"I didn't. That's so touching."

"I don't think he wanted it made general knowledge. The graves and memorial site are going to be closed to the general public next year and not maintained anymore. Lorcan wanted the world to move on after his death."

The mood took a downturn. Perhaps the others felt as Taylan did—that the world had moved on for them too, leaving them behind. Her sense of displacement and alienation had built for months, along with confusion and unhappiness. Carys, her adopted daughter, had left with Talman's fleet long before the *Defiant*'s return. Her parting message had been hurtfully brief and impersonal. Taylan didn't know if she would ever get over the pain she'd felt when reading it or the loss of the girl. She would never see her again, and Carys would never experience the rich pleasures of existence on 'New Earth', as some had taken to calling it. She'd swapped an easy, enjoyable life for the uncertainty and dangers of deep space colonization.

Why?

Taylan would never know. The absence of Carys made the days feel pale and incomplete, and Taylan had another deep unhappiness she couldn't even bring herself to face.

Kekoa said, "Now you two have all the free time in the world you should come and stay with us for a while."

"Uhh…" Iolani seemed annoyed, and Taylan had the impression from the look that passed between them that she'd nudged Kekoa under the table. "You're very welcome but maybe later on, after we've fixed things up a little."

"Did you tell them about the weird stuff happening on the mountain?" Kekoa piped brightly.

"I don't really want to talk about it."

"The mountain?" Wright asked.

"Where we live," Kekoa explained. "Iolani's old house is there and we've been renovating it. The jungle wasn't slow at reclaiming the place, but we're making headway. Or at least we were." She looked at her partner, who had averted her gaze. "Should I show them the pictures? It isn't going to hurt, surely."

"I guess it's okay." Iolani gave an apologetic look. "You guys are like us, just trying to get back to normal, right? Only nothing's normal anymore. I don't want to burden you with more bullshit."

"It's no problem," said Taylan. "I'm interested to hear about it." In truth, any distraction was welcome.

Kekoa pulled a small interface from her bag and placed it screen upward. At a word of instruction, the interface projected a holo about thirty centimeters high of an animal skull. Curved canines hung down from the upper jaw and large eye holes stared. The skull was fresh and bloody.

"Whoa." Taylan reared back. Quickly checking around she said, "I'm glad Kayla isn't here."

"Sorry." Kekoa issued another instruction and the skull was replaced by a rope of colorful beads hanging from a tree branch. "I didn't realize the skull would come up first. That's the worst pic in that file. The really bad ones are somewhere else."

"There are worse things than the skull?" asked Wright.

Iolani sighed. "We've been coming across things like that all over the place. Along tracks, next to streams, and even deep in the forest where hardly anyone ever goes. Skulls and bones, blood wiped on leaves, dolls made of bark and feathers, butterflies impaled on thorns, beetles threaded on animal gut—"

"*That's* what that is?" asked Taylan, viewing the beads with new eyes. She took a swig of wine.

Iolani turned to Kekoa. "I don't think they need to see anymore."

Her partner turned off the holo and returned the interface to her bag. "Iolani lived in that part of the mountain for years and it's the first time she's ever seen anything like it."

"It is very unusual. I don't know what to make of it. Should we be scared and move out? I'd hate to do that. I love it up there. On the other hand, I don't want to stick around if we might be in danger."

Wright asked, "Does it seem like this stuff is targeted at you?"

"We haven't seen anything close to home," replied Kekoa, "and we can't figure out a pattern. The sites appear to be random."

"Then maybe you just have a nutter living locally," said Taylan. "Someone the authorities don't know about yet. Have you told anyone what you've seen?"

Iolani grimaced. "Things aren't as well set up in Suriname as they are in most places. The modern revolution has passed the country by to a large extent. We can't rely on the authorities to do anything about what we've been seeing, especially not way up in the mountains. They won't want to leave their comfortable, environment-controlled offices. Besides, nothing actually illegal has taken place as far as we know. It's just concerning behavior."

"Shit," said Taylan. "I don't know what to suggest. That's sounds awful."

"It *is* awful," Iolani agreed. "It was a bad idea to bring it up. Let's talk about something else."

But the vibe didn't recover after the revelation. A pall seemed to hang over the four companions. When Kayla returned to the table, she noticed it immediately. Looking from face to face, she said, "I would ask who died but I already know."

"Maybe it's time we headed home," suggested Wright. "It's been a long day."

Taylan quickly agreed. Kekoa and Iolani appeared to be ready to leave too. With vague promises to meet up again soon, they departed.

Taking one of the small, neat autocars waiting outside, Taylan, Wright, and Kayla settled in for the journey home. The quiet, somber, post-funeral mood continued, until Kayla said, "Mam, I got talking to another girl at the reception. She goes to a private boarding school in Scotland. It sounds amazing. They do all kinds of things: archery, horse-riding, hiking. And they learn cool stuff, like gene splicing. I know you want me to go back to my old school, but it isn't going to be the same now all my friends have left. Do you think I could go to the boarding school in Scotland?"

Taylan's heart sank. The last thing she wanted was to lose the last of her children.

Perhaps sensing her feelings, Wright replied for her. "Maybe you can find out some more about it first. It sounds like something to think about."

"Okay," said Kayla, returning her gaze to the darkness beyond the car windows.

Taylan looked outside too. Nothing was visible except the lamps lighting the road, but she recalled the wild meadows they'd passed on their journey to the launch site. The scenery was wonderful. Free energy meant that most food was grown underground in vast subterranean fields. All over the globe, the land was reverting to its natural state. Woodlands and forests were sprouting up everywhere and animal life was booming.

The world was beautiful, yet she could find no pleasure in it.

She swallowed the lump in her throat. "If that's what you really want, Kayla, you should do it."

TWO

Kayla left for her new school in September. Taylan tried to not be too emotional as she said goodbye but she didn't succeed. The parting brought back so many bad memories of searching for her children while the world had been at war. Separating from her daughter again challenged the very fiber of her being. Though it was irrational, she couldn't shake the feeling that she was seeing Kayla for the last time.

When it was over, she and Wright journeyed back to West BI. After arriving at the empty house, she went straight to bed but endured many hours of wakefulness, contemplating the empty future, before finally falling into a restless sleep.

It was very early morning when she awoke, not feeling remotely refreshed.

Wright, unusually, was already awake. He draped an arm over her and pulled her close, kissing her cheek. "Do you fancy going for a run?"

"Yeah, why not?" she replied dully.

"I was thinking we could go to your favorite walk on the coast." He meant the place where he'd proposed, twenty-one years ago, Earth time.

"All right."

He was being his usual kind, considerate self, trying to take her mind off things and make her feel better. She doubted a run in a nice spot was going to help, but she appreciated the gesture.

She dressed mechanically, wondering to herself if there was any point in keeping in shape anymore. It made sense when there had been things to do and enemies to fight, but what did physical fitness matter now?

When they arrived a stiff breeze was blowing across the cliff top, salt-laden, moist, and warm. Summer was clinging on in the Britannic Isles. The sun was just rising, chasing night from the western sky, where only the brightest stars faintly glimmered. From the cliff edge inland, no one and nothing was to be seen except turf and low, tough shrubs leaning away from the sea.

Taylan and Wright set off.

Before running even a kilometer she was panting and coated in sweat. It was hard to stay fit in space, and her time on the *Defiant* had taken its toll. They covered another kilometer and then another while the sun slowly rose.

The exercise wasn't having its usual effect. Rather than alleviating her heavy-heartedness it seemed to be making it worse. Perhaps it was because it was here Wright had surprised her with his proposal. Life had seemed perfect then. Her family had been complete, the war long over, and the future appeared rosy. Now...

She collapsed, dropping to the trail mid-step. Her impetus carried her forward onto her elbows and her forehead hit the ground. Sobs welled up, her chest heaved, and her shoulders shook as the tidal wave of emotion spilled out.

"Taylan!" Wright was at her side.

Dimly, she felt his arm around her, pulling her against him. Then she knew little of time passing, only the vague comfort of another human body, the warm wind, and the rhythmic crash of waves on rocks far below.

Eventually, Wright said, "It's Patrin, isn't it?"

She nodded.

Ever since leaving her son at the jousting list on the far-distant alien planet, she hadn't truly faced the inevitable consequence of his decision. Merlin and Morgan had asked him to remain behind when the *Defiant* departed. In return, they had conjured the dead personnel back to life and agreed to cease interfering in humanity's affairs. They had been true to their word. Everyone had retuned to the ship except the chosen four: Patrin, Arthur, and Kala and Perran Orr. The *Defiant* had flown back to Earth without incident, and the skein mappers had reported no further external influences on human society.

There had been no time for a proper goodbye, but Patrin had been sanguine. He hadn't really understood what he'd agreed to, despite Taylan's attempts at explanation. Arthur knew. His expression had been grave, yet he hadn't tried to dissuade the boy. Perhaps, as a king who had dedicated himself to serving his people, he accepted the gesture of sacrifice.

Faced with the impossible choice, so had Taylan. Yet she could not trust the aliens to send Patrin home as they'd promised. They might do it eventually, but their concept of time was skewed by their extreme longevity, perhaps immortality. Also, Morgan and Merlin enjoyed playing with human emotions. If they did comprehend the relatively vast period that would pass for Taylan as she waited, the idea of her spending decades pining for her child would tickle them.

She might never see Patrin again. It was a fact she'd been trying to ignore since their brief farewell. She could never see her son again. She'd only just been able to admit it.

Wright said, "He might—"

"Don't say it. Please don't say it." She didn't want him to spark a ray of hope in her heart. How could she live every day waiting, watching, looking for a sign that Patrin might be back? What kind of life would that be? She couldn't live on dreams, yet she also couldn't live with the knowledge he was gone forever. "I'm sorry."

"Sorry for what?"

"That you aren't enough."

"Taylan, I never expected to be."

Some time later, they got to their feet and began the walk back to the car park, hand in hand. Taylan felt numb. Tomorrow stood out in her mind as a mountain to climb, and the day after, and the day after that. Every day would be the same. The days would melt to weeks, months, and years, all containing a giant, gaping hole. She would not live her life—she would endure it.

Neither of them had thought to order an autocar as they walked back, so they had to wait for one. As they stood in the car park, Wright said, "I have an idea. Why don't we go and visit Iolani and Kekoa in Suriname? It would be a change of scenery and might help take your mind off things."

She shrugged. "If you like."

"We can go by airship. No need to hurry. Kayla won't be back until Christmas."

THREE

The mountains of Suriname spread out below, steep slopes cloaked in deep green, tendrils of cloud wreathing their peaks. As the airship approached a valley it began to descend, drifting gracefully down from the heights. The engine noise was a mere murmur against the background sigh of gentle winds.

The valley floor widened, and a few low buildings came into view. Here was the stopping point of their two-week journey, and it was here Iolani and Kekoa would meet them as pre-arranged. They'd been forced to make the arrangements before they set off. One of the features of the voyage was lack of connectivity to the net. The passengers were supposed to relax and free their minds of worldly cares, and being unable to contact the outside world was a part of that. Unfortunately, Taylan's worries had little to do with the affairs on Earth.

Her concerns aside, the trip had been magnificent. Floating across the Atlantic, they had seen scores of whales, dolphins, the vast Sargasso Sea, flocks of migrating birds, stunning cloudscapes, breathtaking sunrises and sunsets, and at night thousands of brilliant stars reflected in the dark ocean. At several points the airship had drawn to a slow halt and lowered viewing capsules into the water, offering glimpses of life beneath the waves.

The meals had been delicious. Some included ingredients she'd never even heard of. Outside of mealtimes, the passengers read, listened to music, danced, exercised their artistic talents, or simply watched the view and chatted.

If only she could have appreciated the experience. Intellectually, she did. But she could not feel it. All she felt was a hollow dullness. And as the cruise liner of the skies sailed closer to the ground, she feared this holiday visiting Iolani and Kekoa wouldn't change how she felt, that she would have to put on a show so as not to spoil the atmosphere.

They were watching from their balcony as the airship descended. As if sensing her thoughts, Wright put an arm around her. "Let's just see how it works out. If we aren't having fun we can make our excuses and leave. They'll understand. There won't be any hard feelings."

A question that had burned in her mind for a long time surfaced. In her misery she asked it, prodding old scars. "You know when you and Iolani were on the *Dauntless*, did you have a thing going on?"

When Taylan had refused to go on the mission and she and Wright had parted ways, neither knowing if they would see the other again, he'd told her not to wait for him. Yet she *had* waited. Had he waited for her?

He was watching her from the corners of his eyes. "What makes you think that?"

"Nothing in particular. Did you?"

He pulled her closer. "No, Iolani and I did not have a thing going on."

She sensed there was more than he was telling her, but she didn't push it. There were some things it was better not to know.

The gondola hung fifty meters off the ground. A grassy expanse awaited it, along with ten or twelve men in red-and-white striped T-shirts and denim jeans. A shout went out from the ship, and coils of rope unfurled until they dangled at full length.

"They aren't going to *pull* us down, are they?" Taylan asked.

"Only the last twenty meters or so. It's part of the experience."

In other circumstances, she might have chuckled. Naturally, the airship could land perfectly safely under its own steam, but men dressed like fairground roustabouts hauling it in was more quaint and charming.

A man leapt and caught the end of a rope, and in a minute all of them were pulling hand over hand. The gondola kissed the grass and its descent came to an almost-imperceptible halt. The men tied the ropes to pilings with a flourish.

The journey was over. It was time to disembark. Taylan and Wright picked up their suitcases and walked out into the sunshine. Tropical, moist air tinged with floral scents enveloped them. An automated transport awaited to take the luggage to the arrivals terminal. After depositing her suitcase, Taylan took a final look at the immense balloon that had carried them across the ocean, swaying in the breeze, before setting off with Wright across the field.

Environmental controls within the arrivals hall provided short-lived relief from the heat and humidity, and then they were outside again, officially checked into Suriname.

"I thought Iolani and Kekoa would wait for us inside," Taylan commented as they stepped into the sunshine. A few tour operators and hawkers had been awaiting the airship passengers.

Wright was scanning up and down the road that ran across the front of the building. "I thought so too, or they would at least be out here."

Four autocars sat in a bay, and they were quickly taken. Other passengers had gone with the tour operators in their minivans. Only Taylan and Wright had no one to meet them and no transportation.

"I'm sure I told them the correct date and time," he went on, "but with the comm blackout on the airship it wasn't possible to confirm."

"Something's made them a bit late, that's all." Taylan scanned the greenery spreading out all around. Beyond the road the ground dipped into a wide basin thick with trees. The basin was so deep the canopies were level with her eyeline. The jungle ran up the slopes and then rose higher into mountains in the distance. In the Britannic Isles and many other places in the world, wild plants and animals were reclaiming the land, but here she had a sense they had never departed. "Traveling around this place can't be easy."

The airship port was far from the capital and smaller cities and towns, deliberately so, in order to fit in with the 'escape the hustle and bustle' experience. By coincidence, it also happened to be near the mountain where Iolani and Kekoa lived.

Wright fished in his pocket, brought out an ear comm, and popped it in. "It's working. I'll—"

"What's that?" She'd heard the distant whine of an engine from somewhere high up. She searched the skies. It was too soon for the airship to be departing. The noise had been different too.

"There it is." Wright pointed a little south of the sun.

She squinted. A small heli was approaching. "Do you think it's them? What a novel way to pick us up."

"Probably the most convenient, considering the terrain."

The heli swooped overhead and descended rapidly and rather jerkily, landing in the same field as the airship.

"Do you think it's going to be safe traveling in that thing?" Taylan asked. Whoever was flying it, their piloting skills left something to be desired.

Wright didn't answer. Picking up their suitcases, he said, "If it is them, we can meet them inside."

Iolani burst through the double doors on the immigration and customs side of the arrivals hall. Spotting them, she beckoned frantically, her eyes wide and her face flushed. As they got close, she said, "I'm sorry I'm late, but something terrible has happened. I almost forgot you were coming today. This way, quickly." She disappeared through the doors.

Raising her eyebrows at Wright, Taylan followed Iolani into the now-deserted passenger processing section.

"Are you sure this is okay?" Wright asked Iolani's back as she hurriedly led them to the field. What they were doing seemed odd to Taylan too. Surely they couldn't just return the way they'd come. Surely there were security prohibitions.

Iolani gave them a quick glance. "You'll find things are a bit different here. Slacker. Don't worry. No one cares." She passed through the exterior doors running. Then she ran to the heli. By the time Taylan and Wright reached it she'd already started it up and the blades were lazily swinging around.

It wasn't until Taylan had climbed into a seat that she realized someone was missing. "Where's Kekoa?"

As if she'd been shot, Iolani collapsed. She hunched over, her face in her hands. "She's gone! I think she might have been kidnapped. That's why I was late picking you up. I've been looking..." Her sobs overcame her ability to speak, and she huffed, her chest heaving.

Taylan, sitting next to her, put a hand on her shoulder. "Take your time." Sharing a surprised and concerned look with Wright, she added, "Don't worry. We'll help you find her. It might not be anything serious. She might only be lost or—"

"She isn't lost," Iolani wailed. "She's walked the trails around my house hundreds of times." She leaned back in her seat and took a deep breath. "It's possible she only had an accident. That's what I keep telling myself. Something bad enough to disable her and stop her from contacting me, but not so bad that she's in real danger."

"Have you contacted the rescue services?" asked Wright.

"There *are* no rescue services."

"What about the police?"

"It doesn't work like that around here." Iolani took another deep breath and appeared to assert some control over her emotions. "I'll take you home. You'll understand better when we get there."

She manipulated the controls, the rotor blades whirred to a blur, and the heli lifted into the sky. Taylan watched the ground fall away with some concern. She was worried about Kekoa, but also about Iolani, who was also not in a fit state to be piloting anything. Raising her voice over the noise of the engine and blades, she asked, "This doesn't fly on automatic?"

"There's no net for air vehicles, only ground," Iolani explained. "You have to understand, the tech revolution hasn't reached most of Suriname. The topography, climate, and low population work against development. In many ways, this place is the same as it's always been."

The tree canopy sped past beneath them. A mountain approached, and Iolani took them high up its slope. All the while, Taylan hadn't seen any roads since leaving the airship port, though she guessed there had to be trails invisible from above. Iolani had said Kekoa knew the ones around her house.

The heli moved close to the mountain. A flat roof appeared amidst the vegetation, orange and easily visible within the green. A white cross marked the center.

"Buying this heli was one of the first things I did after I got home," Iolani commented as she lowered the aircraft to the landing spot. "I'm so glad I did. It used to be a nightmare to get down the mountain and bring back supplies. This makes everything much easier. It was Kekoa's idea." She trembled and the heli wavered as it hit the pad.

"Take it easy," said Wright from the back seat.

She turned off the engine. "I'm okay. It's going to be okay," she added, as if talking to herself. "There has to be a simple explanation for why she's gone missing, right?"

"Right," Taylan said.

Iolani attached the heli to tethers, and then led them down an outside staircase. Dogs could be heard barking within the house, no doubt understanding their mistress had returned. Taylan walked with her and Wright around to the front. A verandah protruded from it, closed in by mosquito netting. It held a hammock and two reclining chairs. Traces of vines once covering the walls remained, and the vegetation in the yard looked as though it had been hacked by machetes. The jungle had indeed tried to reclaim this place, but the two women had been hard at work taking it back.

The home was a picture of human domesticity deep within the heart of nature—except there was something red and weirdly shaped attached to the front door. Iolani drew to an abrupt halt and began to breathe heavily. The verandah door hung open.

"What *is* that thing?" Taylan asked.

Iolani didn't answer. She seemed transfixed.

Taylan slowly climbed the steps. Now she could see the object more clearly, she also froze.

It was a skull, bloody, with shreds of flesh and hair still clinging to it. The lower jaw was missing, and the sightless eye sockets stared, boring into her soul.

FOUR

"It isn't human," said Wright. He'd walked past Taylan and up to the door. "I'm sure it isn't. It's too small."

Iolani seemed to break from her paralysis. She slowly climbed the stairs, her hand shaking as it glided up the banister rail. When she reached Wright's side, she peered up at the skull, which hung at the height of his head.

Taylan still couldn't move. A single drop of blood fell from the horrible object and hit the planks below, joining other splatters. The skull must have been placed recently. She forced herself to turn and search the shadows beneath the trees, but she saw only darkness. Whoever had brought the skull here had either left or was standing still and in silence, watching for a reaction.

"You're right," Iolani breathed, her tone high-pitched and tremulous. "It's from a monkey. *Shit.* I thought..."

"I feared the same," Taylan said. "Thank the stars we were wrong."

Wright was inspecting the skull closely. "It's fresh. Someone's only just put it here." He made a move toward the outer door. "I'll—"

"No, stay here." Taylan touched his arm. "We don't know how many of them there are." The pictures Kekoa had shown them at

Lorcan's memorial reception were flashing back—animal heads, necklaces made from dead insects—there was no question in her mind these were linked to Kekoa's disappearance and the skull on the door.

Inside the house, the dogs were going crazy, barking, whining, and scratching at the door.

Iolani reached up and gingerly prodded the skull. "My dogs must be able to smell it, and they'll be on alert from a stranger being here. Can you wait a moment? I'll go in and calm them down." She slipped inside.

"Poor Kekoa," Taylan murmured. "I hope she's okay."

"Iolani needs to contact the police," Wright said. "I can't believe they wouldn't do something about *this*, even here."

Taylan shrugged. "She must know what she's talking about."

A few moments later Iolani reappeared, smiling tightly. "The dogs want to say hello. Lorcan and Talman are boisterous but they won't hurt you. They'll understand you're my friends."

"Lorcan and Talman?" Taylan asked.

"He was the scariest person I knew, for a while. I couldn't resist naming them after him."

She opened the door.

Two large, black, short-haired hounds bounded out. The first place they went was the skull but Iolani ordered them away. Next, they sniffed Taylan and Wright thoroughly, though they were sufficiently well-disciplined to not jump up. The head of the tallest one reached Taylan's waist. She didn't know their breed and speculated they weren't pure-bred. Iolani must have chosen them for their ability to intimidate, which they had in spades.

"Kekoa usually takes them with her when she goes for a walk," Iolani said sadly. "She didn't today. They ate something they shouldn't have in the forest and they were suffering the repercussions all night. If only they'd gone with her..."

"Let's go in," said Taylan.

Iolani's home had a natural simplicity to it that, having come to know her well during the *Defiant*'s voyage, Taylan would have expected. It was compact too. The main area combined a kitchen, living, and dining room. The furnishings were plain but good quality, and fresh, tropical flowers were the principal decorations.

"Sit down," Iolani said. "You must be tired after—"

"You need to contact the police," Wright interrupted. "Now. Whoever put that skull on your door won't be far away. If they hurry they might still catch them and find out what's happened to Kekoa."

Iolani's shoulders slumped. "I suppose it's the only thing I *can* do, but it won't do any good. You'll see." She left through one of the inner doors.

"I don't get it," Wright said. "In any other place in the world contacting the authorities would be the automatic action if a loved one went missing. Why is she so reluctant?"

"I guess she knows how things operate here better than us."

"Then what else is there? I mean, we can look, but our chances of finding Kekoa without outside help are next to nothing."

"I wish Arthur was here," Taylan ruminated. "He can read a trail like no one's business."

"*I* wish we had guns."

Iolani returned, looking even more forlorn. "They're on their way. They should arrive in a couple of hours."

"Two hours?!" Wright echoed.

"As I keep telling you," Iolani said with uncharacteristic vehemence, "things work differently in this country. Besides, the police have to bike up the mountain and then hike in. They don't have air transport."

"Can't you collect them in your heli?" Taylan asked.

Iolani turned despairing eyes to her. "They would refuse. It would be an insult to them. They would take it as an implication they couldn't do their job. If I offered, they would be even less inclined to help me."

"That's insane," said Wright.

"I agree. It doesn't change anything." She sighed and sank into a seat. The dogs circled and then plonked themselves on the floor at her feet, glancing up adoringly. "Please, sit down." When Taylan and

Wright complied she went on, "It's partly to do with my rep. When I lived here before, I was "the madwoman who lives on the mountain". The local people didn't know about the work I was doing, or if they did know they didn't understand or appreciate it. To them, living up here when you have the option to live in the city in a nice, modern house with access to all the amenities is crazy. Only the very poor or very stupid do it. I don't know which they thought I was, but most people I dealt with treated me with condescension or contempt."

She smiled wanly. "To the locals, I wasn't a world-renowned scientist doing vital research to help save the planet, I was a weirdo, a moronic hermit. And my reputation has stuck. Even now, decades after I left, they still see me the same way, though now their feelings about me are also riddled with deep suspicion. How did I stay young for so long? Am I the daughter of the previous madwoman? I get questions like that whenever I show my face in town. I could hear the suspicion and disbelief in the dispatcher's voice just now when I explained the situation. The police will come, but they won't hurry. They most likely believe I'm making it all up for attention. And, regardless, they're generally so incompetent they wouldn't be able to help anyway." She stood up. "We're going to be waiting a while. Let me get you a drink."

"Iolani," said Taylan, "the love of your life is missing and you have maniacs attaching monkey skulls to your door. You don't need to be the gracious host."

"You're right." Her chin trembled. "I know you're right. But I don't know what else to do."

"I'm going into the forest," Wright announced. "If we wait two hours whoever's doing this will be long gone."

"But they're dangerous," said Taylan, "and you aren't armed. Anything could happen."

"We can't sit by and do nothing."

"All right, but you shouldn't go alone and I don't think we should leave Iolani by herself."

"Then stay with her. You know I can look after myself."

"You don't know—"

"Lorcan and Talman will protect me," said Iolani. "There's no need to worry. That's why whoever's taken Kekoa waited until she was alone."

"Wait," Wright said, "Did you try sending the dogs out to find her?"

"It was the first thing I did, but they got halfway down the main track and began sneezing. Then they wandered around as if they were confused."

"Sneezing? Do you think someone put something down to mask Kekoa's scent trail?"

"It's possible, but there's a lot of weird stuff out there too. Besides, Lorcan and Talman aren't trained to follow scents. I'm not sure they knew what they were doing."

"Okay," said Taylan decisively, rising to her feet. "I'm coming too."

FIVE

They checked they were in full comm contact before leaving. Even in Suriname, comms worked effectively. The fact eased Taylan's concerns about Iolani being alone, albeit with two massive hounds between her and potential attackers.

"Those dogs, huh?" Wright remarked as they crossed the open patch of ground in front of Iolani's house.

"I was just thinking about them too. Lorcan and Talman?" She chuckled. But then the seriousness of the situation hit. "Do you have any ideas on what might be going on?"

He halted at the edge of the jungle. "What Iolani said about her reputation makes me wonder if this is intended to get her and Kekoa to leave. Maybe they'll release Kekoa soon, now that they've given her a fright."

"I hope that's all it is. I certainly wouldn't want to stick around here after everything that's happened."

They stepped under the canopy. There was a clear track leading away from the house, which they followed. The heat and humidity quickly closed in, and the air buzzed with insect life. As Taylan became coated with sweat, she too questioned the wisdom of living in this inhospitable, isolated, lonely place. The cool climate of West BI was far preferable.

A second, narrower track led away from the first. They decided to take it, reasoning the kidnappers wouldn't stay on the main path. The ground had been sloping downward ever since they'd entered the forest, and in this section the incline was steeper. They were soon grasping vines and tree roots for safety.

A third track appeared. It was little more than a trace of slightly clearer ground. In her previous life, Taylan might not have even noticed it, but accompanying Arthur on journeys through wild places had taught her to be more observant. Wright agreed it was worth a closer look, and they took it.

As they'd descended, the sounds of jungle life had been growing louder—rustling in the undergrowth and high in tree branches, the calls of birds and perhaps other things, the flash of a disappearing reptilian tail. But there was no sign of human activity, current or recent.

"Maybe they didn't come this way," said Taylan. "Iolani mentioned that Kekoa knew all the trails around their house so there must be lots of them."

"We're only twenty minutes out. Let's go a little farth—Uhh!"

He'd slipped.

Wright slid away down the moist slope before Taylan could grab him. He fell meters, bumping against roots and protruding nodules of ground, reaching for but failing to grab anything that might stop his descent. Taylan looked on in horror, unable to help. He disappeared from sight. She called after him, rapidly climbing down the track and nearly falling too. Then the sounds of his progress stopped. "Wright? Are you okay? Where are you?"

"I'm...Oh, shit!"

"Wright! What's happening?"

He didn't answer. She could hear him moving, however, and headed toward the sound.

"I'm down here," he finally said. "Be careful. It's really steep. Actually, it's better you don't come down. I'll climb back up."

"No way. Wait there. I'm coming." She still couldn't see him but she could guess where he was. The faint trail they'd been following had been made clearer by his passage. Bruised foliage, bent stems, and patches where the moss had been scraped away, revealing the almost-black, earthy leaf mold, marked the path.

"Taylan, stay where you are. You don't want to see this."

"I don't want to see what?! I thought you weren't hurt."

"I'm not, except I'm going to have some spectacular bruises, but I found something and it isn't nice."

She could see him now. He'd reached a level piece of ground and was sitting in the hollow at the base of a huge tree root snaking over the path. He was side-on to her and was looking at something, but he seemed to hear her approach and looked up. "I told you to stay where you were."

"You know how good I am at following orders, and, besides, you're not my CO anymore, Major Wright." He'd been promoted, but *Major Wright* was her go-to tease. He was covered in mud and green streaks of moss, and also...

"Is that blood?!" she exclaimed. "Stars, you *are* hurt."

"I'm not. It isn't mine." He gave a huff of frustration. "Come on down then, since you insist."

She descended the track. What she hadn't been able to see from above, what he'd tried to keep her from seeing, was the body of a dead monkey, or more like a gibbon or baboon. It was draped over the root as if casually tossed aside. The corpse had been decapitated.

She drew in a breath. Wright was looking at her with his *I told you so* expression.

"You fell onto it?"

"Yes."

"So it's the monkey's blood, not yours?"

"Yes."

She swallowed. "Well, we know they came this way."

"We do." He clambered upright, using the tree trunk for support. "We should leave it for the police. I think the kidnappers probably killed the animal here, and then cut off the head to carry it to the house. Let's look around some more."

"Do you think they came back this way?"

"Who knows? But even if they're nearby I doubt they would try anything. Kekoa's small, like Iolani. You don't have to be brave to snatch a small, weak woman out by herself."

As they continued downward the sound of running water supplemented the noises of the forest. They came upon the source quite suddenly. A fast-running stream crossed their path. A log had been placed across it, but the log was wet and slimy and seemed extremely likely to aid passage *into* the water rather than over it. Beyond the stream the jungle grew even thicker and the track appeared to entirely fail.

As they debated whether to attempt a crossing, a comm request arrived for Taylan.

It was Iolani. "The police are here."

"But you said it would take them a couple of hours?"

"I thought about it and decided to offer to fly them up anyway. They accepted, surprisingly. The chief of police came along too, so he must be taking it seriously. I guess I'm less notorious and more famous than I thought."

"You must be. We'll be there soon. We found something they'll be interested to hear about."

She and Wright began the climb back.

The local chief of police was a tall man in his fifties, well-muscled but running a little to fat. He grasped Taylan's hand tightly as he introduced himself and stared fixedly into her eyes. She stared back, unfazed by the power play. According to Iolani, his force wasn't that great at its job. She would decide whether Chief Mohan deserved her respect when she'd seen him in action.

He turned to Wright, offering his hand. "And you must be Lieutenant-Colonel Wright."

"Uhh, no..." Wright frowned. "I'm no longer with the Royal Marines. You can call me TJ." He looked questioningly at Iolani, but she shrugged.

"Ms Hale didn't reveal your identity," Chief Mohan explained. "Everyone knows about the famous Lieutenant-Colonel Wright of the *Defiant*, who led the team that freed Earth from alien control."

Wright seemed even more puzzled, and so was Taylan. How did he know who Wright was? What was more, if anyone could be said to have 'led the team' it was Fleet Admiral Yorkson. At least, as far as the public were aware, that was the case. In reality, Yorkson had been at a loss when it came to the battle on the alien planet. Abacha had thought up the tactics, and it had been Patrin who had defeated Merlin in the joust.

Perhaps Mohan knew Wright from the airship manifest. They'd had to state where they were staying when passing through immigration control, and the chief had put two and two together. In some ways, the local police weren't as inefficient as Iolani thought. Taylan hoped her husband's apparent fame would spur Chief Mohan to do his best to find Kekoa.

Iolani had put her dogs in another room. She looked overwhelmed and near tears. Whines, scratches, and other occasional sounds of canine dissatisfaction leaked out from behind the closed door. The chief had brought three subordinates with him, two of whom were inspecting the monkey skull, their hands encased in latex gloves.

"We found the rest of that in the forest," Taylan said, gesturing at the skull. "Or rather, Lieutenant-Colonel Wright did."

Wright threw her a withering look. "I fell onto it, unfortunately. We left it where we found it."

"Interesting," said Mohan. "You remember where it is?"

"Certainly."

"I'll conduct a coordinated search. If it weren't for the monkey skull, I would suspect this was just another case of an unwary hiker getting lost or getting themselves into trouble. But there may be something else going on."

"No shit," Taylan muttered, louder than she'd intended, drawing the gazes of everyone in the room. She gave a small cough.

Wright rolled his eyes.

"First," said Mohan, "I'd like to take a look at the monkey's body. If you wouldn't mind, TJ?"

"I'll stay here with Iolani," Taylan announced.

Wright and Mohan left, the three officers accompanying them. They'd put the monkey skull into an evidence bag and then inside a cooler. Iolani placed the cooler on the verandah, closed the door, and then let her dogs out.

Taylan made her sit down while she prepared drinks for both of them in the small kitchen. Iolani was weeping by the time she returned, carrying their glasses. Lorcan and Talman had rested their heads on her knees and were watching her mournfully.

"I can't help thinking I'll never see her again," Iolani said between sobs.

"Whoever's done this is probably only trying to scare you and Kekoa. Don't give up hope. Is there any reason someone might want you to move out?"

Iolani sniffed. "Not that I can think of. Believe me, I've done a lot of thinking, trying to figure out who it might be and why they're targeting Kekoa and me, but I can't come up with anything. We literally have no face-to-face contact with anyone except shopkeepers in town. All our other contacts are online. And though this area is beautiful it has no practical value. It's too wild and inaccessible for tourists, and the days of exploiting mineral deposits on Earth are over. I don't see why anyone would want to force us to leave."

Taylan was stumped too. The only possible conclusion seemed to be that Kekoa's kidnappers were nutters, pure and simple. If she was right, there was no telling what they might have done.

Later, when Wright and Chief Mohan returned, they brought the monkey's body with them. The sight of it sent Iolani into a fresh fit of fear and unhappiness. Mohan seemed to anticipate a second, longer search, asking her if he and his officers could stay at the house overnight if necessary. His expectation made sense, considering Iolani had already searched everywhere nearby and the nature of the terrain. She told him she had camping equipment they could borrow to sleep in the front yard.

Wright told Taylan, "We found some more of the weird stuff Kekoa and Iolani told us about before."

"Like what?"

He stepped away from Iolani, taking Taylan with him, before saying quietly, "There was the flayed body of some kind of rodent hanging from a branch, with feathers stuck in it. It was awful. And someone had painted symbols on a tree trunk in blood."

"What sort of symbols?"

"Not anything I recognized."

Mohan was briefing the search team, dividing up the ground, and allocating sections. It was now mid-afternoon, with only three or four hours of daylight remaining.

Taylan glanced at Iolani. "I think I should stay here while the search is going on."

"I agree. Iolani shouldn't be on her own at a time like this. I'm going to join the team."

"Be careful." She hugged him, mud, moss, blood, and dirt notwithstanding. Soon, the sounds of the searchers were quickly dissipating as they walked into the forest.

While Taylan waited with Iolani, she tried to distract her from her worries but it was impossible. Iolani was constantly on edge, listening minute by minute for news via her comm.

But no news came.

The dogs grew restless, and Iolani explained it was their dinner time. She fed them, and afterward Taylan helped her take tents out of storage and put them up, hoping they would not be needed.

Twilight fell, and the searchers didn't return. Their tents remained empty in the yard. The forest was dark and silent save for the sounds of the wildlife.

When dusk arrived there was still no sign of the police officers or Wright. Taylan sat with Iolani on the verandah, looking out into the shadows. Lorcan and Talman lay on their stomachs facing the screen door, heads between their paws, ears pricked. The stridulation of insects filled the air. Not a breath of wind moved. Above, brilliant stars pierced the black velvet sky.

"Do you think they've found something?" Iolani asked. "Is that what's taking them so long?"

It was impossible to answer. "I'm sure they'll be back soon." Taylan was growing concerned. Night was falling, and the forest wasn't easy to navigate even in broad daylight. As she decided to comm Wright, Iolani leapt to her feet.

"What's that?"

Something was moving among the trees. Taylan also stood up. The dogs padded to the door and pressed their noses against the netting. Rustles sounded from the vegetation. The glow from the verandah light revealed agitated leaves and fronds. A deeper noise started up, a bass-level rumble. Lorcan and Talman were growling, and the fur on their backs bristled.

Iolani faced Taylan. "Should I let the dogs out?"

A figure stepped into the clearing, quickly followed by others. It was hard to make them out in the darkness, but there was something weird about their heads. Their eyes were impossibly large and they glinted in the light from the verandah.

Iolani gripped Taylan's arm, her fingers digging in painfully. She reached for the verandah door. Her dogs whined and shuffled, anxious to be set free.

Taylan pressed a hand against the door. "Don't."

Wright had appeared. She would have recognized him anywhere. "It's okay," she told Iolani. "It's the police. They're wearing night vision goggles."

"Oh." Iolani's small remark held a world of sadness and disappointment. From the stooped, tired gait of the searchers it was clear Kekoa had not been found, or at least not alive.

Taylan stepped out while Iolani held her dogs' collars. As she walked down the steps to meet Wright, he took off his goggles and shook his head sadly. "No sign of her."

Later that night, while the police bedded down in their tents and Iolani's muted sobs came from her bedroom, Taylan climbed onto the sofa bed in the living room and lay down in Wright's arms, also missing people she loved dearly.

SIX

Taylan decided to join the new search the next day, and Iolani wanted to come too. Perhaps reacting to the desperation in her eyes, Mohan agreed. After a quick breakfast, she locked Lorcan and Talman in the verandah, and the party set out. The dogs gave short, yelping barks as the group moved away.

"Will they be okay?" Taylan asked her friend.

"They'll be fine. They're just worried about me. They sense something's wrong, and they must miss Kekoa too. I offered to bring them with us but Mohan said it's better they stay here. He's probably right. I don't want them to eat something they shouldn't again."

The plan was to extend the search farther afield than yesterday's effort. Everyone was carrying plenty of water as well as food. It was not anticipated anyone would be returning until nightfall. Mohan had outlined the target areas, segments of terrain not checked yet. It was less likely that Kekoa was on the populated, lower slopes, where cries for help could be heard and injured hikers seen more easily, but the chief included them too, wanting to cover all the bases.

The section allotted to Taylan and Iolani was way above the small mountain home, rising right to the peak. Two police officers accompanied them, while Wright was with the other team. As the person most familiar with the territory, the officers suggested that Iolani took the lead. She and Taylan walked ahead of the men, following a trail that began behind the house. It was steep, and Taylan was soon puffing.

"Did Mohan say anything useful last night?" she asked between gasps. The chief had pulled Iolani aside for a private conversation after his return.

"Only that he's leaning toward Kekoa's disappearance being simple misadventure, not linked to the monkey head. He saw the other strange items yesterday and I showed him the pics we'd taken, but he said it's probably kids messing around. The same with the head."

"But there aren't any kids around here, and, anyway, a child could never have hammered that skull into your door. And what about the body of the monkey? Is he seriously suggesting a kid could have killed it? I heard those things can be vicious."

"They can. I certainly wouldn't want to mess with one. He said a jaguar killed it, that someone must have found the head and thought it would be hilarious to play a practical joke. He thinks Kekoa's disappearance is just coincidental."

Taylan wasn't convinced. On the other hand, the local chief of police probably had a better handle on the situation than she did. "What do *you* think? Could a jaguar have killed the monkey?"

"It's possible. There are jaguars around here, though they're very timid and keep out of sight. I didn't take a close look at the body so it's hard for me to say. But if that is what happened the jaguar should have eaten it, not left it lying around in the forest. I hate to mention it, but you and Wright might have disturbed it mid-meal."

"Shit. I didn't even think of that." Taylan took a look over her shoulder.

The two police officers were chatting quietly in their own language a little way below them. Thick vegetation crowded in from every side, and the jungle canopy spread out down the slope. Iolani's house was already obscured and also, naturally, was the other search team. For reassurance, she touched the tracker Chief Mohan had given to everyone. She'd fastened hers to her shirt. It really wouldn't take much to become lost in this wild place.

"Don't worry," said Iolani. "A jaguar would never approach a group of people."

"You don't think...?"

"Kekoa wasn't attacked by a jaguar. I walked these trails for years while I was doing my research, sometimes without dogs. I only caught glimpses of jaguars a handful of times. We're not one of their prey species."

"Any tips on what to look for? Do you remember what Kekoa was wearing when she left?"

As Iolani described the clothing Taylan scanned the undergrowth. It looked impenetrable just meters away. Kekoa could not be far from a trail—unless she'd fallen down a slope, in which case she would be extremely difficult to find.

Iolani began calling her name. Taylan did too, and so did the officers. They were all bent nearly double to scale the incline, grabbing at the greenery for balance and traction. After half an hour Iolani called a halt. It was almost impossible to climb and shout. Everyone needed to catch their breath. Taylan rested a hand on a low-slung branch, drenched in sweat, her chest heaving.

Iolani said, "Just about a hundred meters til we reach the new search area. It's cooler up there."

One of the officers lifted a finger to his ear and bent his head as he listened to a comm. The atmosphere seemed to change. Taylan tensed. Iolani looked at her fearfully. But the officer only nodded in response to an unheard comment.

"Has something happened?" asked Iolani.

"No news," he replied.

They continued their ascent. The atmosphere began to cool as Iolani had predicted. By the time they reached the allotted search zone, they had to stop again. The day promised to be long and gruelling. Taylan hoped with all her heart it was successful. At least with Kekoa there was a chance of finding her. Taylan's own loved ones were beyond reach.

She sank down onto her backside, heedless of the dampness of the ground penetrating her pants, sucking in lungfuls of humid air. Iolani sat beside her. The police officers moved toward their rear.

In her tired state, it took Taylan a moment to register the incongruity of their behavior. There was no reason for them to—

Iolani shrieked. One of the men had grabbed her.

At the same time, hands fastened around Taylan's arms, jerking them behind her back. Her instincts kicked in. Without thinking, she jabbed her elbow backward, hard. A grunt burst out as it met flesh and the grip on her arms loosened. She broke free and swung around, her fist following, and punched the man in the jaw.

Meanwhile, in her peripheral vision she could see Iolani being overpowered. She was on her side, her wrists being tied as she struggled and fought.

Taylan's assailant was on his back, reaching for his gun. She stooped to grab it first, but the momentary distraction of Iolani's plight had been her undoing. The police officer jerked the gun up and aimed at her. She froze. He didn't speak, only held her gaze while his companion completed Iolani's capture.

The man gestured with his gun. "Turn around."

"What's going on? Who are you?"

Were they even the police?

He repeated his command.

Iolani's captor hauled her to her feet.

If it hadn't been for the danger to her friend, Taylan might have risked taking on the officer. But it would be impossible to free herself and Iolani. She faced about and allowed her wrists to be tied. The officer removed her ear comm. A heavy hand descended on her shoulder, forcing her forward.

"Where are you taking us?" When no one replied, she said, "Iolani, do you have any idea what's happening?"

A metal object poked her back—the muzzle of a gun. "No talking."

The officers pushed them higher up the trail until they reached an offshoot. It was as barely noticeable as the one where she and

Wright had found the dead monkey. Thick, wide leaves and looping vines impeded her progress as she stumbled along. What had to be going through Iolani's mind? Was this what had happened to Kekoa? Where was Wright? Had he been hurt?

They went deeper into the forest. The ground sloped downward. They seemed to be returning to the area they'd left behind, but by a different route. Then a thicker, more trodden path appeared.

"That way," the officer commanded, jabbing her again with his gun.

She ducked under overhanging foliage and stepped into a clearing, abruptly drawing to a halt and sucking in a sharp breath.

There was Wright, on his knees, a bag over his head.

And there was Kekoa! She was hooded too. Her clothing was dirty and torn and a deep cut ran down from her shoulder, as if she'd been dragged over something sharp. Where had she been since yesterday morning?

And there was Chief Mohan.

Except he wasn't dressed in his uniform. A blood-red robe fell from his neck to his feet, and a hat of the same color sat on his head, spreading wide from the circle that encased his skull.

Mohan signalled, and Taylan and Iolani were shoved downward to a kneeling position. The chief of police—if that was who he really was—nodded his satisfaction. "Four little birds trapped in a cage. It took a while to get you, but the bonus birds were worth the wait. Bring them to the center!"

Taylan and Iolani had to get to their feet and join Wright and Kekoa. Mohan instructed his men to remove the hoods, and Taylan could make eye contact with Wright at last. He winked, as though trying to reassure her everything would be okay. But she couldn't see a way out of whatever Mohan had in store. It was four armed aggressors against four unarmed, restrained captives, two of whom were not trained to fight or even brawny.

Mohan stepped closer. "Lieutenant-Colonel Wright and Taylan Ellis. What a piece of luck you happened to arrive at the right moment. Oh yes, Ellis, I know who you are, and how important you think you are. Don't think I didn't notice you pouting when I praised your husband." He chuckled. "Hell hath no fury like a woman scorned. Am I right, TJ?"

"What the fuck do you think you're doing?" Wright growled. "Are you insane?"

Taylan was at a loss. What could Mohan's motivation be? He had to be crazy, but he'd persuaded at least three other people to join him. How? Why?

"Let the others go," said Iolani. "You've clearly got a beef with me, but there's no need to drag innocent people into it. Let Kekoa, Wright, and Taylan leave, and I'll do whatever you want."

"No way!" Taylan protested. "I'm not leaving without you, and not until I've made these bastards pay."

"That makes two of us," said Wright.

Mohan smiled. "So, Ms Hale, we have another person full of her own importance. Please, don't flatter yourself. Wright and Ellis are more valuable to me than you. They were just far less reachable, living as they do in civilized lands. *Did*, I should say. Kidnapping is so much easier here."

While he talked, his goons spread themselves out in a rough triangle, facing inward. There was something different about them, a change in their expressions she couldn't quite put her finger on. Was it fear or adoration they showed when they looked toward Mohan? Their expressions reminded her of—

"Let's get down to it," Mohan said. "You know where our beloved leader is and how to get her back. Tell me, and you can live. When she has returned I will release you. Refuse, and you die, one by one, while your companions watch."

"Your beloved leader?" Iolani echoed.

"You have no friends here," Mohan went on. "No one knows you're missing, and no one will be looking for you. I can hold you as long as I like—as long as it takes. And if you don't give up your secrets, I am no worse off than when I started. So, what's it to be? Where is she? What has happened to her? Why didn't she retur—"

"Who?!" Iolani demanded. "Who the hell are you—"

"The Dwyr," Taylan said. "He means Dwyr Orr."

"Holy shit," said Kekoa. "Not that bitch. She's—"

"*Shhh*!" Taylan hissed. If Mohan understood Orr would never return to Earth, that she was unable to, he might kill them all on the spot. What did he have to lose? In this wild place, who would ever find out?

"Of course I mean our beloved Dwyr," Mohan snapped. "What have you done with her? She must have returned with you on the *Defiant*. She would never desert her people. The Britannic Alliance is obviously lying and has imprisoned her somewhere. Perhaps she's been executed. If she has, you'll soon be following her."

"She wasn't executed," Taylan replied. "She's still alive." Her mind raced. What could she tell this maniac to appease him while they figured out a way to escape?

"Very much alive," Wright said, "along with her son."

"Hmpf." Mohan nodded. "I knew it. I knew I would feel it in my bones if she was dead."

"All that junk on the trees," Iolani said, "the bits of dead animals and the insects, that was you all along?"

"Ha! I don't make the offerings. Those are the sacrifices of lesser people. It's my duty to keep the faith alive, and I've done my duty like my father did before me. I've kept our beliefs strong all these years, and now it's time for my reward, for my triumph. I will return the Dwyr to her faithful followers—more are already on their way here—when you tell me where she is."

"Release us and I'll tell you," said Taylan. "Not before. If we tell you now there's nothing to stop you from killing us anyway."

"Maybe you'll just have to trust me," Mohan replied, hooding his eyes.

"If we're dead you'll never find your Dwyr," Taylan insisted. "You'll never get another chance to capture someone from the *Defiant*. You'll never get Orr back, and what will you do then? Just how furious will she be, how disappointed in you, if she discovers you had your chance and fluffed it?"

Doubt momentarily clouded Mohan's features, but then manic

savagery returned. "If I release you, you will never tell me. Why would you when you've worked so hard to prevent her fulfilling her destiny? I will *make* you reveal her location. One by one..." his gaze traveled to each captive "...I will test you. I have many ways. And, finally, one of you will prefer death and an end to the pain, or an end to the suffering of someone you love, and then I will know the truth."

He approached Wright and jabbed a finger at him. Turning to one of the police officers, he said, "Start with thi—"

Wright pistoned to his feet, thrusting the top of his skull into Mohan's jaw. The man's head snapped back and he staggered before collapsing. Taylan ran at another of the officers, driving her knee into his solar plexus. When he was down she booted his temple so hard the judder ran up her leg. He was out cold. Meanwhile, Wright had gone for another of the officers. The men wrestled on the ground, Wright holding down the arm that held the gun with the weight of his body.

The third officer, a woman, aimed her weapon uncertainly at Taylan, fear in her eyes. Taylan stalked toward her, brow lowered. "You wouldn't dare!"

Chief Mohan groaned. He was beginning to come around. The female officer's gaze flicked to him and then back to Taylan, the resolve on her face strengthening.

Taylan ran at her.

The flash of a pulse round lit up the scene like lightning.

Agony exploded.

The grassy ground rushed upward to Taylan's face, and suddenly she was down. All she could feel was pain. It occupied her world, shutting out all sound, all vision. Distantly, she heard herself screaming.

SEVEN

She was alive. By some miracle, she was still alive. The pain had barely abated, but her brain, as if finally understanding there was nothing she could do about it, was allowing in information from her surroundings. She was on her back, a circle of blue sky framed by tree canopy above her. Voices encroached but she couldn't make out what they were saying. With a monumental effort, she turned her head to the side.

Mohan was back on his feet, though he still looked groggy. Blood dribbled from his mouth, his hat had fallen off, and his ridiculous robe was askew. The officer she'd knocked out sprawled on the ground, motionless. Perhaps she'd killed him. The two others flanked Mohan, staring down at...

Shit.

Wright had not got away. The man he'd been fighting with must have overpowered him. Maybe he'd been distracted by her getting shot. He lay between Iolani and Kekoa, his wrists and ankles fastened to stakes.

"We won't be seeing a repeat of that incident," Mohan was saying, "because I will start with you, Lieutenant-Colonel. You will be the first to suffer, and the experience will put you out of action. Will you reveal the Dwyr's location? This is your final chance."

Wright cursed bitterly and his gaze shifted to Taylan, deep grief etching his features. Then they made eye contact. Shock and joy broke out over his face. He shifted. New energy seemed to flood him. He looked up at Mohan and the officers, apparently reassessing the situation.

But what could he do?

His hands and feet were tied. Iolani and Kekoa didn't know how to help him, and she was useless, utterly incapacitated.

"I'm disappointed," Mohan said, "but not too much. Your blood and agony will invigorate the Horned One before you finally give in. No matter how long it takes, in the end the result will be the same. Our Dwyr will return to us and the old ways will begin again." He took a step back. The officers dragged Kekoa and Iolani to the edge of the clearing, leaving Wright by himself in the center. Then they returned. The man took out a knife.

Taylan's heart froze. Wright looked at her again. She knew his meaning.

Look away.

Don't watch.

But her attention was fixed by horror. She couldn't move her head. She couldn't close her eyes.

The man slit Wright's shirt from his pants to the collar, and the woman pulled it over his shoulders, exposing his chest.

Taylan whimpered.

Mohan swivelled, his eyes blazing. "Ellis is still alive? Even better. The Horned One will have two blood sacrifices today."

"You... I'll..." She couldn't get the words out. The tiniest movement sent shards of pain lancing through her, but a worse agony was what was about to happen to the man she loved, the man whose unending kindness, generosity of spirit, and loyalty had kept him by her side, flawed as she was. It didn't matter if Mohan killed her. How could she go on without Wright? She couldn't bear to see him hurt. A growl of frustration, impotence, and despair rose up from her stomach.

Mohan chuckled. He nodded at the male officer. "Begin."

The man crouched and angled the knife downward, pushing the tip into the soft spot at the base of Wright's neck. He drew it slowly along his chest, slitting the skin. Wright's muscles bunched and his jaw tightened but he didn't make a sound. Iolani and Kekoa softly gasped. One of them—Taylan could not see who—began to weep.

Still, Taylan could not look away. The scene was surreal, unbelievable, impossible. How could she have thought her life no longer held any happiness when—

There was a rustle of vegetation, the drum of fast padding, and a black blur flashed into the clearing.

The creature leapt for the male officer. The attack was almost silent as the man fell to the ground. He didn't even manage to scream before his throat was ripped out. A brief gurgle emanated as blood flooded from the wound in gushes.

For a second, Taylan thought a black jaguar had entered the clearing and launched into a predatory frenzy. Would it kill them all?

But it was not a jaguar.

Lorcan and Talman had escaped the verandah.

As the first dog to appear turned from the dying man, the second arrived and instantly went for Mohan, who was a statue of terror watching his officer die. In a flurry of snarls and snaps, Mohan also fell. The dog loomed over him. Futilely, his hands waved and legs kicked as the animal busied itself around his head and throat.

Meanwhile, the first dog focused on the only Crusader who remained standing, the female officer. It lifted its lips to reveal sharp, bloody teeth, a deep growl vibrating the air.

The woman's gun rose, shaking violently, as the whites of her eyes shone out in the shadows. Her other hand rose as if trying to steady her aim.

The dog leapt.

Taylan had not been able to close the distance between her and her assailant before being shot, but the animal had no such problem.

Lorcan and Talman's attack was over within less than a minute. Mohan and two police officers were dead. The third had stayed unconscious throughout the ordeal. Wright was silent, his cut chest quickly rising and falling. Kekoa gaped, her face pale. The dogs trotted to Iolani, tails wagging and ears pricked, their muzzles drenched in blood. They nudged her happily and then sat down, anticipating pats.

"Good boys," she murmured. "Good boys."

EIGHT

Iolani had used her heli to fly Taylan to the nearest hospital. No doctors or nurses asked any questions about who she was or how she'd sustained her wound. It was the way things worked here. The medical professionals told her she should not have survived. A few millimeters deeper penetration of the round would have injured her heart sufficiently to stop it beating, and that would have been that. Certainly, Wright had been correct to conclude she had died. He'd seen enough soldiers killed by pulse fire in his time.

His wound was superficial and quickly healed by application of a gel. Within hours, his body responded and sealed up the cut without even leaving a scar.

Her recovery and recuperation would take longer, but the prognosis was she would suffer no lasting physical effects. The same could not be said for her psychological state. Not by her, anyway. She would never forget the time she'd come within a whisker of seeing the man she loved tortured to death.

Kekoa had also recovered from her ordeal. She'd been hurt by her cultist kidnappers, and the night she'd spent gagged and bound in the jungle had taken its toll, but she emerged unscarred. Lorcan and Talman had required treatment too, for the damage they'd done to their paws and mouths as they broke through the verandah netting.

No dogs ever received more loving attention to their injuries. Iolani wasn't sure what exactly had alerted them, but she guessed they must have heard her or Taylan's screams.

On the day before Taylan was due to be discharged, Iolani and Kekoa came to see her. Wright had stepped out to stretch his legs. He'd barely left her side all the while she'd been in hospital.

"Are you going straight back to the BI?" Kekoa asked.

"I think so. I mean, Suriname's nice, but…"

"I get it," Iolani said. "The Crusader cult hangover is putting you off."

"Something like that."

They chuckled, but then Iolani grew serious. "Taylan, I'm so sor—"

"Don't apologise." She'd been waiting for this. "Don't take responsibility for those maniacs' actions. None of what happened is your or Kekoa's fault. I would hate it if I left here knowing you blamed yourself. So, please, don't."

Iolani sighed. "All right."

"What about you?" Taylan asked. "Are you going to leave the mountain now?"

"We thought about it…" She shared a look with Kekoa. "And we're still thinking about it. We haven't been back to the house yet. We've been staying in a hotel with the dogs while the police complete their investigation."

"The police?! How can you trust them?"

"They've admitted the corruption in their ranks and invited the Global Nations Security Division to oversee an internal enquiry."

"But there's no saying whether Crusaders exist outside the force. Do you remember Mohan telling us more of them were on their way?"

"I do." Iolani looked down and shrugged. "Like I said, we have some thinking to do."

Would the world ever be rid of the influence of the Earth Awareness Crusade? Taylan doubted it. Despite all the improvements that had taken place while she'd been on the *Defiant*, one thing hadn't changed: human nature and its habit of developing weird beliefs. If it wasn't Crusaders, some other strange cult was bound to pop up.

"I know what you should do," Taylan announced.

Iolani looked up.

"Come and stay with me and Wright in West BI. We have plenty of room now Kayla's gone for the autumn term. You can get away from all this heat and humidity and decide what you want to do, depending on what the police discover."

"That sounds like a great idea," said Kekoa.

"But what about Lorcan and Talman?" asked Iolani.

"They, uhh…" in truth, Taylan had some reservations about the dogs now she'd seen them in action, though she would be eternally grateful to them "… they can come too."

Iolani grinned. "Then it's a deal."

Kekoa chuckled. "I think Lorcan Ua Talman finally redeemed himself for kidnapping you, in spirit at least."

Wright returned bearing a coffee in each hand. "Ooops. I didn't know you had visitors. I can go and get some more—"

"Never mind that," said Taylan. "I have some news. Iolani and Kekoa are coming home with us."

"Really? Fantastic. We can show them around."

"I would love it," said Kekoa. "I've never been to the BI."

Now that the next few months of her life were decided, sudden tiredness hit Taylan, and she yawned.

"We should let you rest," Iolani said. "You're still recovering."

"No, it's okay."

But her friends were already standing up.

Kekoa said, "I'll comm you, TJ, about flight tickets, etcetera."

"Sure. We'll be traveling home the fast way this time."

They said their goodbyes, and Taylan and Wright were alone again.

She took his hand. "You know, though we've had a bloody awful time, one good thing has come out of it, for me at least."

"What's that?"

"When we were in the jungle and I really thought we'd had it…

When I thought I was going to lose you and in the most horrible way…" She swallowed the lump that had formed in her throat.

"Let's not talk about it."

"I want to. I just wanted to say, I learned to appreciate what I have. That's what I'm going to focus on from now on—appreciating what I have."

"I see." He put a finger to his lip. "Does that mean I can expect to be waited on hand and foot? Bacon and eggs for breakfast every morning? Back massages every night?"

"Now wait a minute. Don't get ideas above your station, Major Wri—"

He kissed her.

FOUND

ONE

He hadn't been given time to say goodbye, to his great regret. Patrin would never forget the look on Mam's face when he'd announced his decision to remain with the aliens on their planet. It had seemed an obvious choice. What was a few months or even years of his life in exchange for the lives of everyone aboard the *Defiant*, including the people who had died? And the aliens promised to stop interfering in human affairs. Who in their right mind would refuse? Yet when he remembered Mam's reaction, he couldn't help thinking he'd made a huge mistake.

At least Arthur was here too. That was something.

They'd moved to this room in an army barracks as if by magic. He guessed everything the aliens did would seem like magic, though only because they were so much more advanced than humans. Merlin had said he could appear on Earth in an instant, without the use of a starship. Would that be how he would send him back, just like that? He hoped it wouldn't take too long. Mam had said something about time passing differently here.

Arthur turned from the window of their little room. "Soldiers are practicing in the yard. They look real but they must be phantasms like the knights we fought in the battle."

"Must be." Patrin, sitting on one of the two bunks, looked up at the older man. "How long do you think Merlin and Morgan will keep us?" He missed Mam and Kayla already, but he was reluctant to admit it. He didn't want to look weak in front of this famous warrior.

"There is no telling. Both are whimsical and fickle. Morgan especially so. Even when Merlin was my friend I couldn't entirely trust him to follow through with his promises. We cannot rely upon any reassurance they give. We are entirely under their power. Perhaps we can only hope they grow bored of us soon and send us home."

"Did I..." Patrin swallowed "...did I do the right thing, sir? I mean, agreeing to stay."

Arthur smiled warmly and joined him on the bunk. "Patrin, you must call me Arthur. I have never enjoyed the airs and graces accompanying my kingship. It would please me greatly if we could be more like friendly companions than a king and his squire."

Patrin nodded, though he couldn't imagine ever feeling like an equal with this great man.

"As to whether you made the right decision," Arthur continued, "there was no decision to be made. Had you refused you would have died, and so would have all our company. Merlin and Morgan knew this full well. Their proposal had only one possible answer and you gave it, as would any rational person. Don't concern yourself with doubts. Our predicament is very simple. We must face whatever lies in store for us with brave hearts. That is all." Placing a hand on Patrin's shoulder he added, "I have only one caveat, my friend, and it is one that you ignored despite my earlier request."

"Huh? What's that?"

"When we first arrived on this new world and we were waiting for Merlin or Morgan to meet us, I had a great foreboding and I mentioned it to you. Do you remember?"

"Uhh, yes." A heavy feeling settled in Patrin's stomach. "I'm sorry."

"I am glad you have not forgotten. I asked you not to put your life in danger out of loyalty to me, but you did so anyway."

"I know I went back on my promise, but I was so angry about what Merlin had done to you." Recalling the joust, Patrin gained courage. "And if I hadn't forced him to fight again—"

"We would all have been killed. I am aware of the paradox. I forgive you. I understand why you behaved as you did. But my request stands. I do not know what the future holds or what the beings of this world plan to do to us, but I don't want you to repeat your earlier mistake. I want you to swear to me on the lives of your mother and sister that you will not do such a thing again. You must not risk your life to save mine. Though we may be friends I am still your king, and I ask you to make this oath to me as your royal sovereign."

Arthur's features transformed from those of an affable older man to a solemn, dignified elder. His blue eyes held Patrin's gaze sternly.

"I swear, sire, on the lives of my mother and sister."

Arthur's face relaxed. "I am satisfied." He rose to his feet and stretched his arms wide. "Merlin has not re-invigorated me, more's the pity. I would not have objected to that particular charm. My age creeps up on me apace, faster than it would naturally. I fear he will not be affording me any protection in the trials to come."

"But I thought they just wanted to study us?" Patrin's vague idea had been that the aliens might examine them or ask them questions. "They'd said they wanted to understand humans better."

Returning to the window and resting his elbows on the sill, Arthur replied, "I knew Merlin all my life and Morgan for most of it. Even so, I doubt I know them well. But if my past experiences of them are anything to go by, their study will not be the serious examination you expect. They are playful creatures, delighting in intrigue, rivalry, and strife. And, as your mother divined, their greatest delight is to see humans desperately cling to life. It is that aspect of us that most interests them. Which does not bode well for us, unfortunately. That is the reason I made you swear your oath. I know you are not an oath breaker."

The door opened and in walked Merlin. No trace remained of the wound Patrin had inflicted when he pierced the alien's throat with his lance. What was the creature made from? Not flesh and blood. He could melt his body into a pool of liquid and make it solid again. He wore a black robe and a close-fitting cap that covered most of his head and short, silver hair. He knitted his fingers, his gaze drifting from Arthur to Patrin as he seemed to consider his words. "I must confess, I had relished the prospect of punishing the rude visitors who had turned up at our door uninvited, but now I'm of a different mind. Morgan's idea was inspired. This new game promises to be even more engaging than the last."

Patrin stood up. "You said you wanted to get to know us better, not to continue playing with us."

Merlin cocked an eyebrow at Arthur. "Your young friend is rather outspoken, is he not? You should rein him in before he gets himself into trouble."

"Patrin is his own man," Arthur replied. "He is not under my command. And I endorse his sentiment. If you only plan on continuing your old habit of toying with human emotions, then you are keeping us here under false pretences."

"You know better than to hold me to my word," Merlin said darkly.

"Indeed I do, you old fox. If it's to be more of the same, send the boy home. You don't need him."

"Ah, if only I could. Morgan would object, unfortunately."

Arthur snorted in disgust and returned his attention to the view outside the window.

Patrin said, "Maybe there are things you can learn from us, if you're willing."

Merlin's lips creased into a thin smile. "Go on. I'm fascinated."

Counting the words on his fingers Patrin said, "Honesty, trustworthiness, integrity—"

A peal of laughter from the alien interrupted Patrin's recitation. "I lived among humans for hundreds of Earth years, far longer than Arthur's lifetime. The characteristics you mention are not as common as you might think. They are certainly not representative of humanity."

"It's true that not everyone has them, but a lot more than your kind do, that's for sure."

"My kind? Who are my kind? What are they? Do you think you know?" When Patrin didn't answer, Merlin yawned, lifting the back of his hand to his mouth. "I am here to tell you what you can expect. It will make things more interesting if you are prepared. Morgan and I have devised some tasks for you to complete. If you perform them to our satisfaction, you may return to Earth."

"That isn't what we agreed!" Patrin protested.

Merlin smirked. "Then file a complaint with the relevant authority. Ooops, I was forgetting—there isn't one." He gave a small cough. "Seriously, the outcome of our scheme will not be significantly different from the agreed purpose of your stay. By observing what you do we may learn nuances of human psychology we previously overlooked. You see, Kala Orr and her son will be with you. Dissimilarities between your actions and those of the half-breeds may shed light on traits which are uniquely human."

"Tasks?" asked Arthur. "Are they dangerous? You know how fragile our bodies are compared to yours. If something were to happen to Patrin—"

"You would do what? Regardless, Patrin is Morgan's responsibility. She was the one who wanted two of you, and the one spouting all that motherhood nonsense."

Patrin sank onto the bunk.

"Merlin," said Arthur, "I ask you once more, I beg you, return the boy to Earth. I am fully human. I repeat, you have no need to involve another of us in your game."

"Need was never my motivation."

Merlin left.

"Thanks for trying to help," Patrin said, "but I would feel bad if you were here by yourself. And now we know we have to associate with Kala Orr and Perran..." he grimaced "...it would be extra unfair. No one should have to deal with that pair alone."

"I am quite used to the likes of Kala Orr. Do not fear for me in that regard. I am more concerned that you may not survive this unscathed. Your mother went to great lengths to find you and your sister when you were kidnapped by the Crusaders. I must protect you at all costs, but I am not sure exactly how. I will understand more when the tasks are revealed."

TWO

Row upon row and column upon column of buildings ran between them and the horizon, rising and falling, following the lie of the land. Patrin was reminded of the town where he'd grown up, except there were no gardens or trees or parks, nothing green at all, and the buildings varied greatly in size and shape. Some rose so tall they disappeared into the clouds, others spread wide and flat like square pancakes. They were all the same color—a pale blue that matched the patches of sky between the clouds. They had to be constructed from the same material. The uniformity, despite the differing sizes and shapes, was somehow unnerving. The metropolis felt unnatural though Patrin couldn't put his finger on why.

Figures moved between the buildings. Were they people? At the distance it was hard to tell.

"What do you think of this place?" Merlin asked.

They stood on a hill bordering the city. How they'd arrived here, Patrin did not know. One moment he'd been talking to Arthur in the barracks room, the next he was on the hill, the wind stirring his hair.

"This is where your people live?" Arthur asked.

"One place of many."

"It reminds me of the cities of Earth."

Movement in his peripheral vision caught Patrin's attention. Kala Orr and Perran had appeared on the slope of the neighboring hill, accompanied by Morgan le Fay.

"How big do you think it is?" asked Merlin.

Arthur replied, "I cannot see its end."

"Does it seem a friendly place? Safe to traverse?"

Turning his silver-haired head, Arthur faced the alien. "Is that the first task? We must cross the city?"

"That would be far too simple and easy."

Patrin said, "We have to beat Orr and her son, right?"

Merlin smirked. "A pleasant notion. It would certainly add tension to the game."

Arthur nudged him with his elbow. Patrin silently remonstrated with himself. They were in deep enough shit as it was without giving the aliens more ideas on how to make their lives difficult.

"I will consider it for later exercises," Merlin went on. "Today, you must only cross the city, as Arthur guessed, but you must do it before sunset."

Patrin's gaze swung to a bright patch of cloud hiding the sun. The star hung halfway between the horizon and its zenith. He didn't know which direction was north. "Is it morning or afternoon?"

Merlin's smirk widened.

"How long has it been since the *Defiant* departed?" Arthur asked. "It seems many hours but I am not hungry or thirsty."

"Your primitive needs are irrelevant here. The atmosphere nourishes you." Merlin added sarcastically, "You will not need to stop for lunch along the way."

"So it's morning," said Patrin. "How long is a day on this planet?"

"What an inquisitive young human."

On the farther hill, Morgan was speaking with Orr and Perran, no doubt also outlining the rules of the task. Would she give them additional information? It seemed impossible that the two aliens wouldn't set up some sort of competition between the humans and half-humans. It was exactly the kind of thing they seemed to love.

"Is what you're asking us to do achievable?" asked Arthur, his brows lowered.

"Why would I set you a task you cannot possibly complete?"

"To tickle your fancy, of course. If you really want to discover what it means to be human, you only need to observe us, not play these games. But in honesty I believe you have no interest in observing humanity. You only want to prolong the game you began when you came to our planet millennia ago. You want—"

This time it was Patrin who nudged Arthur. He had a feeling that revealing what they thought about the aliens was unwise. Also, time was getting on. If something important hinged on their success, they should get moving. "So we only have to walk across the city before sunset? There are no other conditions?"

"That is all."

"And if we fail?"

"Then we shall see what we shall see."

"Come on, Arthur. Let's go."

It wasn't only a sense of wariness that compelled him to begin immediately, he was also genuinely curious to enter the city. He was one of the first human beings to set foot on an exoplanet, and not any old exoplanet, but one inhabited by an intelligent extra-terrestrial species. The prospect of seeing them up close intrigued him.

Arthur appeared troubled, though he followed as Patrin descended the slope. "It might have been wise to talk with Merlin longer. He could have revealed helpful information."

"He might have fed us lies too, to trip us up, just for fun."

"That is true."

Patrin looked over his shoulder. Merlin was gone. Morgan le Fay had disappeared as well, and Kala Orr and Perran were walking down their hill.

———

They stepped into the shadow of a building, a skyscraper so tall its upper floors were invisible, lost in the misty vapor that overhung the place. Square, blank windows rose up the façade

until they disappeared out of sight.

"No glass," Patrin murmured. The rectangular shapes weren't reflective. They were dark and opaque, and they were flush with the outer surface, almost as if they'd been painted on.

"Let us hurry," said Arthur. "There will be nothing of interest to see in this place and we must reach the other side as quickly as we can. Who knows what punishment Merlin may have in store?" He was already striding down the street.

Patrin hurried after him. He was also unsure what Merlin might do if they failed. The alien seemed to value the presence of humans on his planet, reversing his earlier reaction when he'd almost killed them. But there was one thing Patrin did not want to lose, and that was the agreement to return him to Earth. Mam had been through enough in her time. He didn't want her heart to break from losing him forever.

The thoroughfare was empty. He wasn't sure where Kala Orr and her son had entered the city, but it was somewhere else. Figures were crossing the road at the junction, however. Despite their rush, his footsteps slowed as they neared them. There was something odd about the people. He didn't know what he'd been expecting— possibly creatures who looked similar to Merlin and Morgan—but it wasn't this.

They weren't wearing clothes or shoes.

And they were gray.

Arthur strode ahead, his long legs eating the distance, silver mane flowing in the breeze. Patrin broke from his bemusement and sped up his pace. Then, as he reached Arthur, the old king began to trans- form. His burly body slimmed down and shrank.

"Arthur?"

"What, Patrin? We must make haste." He didn't slow down.

Arthur's clothes disappeared and in their place gray skin grew, the same as the figures in the distance.

Patrin couldn't go on. He halted, his mouth agape. "Arthur, stop! You... You're..."

Arthur must have registered the note of panic in his voice, for this time he halted and turned. But the man who faced Patrin was not his beloved liege. It was a weird creature, naked and hairless. Wide, black eyes with no white and no lids slowly blinked. A lipless mouth opened into an O. "Patrin?! What has become of you?"

"What's become of *me*? What about..." Fear drying up his words, he looked down. Two long, gray, featureless limbs had replaced his legs. He lifted trembling hands. Five fingers had transformed to four, and the digits were the same color as the rest of his new body. "You're the same," he blurted. "What's happened to us?"

Perhaps it was another of Merlin's jokes. Perhaps the shock was intended to slow them down. Whatever the reason for their metamorphosis, there was nothing they could do except to accept it and continue on.

"We won't stand out among the citizens of this place now," Arthur said. "I expect Merlin will return us to our former state later. Let us move on."

How many minutes had already passed since they entered the city?

They ran to the end of the street. A wide avenue traversed it, thronged with the gray folk. They varied in height and weight like humans. Some appeared to be children, holding their parents' hands as they walked. The figures spoke to each other but Patrin didn't know their language. Vehicles also moved along the avenue, two-wheeled and four-wheeled. They even had autobuses.

Arthur darted across the roadway during a break in the traffic. Patrin followed but not quite quickly enough, causing a vehicle to brake. The person sitting in it shouted and shook a four-fingered fist.

As they jogged down the next street, Patrin squinted at the sky. The sun wasn't visible above the buildings yet. They passed a window at street level, and he was surprised to see this one was made of glass. Creatures sitting at tables could be seen inside, chatting and eating—eating! Merlin had said the air contained nutrients, eliminating the need to eat.

"Arthur!" He wanted to show the king the strange phenomenon. What did it mean? But his newly transformed companion ignored him.

Patrin feared he might lose him in the crowd if he didn't keep up. There was little difference between Arthur and the other pedestrians, except for the fact that he was clearly in a hurry. Patrin pushed past a group of the aliens. Was their hairless, bulbous-headed, black-eyed form what Merlin and Morgan really looked like? He ached to stop and try to communicate with one of them. The reason he'd agreed to stay behind was to find out more about this place, but Merlin had deprived him of the opportunity. "Arthur!"

They'd reached the end of the block. It was not a crossroads. The opposite side of the street held no exit.

"Which way?" asked Arthur. "Left or right?"

"Right? I don't think it matters."

They jogged down the street, waiting for a lull in the traffic, and then crossed it. Soon, an alley opened up. As they ran down it, Patrin spotted another glass window. He couldn't resist the urge to look inside. Gray creatures sat at desks, working on interfaces. Surprise made him stop and stare. First a café or restaurant, now an *office*? What was going on? Was life on this planet so remarkably similar to the way humans behaved on Earth?

He wanted to discuss what he was seeing with Arthur, but the alleyway was empty.

"Arthur!" Patrin flew to the end and peered out. The creatures walked and drove the streets the same as before. The effect was unsettling. Put clothes and hair on the aliens and they could almost be people.

Where had his friend gone?

One of the pedestrians was taller and walking faster than the others. Dodging the creatures in his way, Patrin ran to the potential Arthur and grabbed its shoulder. It spun around, and for a fraction of a second Patrin thought he'd made a mistake. Could this no-nose being really be the king?

"Patrin? Is that you?"

"Thank the stars! I nearly lost you."

"You must keep up! Don't make me remind you again."

The end of a broad street faced them.

"I think this may lead us a long way into this horrible place," Arthur said.

They ran along the edge of the pavement, avoiding the vehicles and the pedestrians. Arthur had made Patrin go in front—to keep an eye on him, presumably. The king had a remarkable ability to focus on a task, regardless of what was going on in his surroundings. Patrin tried to emulate him but again and again his gaze was drawn to scenes playing out around them.

A small version of one of the creatures fell over and its larger 'parent' picked it up and patted it soothingly. A couple of aliens walking arm-in-arm suddenly faced each other and pressed their mouths together. *Kissing*?! A gray being halted at the edge of the road and waved at the traffic. One of the vehicles peeled out of the flow and parked, collecting a passenger before moving on.

"That way!" Arthur shouted.

A diagonal thoroughfare led off to the left. Arthur probably thought it would get them across the city faster. Patrin had long since lost all sense of direction. He looked up. The sun peeked over the roof of a tall building. Nearly midday already? He could have sworn less than an hour had passed. But this planet might have a faster rotation than Earth. Merlin had been careful to avoid telling them anything about it.

After taking the new direction, they were in shadow, tall constructions looming on each side. For the first time, gray creatures who were running appeared, and they were running directly toward them. The creatures stared as they ran, making eye contact. Another first. Up until now, they'd been mostly ignored.

"Do not speak to them," Arthur warned. "I fear they mean to delay us."

Like the rest of the aliens, there was little to tell between them except for their body size. One was nearly as tall as Arthur. The other was shorter and slimmer. The latter's smaller stature made what it did next extra surprising. As it neared Arthur it diverted its path to come closer to the king. Arthur tried to run around it, but the alien drew back a fist and punched him in the stomach.

Clearly taken entirely by surprise, the king gave out an *Ooof*! and doubled over. Patrin raced to his aid, but the taller alien had made a beeline for him. He ducked and only narrowly avoided the fist that swung where his head had been. Why were they being attacked? Were the aliens trying to prevent them reaching their goal?

Patrin punched upward, catching his attacker under his chin. His knuckles sank horribly into soft gray flesh. Did these things even have bones? His opponent stumbled and fell. Meanwhile, Arthur had managed to get his assailant into a headlock.

"Leave me alone, you bastard," the thing hissed.

It spoke English? But, wait, Patrin recognized the voice.

"Kala Orr," Arthur growled. "How like you to try to make us fail at our task, even at the expense of your own failure."

"Let me go!"

"You started this. I've half a mind to twist your head off. These strange new bodies we have may make it possible."

The creature who had swung at Patrin—Perran Orr, he presumed—was rising to his feet. Patrin kicked his legs out from under him, causing him to land hard on his butt. Except none of them had butts anymore. He pushed Perran onto his back and put a foot on his chest to keep him down.

"If you wait here any longer," Kala said, "you *will* fail."

"If I set you free you will attack us again."

Perran gasped, "We won't, I promise. I tried to persuade Mother against it, but she insisted. She says this is what Morgan really wants —for us to make you lose."

"She may be right," said Arthur. "All the more reason for me to put an end to your darling parent." He grabbed one side of Kala's head with his large paw. His fingers sinking into the gray flesh, he dragged it around.

Kala screamed.

"Don't do it!" yelled Perran. "I'll make her leave you alone. You won't see us again. I guarantee it."

"Arthur," said Patrin. "We should give them a chance. They are half human after all, and they're trapped here. They will never be allowed to return to Earth."

The king didn't relinquish his hold at first, but seconds later he threw Kala Orr to the ground. "Hurry, Patrin."

During the short fight, the sun had surmounted the sky. It shone directly down the road, illuminating the gray figures of Kala and Perran as they left them behind.

They reached the corner and the king slowed down. His breath was coming in short puffs. Patrin was feeling the pace too, yet they seemed to be nowhere near the edge of the city. Buildings surrounded them on all sides.

"Which way?" asked the king.

"I don't know. Let's try down there." The new direction seemed as good as any. From Patrin's memory of the view of the city and the position of the sun, they would definitely be heading away from the hills. It also felt better to keep moving than to come to a complete halt and try to assess their surroundings. Everything looked the same anyway—oddly Earth-like.

As they jogged along, Arthur said, "You were right to remind me to show pity and mercy. Sometimes, when faced with evil in the guise of Kala Orr, it's easy to forget."

"I don't know if we did the right thing. I've a feeling it won't be long before we see them again, despite Perran's promise."

"Maybe so, but that would be their fault, not ours."

After a while, Patrin's lungs began to burn. His leg muscles already ached. They'd been running at a fast pace, and he'd grown unfit during his time on the *Defiant*. Where was the end to the city?

They ran on.

As his fatigue increased, Patrin began to imagine he could see

Kala Orr and her son again amongst the crowd. Any pair unevenly matched in height could be them. Perhaps he did see them, but no more of the gray creatures approached. In fact, they seemed uninterested in the two runners.

When the task was over, would Merlin change them back into their original form? Surely he would not allow them to remain like this forever. Was that the reward for success, to become human once more? Was the punishment for failure to remain as they were? How would he live on Earth looking like this?

The sun had disappeared from overhead ages ago and now the light was dimming. Time was running out. His throat sore from panting and his legs on fire, he began to long for a glimpse of the city boundary. What lay at the farther edge? More hills?

Arthur had been running slower for a while and Patrin had eased his pace to match the older man, but suddenly the king drew to a complete stop. His hands on his knees and his odd features strained with effort, he squeezed out a few words. "Go on without me. I cannot run any farther."

"No way." Patrin put an arm over Arthur's shoulders, his own chest sucking in huge lungfuls of air. "You can make it."

"I cannot. I am at the end of my strength."

"You can walk at least. Let's walk."

Arthur stepped forward slowly. "There is no point. You must continue alone."

"I won't do it."

"Patrin," he wheezed, "you took an oath, remember?"

"I know, but this isn't a life and death situation. We don't know if I'm giving my life for yours by staying with you."

They staggered on. Arthur appeared too exhausted to argue.

The streets stretched out, lacking any apparent limit. The sky was darkening.

"You know," said Patrin, beginning to catch his breath, "I don't think there is an end to this city. I think it goes on forever."

"You may be right. It would be exactly the kind of joke Merlin would love."

The atmosphere was growing chilly and a rose tint lit the sky. The endless stream of pedestrians and vehicles was lessening. They turned a corner, one of so many Patrin had lost count. A thoroughfare opened up, similar to all the others. It was as if they were trapped in a gigantic labyrinth with no beginning or end.

Then the rose tint above them swiftly faded and was replaced by twilight.

They had failed.

A figure appeared from nowhere at the end of the street. Clad in his black gown and cap, Merlin smiled superciliously. Arthur and Patrin slowly hobbled up to him. There was no point in trying to avoid their fate, whatever it might be. They were entirely under the creature's control.

"Tut tut, my boys," Merlin chided. "A good effort, but not good enough. It's time to pay the price." He lifted a hand dramatically and flicked his fingers upward.

Patrin flew into the air. He rose high above the city, through the misty clouds and into the upper atmosphere. He choked in the freezing, thin air and flailed about. The icy temperature began to bite. Was this how he would die, asphyxiated and frozen? He began to move sideways. Craning his neck, he saw Arthur following, though the king's head hung down as if he was already unconscious.

Dark clouds moved beneath, obscuring the land below.

Abruptly, whatever force was keeping him aloft vanished. He plummeted, falling so fast he barely registered his passage through the clouds. A black expanse rushed up at him. He briefly recognized the indistinct forms of waves before he dropped feet-first into water and it closed over his head.

Somehow, the impact didn't kill him. He sank deep. Gradually, his momentum slowed and he floated in the depths of the ocean. *Up* had to be above his head. He kicked, his lungs straining for air. He swam on and on but didn't emerge from the water. Everything was forgotten—Arthur, Mam, Kayla, and Wright, Earth, Merlin, Morgan, Kala and Perran Orr—all slipped from his mind except the single focus of being able to breathe.

Yet no matter how hard he kicked or how high his arms reached, he couldn't get to the surface. His body rebelled against his control, yearning for sweet oxygen.

Finally, exhausted and despairing, his mouth automatically opened. He couldn't help it.

He breathed in.

THREE

The water penetrated his lungs deeply. He could feel its liquid coolness inside his chest, but for some reason he didn't cough, gag, or choke. He exhaled, and slightly warmer water flowed out of his mouth accompanied by a fountain of bubbles.

His feelings of panic and fear receded. He wasn't losing consciousness. He wasn't dying.

He hung in the misty dark, confused. Experimentally, he filled his lungs and then breathed out. The water flowed in and out as naturally as air. Was he imagining it? Was he actually dying and this was a projection of his fading mind?

He didn't think so. After all, he and Arthur had been transmogrified into strange alien creatures only a few hours ago. Was he still a strange alien creature? He couldn't see a thing. He was either too deep or the water was too murky. He felt for one of his hands with the other.

Four fingers and a thumb.

He was human again. Except, not quite. Not unless you counted the ability to breathe water, which had never been a human capability, not naturally nor even by design as far as he was aware. Merlin had altered his body again, the same as he'd made him gray and hairless and given him a bulbous head and fully black eyes.

What should he do? What was the point of this new transformation? Where was he, even?

He swam a few strokes aimlessly. The direction of the surface didn't matter now. If he reached it, he didn't know if he would be able to breathe air. Was this a new task, and, if so, what exactly did he have to do?

Merlin was probably observing him right now and laughing at his bewilderment. Morgan too.

The only positive side to this new state of affairs was that he remained alive. No, there were two positive sides: if he was alive, so was Arthur, most likely. Was he around here somewhere?

Without thinking, he tried to shout the king's name, but only a burst of warm water came out of his mouth, without a gurgle or a bubble. Speaking wouldn't work in this undersea realm. Could he find Arthur by touch? He reached out with his hands and feet but encountered nothing. He thought back to his brief time in the sky, but he couldn't recall seeing what had happened to his companion.

He swam some more, slow, lazy strokes, not caring where he went but needing to do something. The exhaustion of his long run through the city seemed to have entirely disappeared, as if when giving him the ability to breathe underwater, Merlin had also alleviated his fatigue. Or perhaps a long time had passed without him noticing and he'd recovered.

According to what Merlin had told them and the challenge he'd set, they'd failed the first task. Was this the punishment? A burst of fear shot through him—was this experience going to be neverending? Was he to spend the rest of his life swimming alone in this abyss?

But he couldn't believe it. He could not believe that Merlin, so bored with his own existence that he engineered strife and mayhem on a whole planet just for his amusement, would pass up the opportunity to have some more fun. Sooner or later, something would happen.

Silver flashed in the darkness.

Huh! I thought so. Are you listening in on my mind, you nasty old goat?

A shape was moving toward him, sliding through the water like an indolent ripple. It had to be reflecting light from somewhere. Patrin gazed in the direction he assumed was 'up' and then all around. A faint glow shone in the distance, a band of light resembling the Milky Way.

Patrin?

Though the voice sounded in his head and not his ears he recognized it immediately. *Arthur?*

I've found you at last. I guessed it must be you. Merlin has altered us once more, but you are the only other thing I've encountered.

Where are you? As Patrin asked the question, he knew the answer. The silver creature had swum closer and now floated in front of him. It was the largest eel he ever saw, except it was narrow and its scales shone like liquid mercury. The head was flat with holes for ears, and it held a gaping, many-toothed mouth and shark eyes. *What do you mean, Merlin altered **us***? He reached for his other hand as he had before, only to feel a sinuous, muscular wave pass through him.

His hands were gone.

Shit! I hate this. What's the point of morphing us into these different life forms?

I have come to know Merlin well over the years, Arthur replied. *I believe nearly everything he does is for his amusement.*

I have to agree. What now?

Ah, I hoped Merlin might have told you.

I haven't seen him either. How to point when you don't have hands? *There's something over there.* He nodded in the direction of the band of light.

Then let us investigate.

Somehow, what would have been the movement of Patrin's legs was translated into moving in the undulating motion of a sea snake. He propelled himself with Arthur toward the light. Might it in fact be the Milky Way, shining down through the water? But then he recalled he was far from Earth and the band of stars might not shine in this sky. The *Defiant* had traveled a long way, slipping faster than light speed through dark paths of spacetime. This planet could be closer to the core of the galaxy and part of that gleaming ribbon in Earth's night sky.

But what grew clearer the closer he swam was not the glimmer of celestial bodies but a fiery furnace, oozing lava, turning the water hazy with intense heat. Great gaseous gouts belched from a jagged wound in the ocean floor. Brilliant colors—red, orange, pink, purple, and yellow—etched the edge of the fissure and spilled out onto rocks and sand.

I know this place, Arthur said, *and I cannot go there. I will not.*

The king turned and began to swim away.

Arthur, where are you going? What do you mean, you know this place? How do you know where we are? There's no way you were here before. Patrin swam after him.

Merlin must have sent them to the bottom of the ocean to perform the second task. He might not have revealed it yet but that had to be the reason for their fish bodies.

Arthur! Wait! He caught up to the king and matched his speed. *Stop. Talk to me.*

Arthur's swimming slowed. *You must know it too. Though you are from a different time than I, all humans know of it.*

But I don't. I really don't. I don't underst—

It is Hell! How do you not recognize it? I do not wish to witness the eternal torment of human souls.

It's...? Patrin halted.

The king swam on.

It isn't Hell, Arthur. It can't be. We're on an alien planet. Patrin set off again. *I get what you mean, but Hell is an idea in human religions. I don't know what that place is, but there's no way it's...* When his companion didn't respond, Patrin went on, *Please, we have to go there. If we don't try to complete this task we might never go home. I'll never see my family again.*

*We have already failed a task. I don't think it makes any differ-
ence whether we attempt this one.*

But, still, what else can we do? Swim around underwater forever?

The sea creature that was Arthur slowed down and then turned
in a smooth arc. *Very well. I will attempt the task so that you might see
your mother and sister again, but I fear it will come to nothing.*

They returned to the gash in the ocean floor. The water around
Patrin's body grew warmer the closer they swam. At some point, it
would grow unbearably hot and his skin would begin to cook. They
could not go right up to the fault line—that was what it had to be.
He'd learned about plate tectonics at school. This super-heated crack
had to be the line where two plates met. Either they were pulling
apart or pushing together, and in the gap magma could leak out.

So this planet was similar to Earth in that way?

Or perhaps it was just a conjuring of Merlin or Morgan's mind.

There are beings! Arthur exclaimed. *It is Hell! I was right!*

Patrin scanned the cleft. It was hard to see anything in the glare,
but he caught sight of movement. There were creatures here, as
Arthur had spotted. They were mottled brown, well-camouflaged
against the seabed they crawled over. Some kind of arthropod, they
marched steadily toward the fault line—steadily and irrationally.
Why would any life form choose to approach the deathly heat?

Then he saw better what was happening and understood
Arthur's deduction. The creatures were not choosing their fatal path,
they were being driven along it by others of their kind. Jabbing them
with long, steel needles, the torturers or executioners surrounded the
victims, cutting off all avenues of escape. It did look like a scene from
Hell.

"Save them."

The words had not been spoken inside Patrin's mind, they had
arrived externally, echoing through the water. They were unmistak-
ably Merlin's.

Save the creatures who were about to die?

How? Patrin asked.

Predictably, no answer came.

Arthur said, *Another impossible task. I begin to wonder if we have been in Hell ourselves all along. If so, there is no doubt I deserve it. I have committed enough sin in my life. But you are innocent, Patrin. That is why you succeeded in the joust. You are pure and noble of heart. You should not be here.*

Patrin didn't know what the king was talking about. It was hard to relate to someone who had lived thousands of years ago, and he was pretty sure it had been Mam distracting Merlin that had allowed him to win the joust, not his 'purity' or 'nobility'. *I am here, though, so I want to try.*

Try we must. There is no alternative. And perhaps Kala Orr and her son may arrive soon to complicate our efforts.

They swam closer, slipping through the water in unison. The heat began to grow uncomfortable. A burning, stinging sensation came from all over his body. Even his eyes hurt.

The creatures holding the spikes had noticed them. As their gazes turned upward, their victims took their chance and tried to break through the ranks of stabbers. The line of marchers was breaking up. Maybe a distraction was all that was needed and the captives would escape without further intervention. But then the torturers realized what was happening and pricked the escapees back into line.

Trying to ignore his increasing discomfort, Patrin glided downward. The heat from the vent was becoming unbearable. He dove at a group of needle-wielding creatures, snapping at them threateningly. They aimed their weapons at him to fend him off. Arthur harried the opposite side of the line. He was even closer to the heat source. Patrin didn't know how he could stand it.

A batch of prisoners broke free and scrabbled hastily over the ocean floor. Patrin continued to distract their captors, feinting left and striking right, the needle points barely missing him.

Arthur was not faring so well. He'd been stabbed. Liquid spurted from his side—blood, no doubt, but in the low light it looked black as oil. Patrin wanted to go to his aid, but if he left his position the escapees would be rounded up again.

A second spike slipped beneath the king's scales and more blood leaked out.

Arthur, come here! I will protect you.

I must fulfill the task.

The task doesn't matter. We can do it together. His statements didn't make sense, but avoiding the jabs and seeing Arthur wounded was confusing him. *Come to my side.*

I must—Arghh!

A third wound opened in the king's side.

Patrin abandoned his location. The alien creatures could go to Hell as far as he was concerned. He would not allow Arthur to be hurt.

Go back! You cannot save me.

Perhaps through loss of blood or due to pain from the scalding water, Arthur was sinking closer to his attackers. The prisoners they'd been herding to their deaths were fleeing, but they were ignored in favor of killing the great fish creature.

Arthur!

Go back! Leave, Patrin. The king's voice was growing quieter. *You have completed the task. You saved some of these strange beings. Leave. Go home to your family.*

NO! He rushed forward. A sharp pain pulsed from his thigh—except it could not be his thigh. He'd been wounded.

Patrin. Arthur's tone was solemn. *Remember your oath.*

The king reached the ocean floor. The stabbing creatures closed in.

Patrin turned from the scene, unable to watch.

As he did so, he caught sight of the prisoners he had freed. They hadn't run away. They had returned and were attacking the jabbers, grappling with them and tearing the spikes from their claws. As soon as they were armed, they poked their former executioners, driving the needle tips into joints and eyes, forcing them closer to a fiery death.

The tables had turned. The condemned had become slayers. Nothing had changed. His effort had been useless, and Arthur was dead.

FOUR

Cool air bathed his skin and the light was unbearably bright. Patrin shut his eyes. He was lying on a hard surface, cold and smooth like marble.

If he was no longer in water, was he human again? Opening his eyes to a slit, he lifted a hand above his face. The familiar color of his skin, the digits, the fine hair, the scuffed knuckles from the battle—all these things warmed his heart. But then a terrible memory struck. In his mind's eye he saw again the sea animal that had been Arthur, set upon by stabbing creatures.

He squeezed his eyes shut and tears escaped from beneath the lids.

Arthur was gone.

His mentor, his friend, the father he'd never had, his king, was dead.

Gaping sorrow opened up in his chest.

But it was quickly replaced by fury.

Arthur's death was Merlin's fault. If he hadn't set the tasks, if he'd just allowed everyone from the *Defiant* to leave, the King of the Britons would still be alive. He would not be a corpse lying at the bottom of the ocean, not even in his natural form.

Patrin leapt to his feet. Wherever and whatever this new place was, he would seek out Merlin and kill him.

"Now then," said a smooth voice. "Be careful."

Patrin spun around, trying to find the speaker. His eyes were gradually adjusting to the glare. A tall figure in a dark robe stood before him. His hands jerked out and grasped Merlin's neck.

"You killed him," Patrin breathed. "You killed him, you bastard."

The neck collapsed beneath his fingers like a bath sponge. He half-expected to see water or blood flow out. But nothing appeared and Merlin only smiled condescendingly. "Press away, young man. Press away. The sensation is quite pleasant."

Patrin released his hold and clenched his fists impotently. He imagined smashing Merlin's face in, throwing him to the ground and stomping on his head, ripping out his entrails with his bare hands and stuffing them in his mouth.

But the alien would not be harmed. His elastic body would only reform to its previous shape.

Merlin's eyebrow lifted. "You seem upset, Patrin. Tell me, what it is that angers you."

"Fuck off. I'm not telling you anything. You'll only feed off my emotions like the parasitic creep you are."

Another memory hit. He was on the battlefield again, and Merlin and Morgan were bargaining with Mam and Wright. One of the brothers from West BI, the youngest one, who had been killed in the battle, walked out of a tent, alive.

"Bring him back to life!" Patrin demanded. "Bring Arthur back. I know you can do it."

The corner of Merlin's lip lifted. "What makes you think I have not?"

"Huh?" Could it be true? Patrin swiveled again.

Arthur was lying only a few meters away, unconscious, but his chest rose and fell. Patrin ran to his side and collapsed to his knees, resting his hands on the broad chest to reassure himself that what he was seeing was real.

"What? No thanks? Not a word of gratitude?" Merlin had moved silently closer.

"We did your tasks. You've played with us enough. Let us go. Send us back to Earth, you evil maniac."

"Absolutely not. The terms of your stay here were not specified, and neither were the number of tasks you must undertake. You could be here a very long time."

"You were never interested in learning about humans, were you? You just wanted a couple of us on hand to torture for fits and giggles, right?" Patrin rose to his feet.

He stood a head taller than Merlin. Making use of his additional height, he loomed over the slim alien, bringing his face so close their noses were almost touching. "You're disgusting and pathetic. Your life is so meaningless, so empty of love and friendship, so lacking in purpose, you have to torment other species just to give yourself a reason to carry on. You might look down on humans, but the poorest, weakest, most disadvantaged of us has a life full of more emotion and significance than yours is or will ever be. You're a waste of space, a blight, a void that only takes and never gives anything back."

Merlin's gaze was fixed on his, but his expression was inscrutable.

"I don't care what you do with me," Patrin declared. "I don't even care what you do with Arthur. We've already lived more than you ever did or ever will. Kill me now. Kill us both. I'll die knowing that you didn't win. I've won. I've won because my mam, my sister, Arthur, and TJ loved me. Who loves you, huh, Merlin? *Who loves you?*"

"Touching," Merlin murmured in his usual sarcastic tone.

Yet Patrin was sure he detected a tremulous note, as if the alien was rattled. Had he really unnerved him? It was hard to believe. He'd only spoken from his heart, but as the words left his mouth he'd known every one was true.

"But," the alien continued, "though you seem intent on dying, that was not part of my plan. A single task remains. Will you attempt it?"

Somewhat deflated, Patrin replied, "Only one more? What is it?"

"Look around. Can you guess?"

The surroundings hadn't fully registered on Patrin. At first, he'd been too blinded by the high intensity light. Then, he'd been too worried about Arthur and angry at Merlin.

He broke eye contact with the alien and assessed this new place. The floor confirmed his first impression. It did appear to be made from a substance like marble. White, smooth, and faintly shiny, it spread in all directions until it reached...

A white vapor obscured the farthest reaches of the floor. They were outside. The sky was entirely clear and the sun was a brilliant orb, too bright to behold. The air was chilly and it felt thin. It struck him that he couldn't see any other parts of the landscape, no hills or fields, no rivers or oceans. "Are we high up?"

"Very high up. We are higher than the highest mountain on your planet. Naturally, I am helping you to breathe."

"That white stuff in the distance—those are clouds?"

"Well spotted. Remember this: there are no barriers to prevent you falling, and nothing to indicate the edges of the platform."

Arthur groaned and lifted a hand to his head.

Patrin moved to his side and squatted down. "How are you feeling? Are you okay?"

The king opened bleary eyes and then quickly shut them again.

"The light's bright here. You'll get used to it in a minute. Thank the stars you didn't die."

"Merlin will wait until he is fully ready before he kills me. Our most recent challenge was not the time."

"We only have one more task. Then we can go home."

Arthur's eyes opened again and he sought Patrin's face. "Only one? What must we do?"

Patrin turned to ask Merlin, but the platform was empty. The alien had vanished.

"*Damn*. He's gone. He didn't say."

"Of course he didn't. Help me up."

When Arthur was standing they surveyed the new place together.

"We're up in the clouds and there's nothing to stop us from falling," Patrin informed him, "so we have to be careful."

Arthur shrugged. "If Merlin wishes, he could catch us."

"Or he could just let us fall."

"Exactly."

"Do you think that's the task—to avoid falling off?"

"That seems too easy. Perhaps we must cast ourselves to our supposed deaths. Who knows? There is no telling."

They walked.

"I am glad I am in human form," said Arthur. "I did not enjoy being a fish."

"Me neither." Patrin didn't ask him what it had felt like to die. He didn't want to remind Arthur of the experience or, in truth, to hear about it. He would find out one day for himself, hopefully a very long time from now. "I saved some of those creatures, you know. I created a diversion so they could escape."

"Well done. You succeeded in the task and you may have saved our lives."

"I don't think so. The creatures I saved didn't run away, they turned on their executioners. They stole their weapons and forced them into the fiery place instead."

"So no good came from your intervention?"

"None at all as far as I could tell, except...maybe the worse of the two types of creature died?"

"I don't understand it. But then, nothing here makes any sense. Who were the beings in the city? Why did Merlin set us the challenge to cross it in a day?"

"The first task was impossible and the second one was pointless."

"I see something." Arthur pointed ahead.

A tiered structure rose from a white base, like a small, cone-shaped tower. Wreathed in mist, it was hard to make out, but then a breeze turned the vapor to threads, revealing a structure that held six seats. Three made up the triangular base, one at each point, two seats were on opposite sides above, and a single seat formed the tip. The seats at the base and middle tiers faced outwards. The person sitting at the tip looked directly at them. It was Morgan le Fay.

She stood up, took a step forward, and floated to the floor.

"Arthur, Patrin. How nice to see you. Have you been enjoying yourselves? Has Merlin shown you a good time?" She winked. "What am I saying? Of course he hasn't. He's far too dark and twisted."

Patrin saw no reason to gratify her with a reply. Besides, he'd just recognized the people sitting in the middle-tier seats. His gaze locked with Perran Orr and then slid to his mother. After a brief discussion, they clambered down. Without Morgan's ability to gracefully float, they were forced to climb on the backs of the seats below, disturbing their occupants, two gray-haired women and a gray-haired man.

Perran asked, "What was your second task?"

"We're not here to compare notes," Patrin retorted.

"What do you get if you win?" asked Kala. "Will you return to Earth?"

"I'm returning to Earth anyway." He turned to Morgan. "That's what you promised, right? I want to go there now, with Arthur. My mam will be worried about me. You said I wouldn't be here long. You didn't say anything about these bullshit tasks and challenges."

"You haven't been here long," Morgan replied slyly.

"I want to go back with them!" demanded Kala.

"*I*?" Perran glared at her. "Don't you mean *we*?"

"Neither of you is going anywhere," Morgan snapped. "Except..." Her attention turned to the cloudy haze.

One of the gray-haired figures at the base of the tower rose to her feet and hobbled toward them.

"Who's that?" Patrin asked.

"Who do you think?" Kala snapped. "Another one of *them*."

The woman was ancient, looking as old as Arthur should have looked. Her head was little more than a skull, wispy strands of white hair clinging to it. Her white robe hung from her skeletal body like a funeral gown. Yet as she shuffled closer, she grew younger. Her hunched body straightened, lustrous, dark brown hair sprouted from her head and cascaded down her back, and her clouded eyes grew bright and vital. By the time she reached them she resembled a woman only just out of adolescence, her skin plump and wrinkle-free.

"You are the humans." She faced Arthur. "You are the oldest, though the time of your existence is equal to only a single exhalation of my kind."

"I am the oldest," the king confirmed. "Who are you and your people? Why have you plagued my world?"

Patrin had a sense of kindred spirits meeting for the first time. This new alien didn't regard Arthur with the same arrogance and haughtiness as Morgan and Merlin did. She looked at him with an expression of respect. Patrin wasn't sure why. Perhaps she perceived the same things in Arthur that so many others did, that maybe Merlin had seen long ago.

"We visit many new worlds and new species. It adds interest to our lives."

"Who cares about that?" Patrin snapped. "What gives you the right to interfere with human affairs?"

"What gives anyone the right to do anything? What are rights? Who decides them and upholds them? These questions have no answers. Believe me, we know. We have considered them for longer than your planet has existed. There is no meaning to life. There are no rights or wrongs. Everything is relative."

"If you believe that why even bother going on? If there's no point to anything, why not kill yourselves?"

"Do you think we have not tried?"

It was not the response Patrin was expecting. He'd anticipated some woolly reasoning, justifying their appalling behavior.

Arthur said, "Please, explain."

"The explanation is simple. We cannot die. We do not grow old and wither as your species does. We can alter our forms, travel through the vacuum of space without protection, dive into stars and emerge unscathed. We can be exploded into atoms, but eventually the atoms will find each other, coalesce, and become whole again."

"How long have you been like this?" Arthur asked. "There must have been a time you were mortal, like us."

"Logically, there must, but it was so long ago we have no record of it. We do not even know the appearance or anatomy of our original form. At some point in our evolution, we must have discovered how to put a stop to ageing. Then we learned how to shapeshift. Perhaps after that, perhaps before, we also devised a method for making ourselves indestructible. At the time these medical developments must have seemed amazing, but there has been a bitter legacy."

"Boredom," said Patrin.

"And all that comes with it. Apathy, lethargy, indifference. We long to feel. We lust to care about something, anything. We desire deeply to believe that one thing holds more importance than another, as you do. But we cannot. We cannot care about anything anymore."

"Those gray creatures in the city," said Patrin, "who were they? Have you trapped other life forms here as well as us?"

"The people in the city are my kind. I may have been one of them. That place is modelled on your planet. We sometimes go there to mimic the way you live, hoping to experience even a sliver of your feelings."

"What about the life forms on the ocean floor?" Patrin pressed. "Don't tell me that was your species too."

"Being forced to an agonized, though brief, death is one of the few ordeals that registers in our emotions."

While they had been talking Morgan stood by listlessly, looking disinterested. Occasionally, she would throw a glance at Perran and then beyond him to the cloudy expanse.

Merlin stepped out of the mist. "Arthur, Patrin, I see you found your fellow humans."

"Half-humans," Morgan corrected. She placed an arm around Perran's shoulder affectionately.

He grimaced but did not remove it.

"We have been learning about your people," Arthur replied to

Merlin. "I must say, despite all the harm that you have caused and the terrible deeds you have committed, pity for you stirs in my heart."

"*You* pity *me*?!"

"He's right," Patrin said. "I pity you too. All of you. My life is rich. Yours is empty. I would rather be human, even though my time is over in a blink of an eye in your terms, than endure the living hell of your existence."

"What are you doing?!" Perran yelled.

Morgan was wrestling one of his arms behind his back, evil delight wreathing her features. Though she was small and slight she was surprisingly powerful. She easily completed her move. Perran was helpless, his face contorted with pain.

She pushed him toward the edge.

"Shit!" Patrin exclaimed. "She's going to throw him off."

Morgan was doing it for fun. She'd clearly grown bored of the conversation and wanted a small diversion. If she did push Perran over the edge, she could save his life regardless. But would she? Would Merlin or any of the others? They probably envied Perran's ability to die. They would be jealous of the few seconds of intense feeling that would course through him as he fell to his demise.

Patrin raced over to the struggling couple. He seized Morgan's hand and tried to peel it off Perran's arm, but she was too strong. She grinned wickedly up at him. Perran was only a meter from the drop-off.

"Don't do it!" Patrin yelled. "He's terrified." He'd never liked Perran. No one could grow up with Kala Orr as their mother and turn out normal, but the young man didn't deserve to be put through terror, not knowing if he was living his final moments.

Morgan gave a grunt as she shoved Perran away from her. He stumbled backward. She giggled like a child as, eyes round and mouth agape, he tumbled over the edge.

Patrin leapt and reached out, blindly swiping through air.

His hand smacked into something solid and he gripped it, fingers digging in for dear life.

He'd caught Patrin's arm, but he couldn't hold onto the platform. The edge was smooth and curved. He slid forward on his belly, the weight of the other man dragging him down. The only way to save himself was to let go.

He couldn't.

He couldn't release his hold.

In a split second he would be falling to the surface along with Kala Orr's odious offspring.

But then strong hands grasped his waist, halting his slide.

"Not so fast, Patrin," said Arthur. "You are not going flying today. Your mother would never let me hear the end of it."

FIVE

From his standing position, Arthur had managed to gain traction on the platform with his feet, dragging Patrin and then Perran to safety. Kala hugged her son, though listlessly. Morgan didn't even look contrite.

Merlin gave his trademark smirk.

The third alien didn't even seem to have registered the event. Her expression remained neutral.

"Was that the last of the trials you set us, Merlin?" Patrin asked. "Were you in cahoots with Morgan, figuring out a prank to play? Wait. Don't bother answering. I don't care. I demand you send me to Earth immediately. I thought it would be fun to learn about your planet and another intelligent species, but I hate it here. You're half-crazy. What am I saying? You're fully crazy. You don't have anything to teach me. I want to go home."

"Humans do not dictate our actions," Merlin retorted. "You listen and you obey. That is all."

"If you don't send me back I'll just refuse to do anything. You won't get any more entertainment out of me."

"I could put an end to your life. At this very instant, I could remove the modification that allows you to survive in this rarefied atmosphere. You would asphyxiate in minutes."

"Then do it. I won't be your plaything any longer."

Morgan pouted. "But your beloved mother would miss you so much if you never returned. She is missing you right now, you know."

"Mam would understand. She wouldn't want me to give up my dignity and self-respect. She taught me my own worth. You're only saying that to manipulate me anyway. You want to feed off my despair, like the parasite you are. Send me back to Earth, and Arthur too."

"Patrin," the king said gently, "I am not sure I should return to our world, or that I want to."

"What?" He stared into Arthur's eyes. The king was serious. "What do you mean? Of course you have to return to Earth with me. What else could you do?"

But his friend's features remained grave, and for several moments he was silent.

Dreams of going home to West BI with Arthur melted in Patrin's mind. Images of the two of them riding through forests, of the king teaching him woodcraft, of listening to tales of olden times... everything was fading like foam from waves on a beach.

"It seems to me," Arthur finally said, "that these creatures who have tortured humans for so long are also in torment. I would like to find a way to help them, if not for their own sake then to prevent other peoples from enduring the experiences of humanity."

"Ha!" Merlin burst out. "The arrogance!"

"I would like to hear what the oldest human has to say," said the nameless alien, her youthful brow wrinkling.

"I have learned much since I was awoken in this new age of humankind." Arthur explained. "I have learned that the stars are hundreds of thousands of worlds existing in the night sky, and they are unimaginably old. I have also learned that many of these worlds may sustain intelligent living beings, like and yet unlike humans."

He turned his kind, patient eyes to the anonymous alien. "It may be that somewhere among these worlds and civilizations lies the answer to your predicament. There could be beings even older than yourselves, creatures you have not yet encountered, who know how to give you the peace of a final ending. I propose that Merlin and I travel the stars to look for this answer. I yearn to see the miracles awaiting within the great expanse and the strange people who live within it."

Arthur faced Merlin. "What do you say, old friend? I care not for the final task you had in mind for us, but we had many exciting and daring adventures together once. Perhaps, over time, we can recapture the engagement and camaraderie of those moments. Perhaps one day you may even look upon me as your equal. I am willing to devote my life to this quest."

"But Arthur," Patrin pleaded, unwilling to let go of this man he'd grown to love, "you're a Briton. We need you."

"Our country is at peace and will hopefully be so for a long time to come. It will hurt me sorely for us to part, but you have a family awaiting you and, eventually, children of your own. Your world is familiar to you. It is your home, but it is not my home. My world faded from existence long ago and will never return. Therefore, I would like to seek out a new life and a worthy cause. This one, which has presented itself by many circuitous, meandering paths, seems fated to be mine."

"You can't..." Patrin thrust the heels of his hands into his eyes and his chest tightened. "I'll miss you if you go," he murmured, struggling to stay in control of his emotions.

"And I will miss you too, deeply. Delight in the sweet sorrow, my friend. These poor creatures cannot feel it nor any of the other emotions that make us what we are."

Morgan had wandered away, as if disinterested.

The nameless alien said, "I have no objection to your scheme. Though we have long searched for an escape from our fate, the galaxy is vast. An answer may exist somewhere out there in the expanse of space."

A pause fell. Patrin's heart seemed to cease beating. He was on the verge of being torn from and, at the same time, returned to the people he loved.

Kala Orr took her chance. One eye on Morgan, who stood at a little distance, gazing out into the mist, she whispered to Merlin fiercely and jabbed a finger at Patrin, "If you're returning him to Earth, send me and Perran too."

"No!" Morgan had overheard. She came striding back. "These two are mine and I'm keeping them." She glared at Kala. "You're staying here, you ungrateful bitch. You begged me to let you stay, and that's what's happening."

"I thought I was going to die with the rest of them! The situation's different now. I've changed my mind."

"Well I haven't. If Earth is off limits I need something to amuse myself with, and you and your precious son are it."

Kala clenched her fists and appeared about to slap Morgan.

The scene was descending into chaos. Who knew what stunt Morgan would pull next?

Patrin swallowed. "Arthur, if that's what you want to do, you must do it. But I have to go home to Mam and Kayla."

"I understand. Merlin, give me your answer. Will you journey with me through the galaxy, seeking an end to your people's torment? And if your answer is yes, will you transport this young man back to his family?"

Merlin lifted a knuckle to his lips and his dark-eyed gaze flicked between Patrin and Arthur. "I suppose I don't have anything to lose," he muttered with disdain. He lifted a hand.

"Wait!" Patrin exclaimed. This was it. There wasn't even going to be time to say goodbye.

Merlin hooded his eyes. "It's now or never, young man."

"No!" Kala spat. "Me too. Send me back too!" She gripped Patrin's arm, as if she might be dragged back to Earth with him.

He peeled her hand off, pushed her away, and grabbed Arthur into a hug, saying thickly, "I was honored to know you, my king,"

"And I you, my faithful squire," Arthur replied, grasping him tightly. "Tell the Britons, if they need me again, I will return."

"Say hi to Taylan for me," Morgan snickered. She was holding onto Kala by her hair. "*If* she's still around."

Patrin took a breath.

The light had changed. Cool, moist air rich with woodland scents hit him. Deep green grass stood beneath his feet and trees rose to the sky.

Merlin had transported him. He was on Earth. He could have been in any temperate forest, but he knew this was West BI. He could feel it.

He was home.

READ TAYLAN AND WRIGHT'S STORY IN STAR LEGEND